D1516248

For a small New England town, Shadow Grove has an uncanny ability to attract the worst kind of trouble. Not that the residents are too concerned about the various horrors living among them.

As the leaves change color and the weather grows colder, a foul presence is making itself known by leaving peculiar gifts for the students of Ridge Crest High. At first, the presents seem harmless—and a rash of accidents seem coincidental—but when seniors Rachel Cleary and her Scottish cousin, Dougal Mackay, find a boneless body in the boiler room, things take an ominous turn.

Something vicious is on the loose in Shadow Grove, but with Orion Nebulius gone, Rachel has little hope of anyone getting out alive.

Other Books by Monique Snyman

The Night Weaver Series
The Night Weaver (The Night Weaver, Book 1)

Forthcoming from Monique Snyman

Dark Country

Awards for The Night Weaver (Book 1)

Bram Stoker Awards Nominee
Superior Achievement in a Young Adult Novel

Independent Publisher Book Awards (IPPY)
Silver Medal Winner: Horror

Foreword Reviews
Indies Book of the Year Awards
Finalist for Young Adult Fiction

OZMA Book Awards
(Genre division of the Chanticleer International Book Awards)
Semi-finalist

Screencraft CINEMATIC BOOK Competition
Quarterfinalist, The Red List #3 in Horror

Praise for *The Night Weaver* (Book 1)

"Stephen King's *It* meets Stephenie Meyer's *Twilight* in this frightening story of horror and fantasy woven together to create a delectable tale of the macabre, romance, and action. Snyman's storytelling will have people lining up for the next book in the series." ~*School Library Journal*

"A sinister and satisfying fantasy that is unique as well as creepy and unsettling. *The Night Weaver* introduces a world of myth, intrigue, and darkness with considerable technique."
~*Foreword Reviews*

"An enjoyable, frenetically paced fantasy." ~*Publishers Weekly*

"If YA dark fantasy is your fare, then *The Night Weaver* is right up your alley. Snyman has begun to build a promising world of intrigue and monsters in the dark. Though don't assume all that hides in shadows is beastly." ~*HorrorFuel*

"There's a clear M. Night Shyamalan vibe … a spine-chilling sense of dread on every page of this truly excellent work."
~*Readers' Favorite*

"… weaves together small-town horror with an intricate otherworldly fairytale to deliver a blend of horror and fantasy that captures the essence of young adult terror seasoned with the stuff of grown-up nightmares." ~*The Nerd Daily*

THE BONE CARVER

Bram Stoker Awards Nominee

MONIQUE SNYMAN

The Bone Carver

Copyright © 2020 Monique Snyman
All rights reserved.

Original Cover Art by Marcela Bolívar
www.MarcelaBolivar.com/about/

Cover Design by Michael J. Canales
www.MJCImageWorks.com

ISBN: 978-1-64548-008-2

VESUVIAN BOOKS

Published by Vesuvian Books
www.VesuvianBooks.com

Printed in the United States of America

10 9 8 7 6 5 4 3 2 1

This one goes out to all the girls who've ever felt powerless.
You're stronger than you think.

Table of Contents

Chapter One—Skull And Bones 1

Chapter Two—Hip2B² 12

Chapter Three—Chilled to the Marrow................................... 27

Chapter Four—The Skeleton Key... 41

Chapter Five—Rickety Old Things... 49

Chapter Six—A Real Pain in the Patella................................. 62

Chapter Seven—Fractured Sense of Self................................. 79

Chapter Eight—Bones Don't Scry 86

Chapter Nine—Badlands 100

Chapter Ten—Brittle But Not Broken 116

Chapter Eleven—Sidetracked.. 129

Chapter Twelve—Blood of my Blood 145

Chapter Thirteen—Charnel Melancholy............................... 155

Chapter Fourteen—Skull Cracker... 167

Chapter Fifteen—Step on a Crack, Break your Mother's Back... 177

Chapter Sixteen—Jaw Dropper.. 187

Chapter Seventeen—Bad to the Bone 196

Chapter Eighteen—We are the Hollowed Ones..................... 207

Chapter Nineteen—Right in the Sternum 213

Chapter Twenty—Calcification 225

Chapter Twenty-One—Body of Work.................................... 238

Chapter Twenty-Two—The Ghost Boy.................................. 248

Chapter Twenty-Three—A Royal Hunt................................. 257

Chapter Twenty-Four—Death Knell 269

Chapter Twenty-Five—Sticks and Stones 280

Chapter Twenty-Six—We Are What We Are.......................... 289

Chapter One
Skull And Bones

The amplified ticking of the auditorium clock grates against Rachel Cleary's already frayed nerves. Sluggish yet deliberate, every second mocks her inadequacies. A pencil taps rapidly against a desk, shoes either squeak or click or scuff against the linoleum floors, fabric moves as bodies shift to get comfortable. Someone coughs. A sneeze. Then there's the scratching—fingernails gouge at scalps, drag across skin. *Skritch-skritch-skritch.*

Every sound adds to Rachel's annoyance.

The dull thud behind her left eye grows stronger as the noise intensifies. She squeezes her eyes shut, pinches the bridge of her nose to alleviate the pain. It doesn't help. Panic sets in. Her heartrate picks up speed.

This is it. Bile rise into her throat. *This is how I get stuck in this hellhole town for the rest of my life.*

When she opens her eyes, the world is unrecognizable—a blurry and misshapen blotch. Colors blend into each other, faces are distorted. Whether this is due to tears in her eyes or the headache pounding against her skull, she doesn't know. Battling against her impaired state, Rachel blindly reaches for her sling bag on the floor. She stands abruptly, the chair screeching and

1

clattering as it topples. Ignoring this, Rachel navigates her way through the rows of desks.

The walls seem to close in on her, ceiling seems to drop lower.

Someone calls out her name. The voice is muted amongst the various other sounds, unable to break through the anxiety encasing her mind. The air grows thick, unbreathable, tastes toxic.

Her legs are sluggish, making it feel like she's wading through mud.

When Rachel emerges from the auditorium, sweat clings to her skin and her clothes stick to her body.

She rushes for the closest trashcan, located near the school's back exit, and grips the sides with trembling hands. Her stomach roils. Stomach acid burns her esophagus, pushing her over the edge. The contents of the omega-3 and protein-rich breakfast evacuate her body, until there's nothing left but a sour aftertaste.

Retching gives way to dry heaves.

Rachel squats beside the trashcan, still gripping it for all she's worth. She inhales deeply, exhales slowly, hoping to calm her queasiness.

A ridiculous breathing exercise she learned online won't work today. Calm? She's never had the privilege of feeling calm where college is concerned. For the past six years, she's done everything she could to make herself look good on paper for Ivy League admission boards—all of them searching for "well-rounded individuals." For two years, she's been prepping for the SATs, going so far as to take the ACTs as a practice run. She aced those tests.

Officially, all the Ivy League schools she's applied to should consider ACT scores. Unofficially, though, she's screwed. There's no sugarcoating it. She. Is. Screwed.

How could I choke on the most important day of my life? Today was supposed to be easy.

Rachel voices her frustration with a low, guttural scream as she shoots upright. She kicks at the trashcan, wishing she could fling it across the corridor. Fortunately, Ridge Crest High had bolted all the trashcans firmly to the floor to prevent this exact response from students.

She raises her hands to her head as the shock takes hold.

"What have I done?"

When she left the auditorium without permission, her life's course had taken an unforeseen detour. This morning, she'd still been certain of her future, but now … Now, she has to wait months before she can retake the SATs. Months wasted and for what? Because of a stupid panic attack?

"What am I going to do?" she whispers, her voice thick.

She can't answer the question.

I can't stay here. She covers her mouth to stifle a sob and squeezes her eyes shut. There's no getting away from reality, though. Not this time. *This is a minor inconvenience.* Rachel sucks air into her lungs and holds her breath a moment before exhaling slowly. *I can overcome this.* Another deep breath. She opens her eyes and squares her shoulders. *If all is well and truly lost* then *you cry.* Resolve forces her to pick up her feet, to move forward. She makes her way out of the auditorium's lobby and into the courtyard, the afternoon sun glaring as the rays rebound from the grayish pavement.

Students sit outside, eating their lunches, oblivious to the turmoil raging inside her. There's a giggle, some laughter, a lot of chitchatting. A regular day at Ridge Crest High.

Rachel holds her head high as she walks past the benches.

The news will reach them about her spectacular failure soon enough, so there's no need for her to have a public breakdown, too.

Rachel enters the cafeteria. Voices rebound from the stark white walls and oversized windows. She hurries to the exit, sidestepping the red and black cafeteria tables, evading the students loitering in front of the open red doors leading into the main building. She hones in on the long, almost deserted hallway. Lockers line both walls, large banners with 'Go Devils Go!'— painted in the school's chokeberry-red and charcoal-black—hang across the hallway, and posters targeting teenage-related issues decorate the notice boards.

Rachel stops at a water fountain, both to catch her breath and to rinse her mouth. She takes her time, repeating a single thought all the while: *Keep it together.* Only when she's pulled herself together again does she continue her trek down the hallway.

Leaning against the locker beside hers is the other new guy, Cameron Mayer. Her cousin, Dougal Mackay, and Cam Mayer were both enrolled at Ridge Crest at the start of the year, but because Dougal is the more popular new student, Cam became known as the "other new guy."

Cameron is somewhat rugged, favoring a faded leather jacket, biker boots, and ripped jeans. He doesn't quite fit into Ridge Crest High, at least not in the traditional sense. Sure, he's figured out how to navigate his way around the various cliques, but he doesn't seem to be especially friendly with anyone.

Cam isn't a bad-looking guy, though. He's a little rough

around the edges, but that's exactly what Rachel likes in her dating portfolio. Bad boys who are still nice to look at. Yup. That's her favorite type. With his blond hair and olive complexion, those soulful blue eyes, not to mention the enigmatic air surrounding him, he definitely ticks all the boxes on her list.

One small setback and you're ready to push the self-destruct button? Shame on you, Rachel Cleary.

She couldn't, however, overlook the fact that Cameron was always *there*. He usually lingered in the background, just watching her. Granted, this could've been her imagination, some residual paranoia after the Night Weaver had stalked her. Either way, Rachel didn't know what to make of him.

He turns his attention to her, eyes narrowing.

"We meet again," he says.

Rachel reaches up to enter the combination code on her locker. "Indeed." She pulls the red metal door open. In the small mirror fastened to the inside of the door, she sees her eyes are bloodshot, red-rimmed.

"You okay?" Cam asks.

"Everything's just dandy," Rachel says. She grabs her SAT revisions from the locker—every binder color-coded and every chapter highlighted for optimum results. She'd squandered her opportunity, though. Choked on the most important day of her life.

Keep it together.

A group of cheerleaders and girls on the homecoming committee make their way past, carrying a large banner between them. Rachel glances their way. On the orange banner, black, bold letters: HALLOWEEN DANCE float among glitter.

Obligatory jack-o-lanterns, witches on broomsticks, and silhouetted black cats decorate the announcement. She turns away, focusing on the interior of the locker.

"You going?" Cam asks.

"I never go to dances," Rachel mumbles.

"Why not?"

She huffs a laugh.

"I'll see you around." She shuts the locker door and gives him a half-smile as she takes a step away.

Cam responds with a grin that promises a whole lot of trouble, and pushes his hands into his jean's pockets. "Don't be a stranger."

"I'll try." Rachel walks past, glancing back only to find him still watching her. Despite the SAT disaster, in spite of her own chastising, she appreciates the attention.

Rachel turns down another hallway, heading toward the original schoolhouse.

Ridge Crest High started off as a tiny schoolhouse with three classrooms and an outhouse. As Shadow Grove's population grew, so did the school. First, more classes had been added onto the original building, then an office. Before long, and thanks to the generous donations of alumni, Ridge Crest High had expanded into a U-shaped double-story building which sports an auditorium, cafeteria, Olympic-sized indoor swimming pool, and enough classes to easily fit three-thousand students. Since there *aren't* three-thousand high schoolers in town, a lot of space goes unused, falls into disrepair, and quickly becomes forgotten.

The pool, for example, hasn't been filled once in Rachel's high school career. There is no swim team, no coach, and certainly no funding for the upkeep.

She repositions her bag on her shoulder as she slips into the least popular girls' bathroom—unpopular due to its proximity to the abandoned classrooms *and* because it hasn't been renovated since the 1960s. There's nothing wrong with it, of course. All the toilets flush, every faucet has running water, and it's almost always empty. It's just not as pretty as the other bathrooms.

The door whines as it opens, squeals as it shuts. She makes her way deeper inside, her ankle boots squeaking with every step. The white tiles are cracked in some places, completely missing in others. Graffiti covers the faded pink walls and seaweed-green stalls—messages ranging from someone-hearting-someone to slurs about students from back in the day.

Labored breathing catches her attention, coming from inside one of the stalls. It's either panicked panting or heavy petting. Rachel isn't completely sure which scenario she prefers to have walked in on.

"Hello?" she calls. Rachel cautiously steps toward to the occupied stall. "Are you okay in there?"

A few tiny white pills scatter every which way, and roll to a stop one after the other. Rachel bends down and picks up the nearest pill, upon which twin deer on their hind legs are engraved on either side. She has seen the insignia in Orion's greenhouse. Rachel frowns, returns her attention to the stall.

The breathing grows more desperate. A loud slap against the metallic wall echoes against the tile. A body slides down and a pale hand sticks out through the opening between the floor and door.

Rachel drops her bag and grabs the hand, pulling as hard as she can until the girl is closer to the gap. When her other hand comes into view, a medical ID bracelet hangs around the girl's wrist. She grapples for the girl's wrist, turns the bracelet around and sees the word 'EPILEPSY' engraved into the sterling silver plate. Rachel cusses under her breath. She can't open the locked stall door in time to help. There's also no way anyone will be able to hear her cries for help.

Rachel crawls around to the empty stall beside the occupied one.

Mercia Holstein, the quiet girl who'd suddenly turned 'grade-A hot' overnight a couple of years back, lies on the cracked and discolored tiles, her body still. With her eyes shut, her lips partially open, she stiffens as the spasms set in. Rachel pushes the pill into Mercia's mouth and hopes for the best.

Rachel leans her forehead against the cold stall wall. "Please don't die," she whispers. She presses her fingertips against Mercia's neck to keep track of her pulse.

"I won't die." Mercia slurs her words, eyes flickering open.

Rachel releases a breath she didn't know she's been holding. When they were kids, Mercia's seizures had been traumatizing to witness. As they got older, and kids got meaner, the bullies began using Mercia's fits as social media fodder. Rachel can't recall the last time Mercia had an epileptic episode, though.

Mercia turns around and props herself onto her elbows. "Can you help me find the rest of my pills? There should be three left."

Rachel gets to her feet. "Yeah."

Mercia groans as she pushes herself up on the other side of the partition.

"Are you okay now?" Rachel searches the floor and picks up the first of her spilled medication. No way in hell is this medication FDA approved. Even Orion, with all his charms and magic, couldn't pull that feat off. "Are these—?"

"Goldmint."

"Relaxants, yeah, I know." Rachel bends over to pick up a second pill. The first, and only time she'd ingested goldmint— thanks to Orion's nasty little trick—she hadn't relaxed whatsoever. If anything, Rachel had become Ritalin-focused, which isn't a typical side-effect according to the manufacturer of this otherworldly drug.

The stall door opens and Mercia stumbles out into the open. "They work. They alleviate almost all of my symptoms immediately." She makes her way over to the washbasin. "Don't judge me."

"I'm not judging you." Rachel picks up the last of the pills and walks back to where Mercia leans against the washbasin. Blonde curls frame her face, barely a hair out of place, but they seem lackluster against her abnormally pale skin. "Where'd you get them?"

"There's a dealer on campus, but I'd rather not name any names. The goldmint supply is dwindling and I need it more than most," Mercia's deadpan tone is accompanied by a sigh. She holds out her hand for the pills and Rachel drops them into her open palm. "Thanks."

"No problem." Rachel picks up her discarded sling bag.

"You won't tell anyone, right?"

"It's none of my business what you do. I just came in here to fix myself up."

"I mean about the almost-seizure." Mercia's brows pinch together. Her popularity would definitely take a nosedive if this becomes public knowledge. The cruel jokes would begin anew and then it's bye-bye social life, adios Holland and Ashley, au revoir the perks of being one of Ridge Crest High's elite.

"Like I said, it's none of my business." Rachel makes her way to the farthest empty stall, hoping it will be enough of a hint for Mercia to leave her alone. As she reaches her destination, something on the floor catches her eye. A four inch figurine, bone white and expertly crafted, positioned in front of the faded porcelain toilet. "Odd."

"You know Greg's paying us to act all gooey and doe-eyed with him to get on your nerves, right?" Mercia says.

Two weeks ago, Mercia had been Greg's pick-o'-the-week and it'd been a stellar performance from both parties. Since summer ended, Greg's gone above and beyond to flaunt his romantic attachments by sucking face with a new girl every week or so.

Not that Rachel really cares what Greg does or doesn't do in his spare time anymore—she just never figured him to be Mercia's type.

"It's not, like, serious or anything. It's a bit creepy if you ask me, especially since he's still obsessed with you. I mean, I'd be careful if I were you, but if you're into that type of thing, so be it."

"I honestly don't care what Greg's up to. It was a mutual break-up." Rachel picks up the weird totem, which resembles Mercia when she's having a seizure a tad too much. "Hey, Mercia, did you drop this?" Rachel asks, exiting the stall.

Mercia takes the figurine and blanches as she inspects the obscene carving. She turns it around in her hands again and again, before she looks up to meet Rachel's gaze. A glower burns bright in her stormy eyes. "Is this some kind of sick joke?"

"I literally just fou—"

Mercia throws the figurine against the wall, shattering it into pieces. The shards ricochet across the bathroom.

Rachel barely ducks in time to avoid one of the pieces hitting her squarely between the eyes. Whatever amicability there'd been between them has been obliterated, just like the creepy figurine.

Speechless, Rachel watches as Mercia picks up her bag, turns on her heels, and storms from the bathroom. The door squeals shut, and an oversized, fading graffiti masterpiece proclaims HIGH SCHOOL SUX.

"Preaching to the choir, here," Rachel whispers, still unsure of how she's gone from hero to zero in a matter of seconds.

Chapter Two

Hip2B²

Red, ochre, and brown leaves dance across Griswold Road on a crisp autumn wind. The convoluted colors liven up the dreariness of the late afternoon but do nothing to alleviate Rachel's mood. A chilly gust of wind nips at her exposed arms, whispering promises of the approaching cold. She pulls the sleeves of her shirt down and pushes her windswept hair out of her face. Her gaze moves toward the ACCESS PROHIBITED sign, where a splatter of the Night Weaver's blood still dapples the faded words, staining the rusted metal edges black.

Nobody in Shadow Grove ever talks about how children had gone missing this past year, but nobody ever talks about it. Not a single person mentions the strange light show in the pitch black sky when Orion and the Night Weaver had battled it out. And while Sheriff Carter knows the children were kidnapped by grieving townsfolk—and offered as sacrifices to the Night Weaver in return for spending time with their departed loved ones—there have been no repercussions for anyone involved.

Granted, if the sheriff doesn't cover up Shadow Grove's countless tragedies and scandals, the town council would certainly have done so.

Rachel purses her lips as she tries not to listen to the faint melody coming from deep inside the forest. The sound is indistinctive, but has a familiarity to it she simply cannot place. Ever since Orion had gone after the Night Weaver, Rachel's been hearing the seductive tune, and she has battled against the song's allure for almost as long.

"Oi, Rach."

Rachel snaps her attention to where the auburn-haired Scotsman walks across the lawn, approaching the porch with his hands pushed into his jacket pockets.

"Yer daydreamin' again," Dougal says in a cheerful tone, but the worry in his ice-blue eyes is unmistakable.

She shifts in the white wicker chair, uncomfortable after having been caught staring at the forest.

The wood creaks as Dougal makes his way up the steps. "Ye all right then?"

"Fine." She drops her gaze to her hands, only to find her thumb's cuticle raw after having picked at it throughout this horrible day.

"I heard—"

"Yeah," she cuts him off before he can remind her of how badly she screwed up.

"Did ye talk to yer ma?"

Rachel shakes her head.

"Greg?" Dougal asks.

The muscles in her brow constrict into a frown. She looks up at Dougal. "Greg and I had some fun over the summer, but that's all it was—fun. So why would I speak with Greg over matters that are none of his concern?"

Ever since the football jocks took a liking to him, Dougal has preferred to spend his time with them. Girls have also taken notice of him, thanks to his tall, muscular physique and icy eyes. His distinctive brogue has faded, too, but not so much that he has lost all his exoticness.

"Why'd you really come over?" Rachel asks.

Dougal shrugs. "Ye looked lonely out here by yerself."

"I'm always by myself," she mumbles.

"Aye." Dougal sighs.

Rachel stands and walks to the porch's railing, surveying the quiet, dense woodlands that lie beyond the ACCESS PROHIBITED sign. Nothing seems out of place in there. It's as disturbingly silent as ever.

Her gaze travels to the Fraser house. "Something's wrong," she says.

"Are we talkin' typical small town wrong or fair folk wrong?" Dougal asks.

Rachel shrugs, not knowing how to explain the sudden dread in the pit of her stomach. It could be residual paranoia from the SATs? No. This is different. She reaches up to hold onto her umbrella pendant, making sure her tether to reality is still in place.

Dougal walks up beside her, studying the area, seeming to gauge the validity of her *feeling*.

"I should get Ziggy," Rachel says, unable to shake the foreboding now crawling across her skin. She heads inside the house, walking with purpose toward the staircase. "Ziggy," she calls out. Her thumb moves over the smooth surface of the pendant, which Orion had forged for her from the Ronamy Stone, an artifact that protects the wearer from Fae Influence. Her thoughts churn with growing unease.

The golden ball of Fae light bounces into view and stops on

the staircase's landing. It hovers in midair for a while before descending.

"Took you long enough," she says. Rachel reaches out to tickle the Fae light's surface, and Ziggy shimmers in delight. She makes her way outside, where she finds Dougal still standing at the porch's railing, now frowning. "See something?"

"No, but I think I heard somethin'."

Rachel turns back to Ziggy. "Will you do a perimeter check for me, please?" The golden sphere responds by flying off the porch. Ziggy flits across the lawn in choppy movements, flying this way and that.

"Och, I still can't get used to the way ye treat yer ball o' light," Dougal mutters.

"We've gone over this already. His name is Ziggy and I'd appreciate it if you stop calling him something else," she says, crossing her arms.

"Ye're stranger than a platypus, ye know?"

"Don't start with me, Scotsman."

Ziggy moves swiftly around the lawn, zigging and zagging in search of whatever may be lurking about. The Fae light halts its progress when it closes in on the ACCESS PROHIBITED sign, hovers in place for a prolonged beat, before rushing across the road. She holds her breath, hoping Ziggy will bypass the Fraser house, but the sphere flies straight toward the porch, knocking into the wooden door before rebounding.

Dougal leaps over the porch railing and lands in the hydrangea bedding. His powerful legs push him forward, toward the rosemary hedges. He hurdles over the hedges, clears Griswold Road at record speed, and runs toward the Fraser house.

"Nan," he shouts, rushing to the front door.

Rachel runs after him, pulling her cell phone out of her pocket as she takes the long way around.

Dougal pulls the front door open and disappears inside the house.

"Call an ambulance," he cries from inside, the fear in his voice chilling her to the core.

Rachel's thumb moves over the screen.

"Nine-one-one, what's your emergency?" the female dispatcher answers after a single ring.

Amy Gilligan, one of the few female deputies at the Sheriff's Department, always gets stuck answering emergency calls. Rachel's certain it's because Sheriff Carter's is a sexist, but he's never publically been called out on his misogyny or bigotry.

"Amy, this is Rachel Cleary. We need an ambulance sent to the Fraser house. Something's happened to Mrs. Crens—"

"Ma'am, I need a street address," Amy interrupts her, sounding almost bored.

"Seriously, Amy? You've lived in Shadow Grove your entire life, *now* you suddenly need a freaking street address spelled out for you? Why don't I draw you a map while I'm at it? Shall I email it to your supervisor or—" Rachel took a deep breath, calmed herself, and rambled off the address.

"I've dispatched an ambulance, ma'am. Stay on the line until they reach you," Amy interrupts again with her unchanging tone.

Rachel rushes up the porch steps and enters the house through the open front door.

Dougal is on his knees beside Mrs. Crenshaw, who lies sprawled at the bottom of the staircase. Her face is twisted in pain, a few bruises bloom on her arms and legs.

"She fell," Dougal states the obvious in a childlike tone. His hands hover above his grandmother, as if he doesn't know where to touch or how to make her pain dissipate. "Nan?" he says, voice cracking with emotion.

Frozen in the doorway, Rachel can only stare at Mrs. Crenshaw—the closest thing she has to a grandmother.

"Ma'am, what is the situation?" Amy's voice is a monotonous murmur, unsuited to the dire circumstances. Why isn't she freaking out? Mrs. Crenshaw, up until this point, has always been a firecracker. Nothing could keep her down, except for the occasional bout of arthritis. "Hello?"

"It appears Mrs. Crenshaw's taken a bad fall down the stairs," Rachel says. She moves to kneel by Dougal's side. "Mrs. Crenshaw? The ambulance is on its way. Hold on, okay."

Her fingertips brush against papery skin that is almost translucent with age as she pushes the Mrs. Crenshaw's white hair from her face. Seeing her like this—the same woman who once called herself a "drop of deadly poison"—is unbearable. Rachel's emotions pummel down the wall of shock, threatening to unravel her from the inside out.

Rachel stands and says, "I'll go wait for the ambulance. Don't move her."

"I'm not an idiot," Dougal snaps, reverting to his thick accent.

She ignores the retort and walks out of the house before she can lose her composure. He's in shock, too, after all. On the porch, she clenches her trembling hands into fists and allows her mind to wander to other things—mundane things—because she can't deal with the present. Maybe later she'll figure out what to do about the SATs and Mrs. Crenshaw's spill, but not *now*. Not here.

The world doesn't feel the way it should. It doesn't seem right.

Ziggy sidles up to her side and nudges her shoulder, begging for attention.

The glowing ball floats at eye-level before moving an inch toward the front door, then back to her. Ziggy repeats the action, as if beckoning her back into the house.

Rachel's shoulders drop in defeat. "I know."

Ziggy weaves around in the air, repeatedly moving between Rachel and the front door.

"What?"

Ziggy doesn't edge closer to the doorway, doesn't enter until Rachel follows. Ziggy slips into the house as she nears the front door. Her gaze drops to where Dougal is holding Mrs. Crenshaw's hand, tears running down his face. This isn't a sight she's prepared herself to witness, even if she knows it's only natural for him to respond this way.

Ziggy flies into her line of vision and blocks Rachel's view, demanding her undivided attention.

"Fine." Her voice quivers with unshed tears.

Ziggy skirts around the living room, flying directly for Mrs. Crenshaw's armchair, and hangs above the side-table.

Rachel makes her way around the furniture, careful to avoid Dougal and his fallen grandmother. The sirens blare as they near the end of Griswold Road, growing louder.

"What is it?"

The Fae light dips to the side-table, sinking slowly to extend the dramatic reveal. Her eyes narrow in annoyance, but Ziggy shoots away before she can chastise him. With Ziggy no longer in view, she spots the strange object sitting next to the TVs remote control and picks it up, both amazed and horrified by the intricate details that went into crafting the ivory depiction of Mrs. Crenshaw. Rachel lays the figurine flat on her palm. She raises her hand high enough to measure the resemblances more accurately, and allow herself to look between Mrs. Crenshaw and the totem.

Just like Mercia this afternoon.

Red lights penetrate the house through the lace curtains. "Hide yer will-o'-the-wisp," Dougal says over his shoulder.

Rachel pockets the totem. "Ziggy, go upstairs," she says just as two EMTs, carrying their gear, enter Fraser house to tend to the injured, unconscious woman. Rachel doesn't hear the exchange between Dougal and the medics, barely hears her own thoughts anymore. The disturbing implication of the ominous carving is enough to silence the world.

"Rach," Dougal screams, shaking her by her shoulders. She blinks and meets his icy blue gaze, eyes he'd inherited from his grandmother. "I'm goin' with Nan," he says.

"Okay, I'll pack an overnight bag for her and find you at the hospital in a bit," Rachel says, her pragmatism kicking into gear. "Do you have your phone?"

"Aye," Dougal says, already moving away to where the EMTs are strapping his frail grandmother to a stretcher and stabilizing her blood pressure. "Phone yer ma, Rach. Tell her what happened."

The EMTs lift and carry his grandmother out of the house and toward the waiting ambulance, oozing professionalism as they set to work. Dougal climbs inside. He takes his grandmother's hand in his own as the door shuts, before the ambulance races off to the hospital.

"You can come out now," she says loud enough for Ziggy to

hear.

The Fae light returns to the living room, his surface rippling various shades of gold.

Rachel regards Ziggy, her only ally left at the end of Griswold Road, then looks back to the space Mrs. Crenshaw had occupied.

"Ziggy, do you want to play a game?" Her gaze returns to the Fae light. Ziggy moves in choppy movements in front of her, conveying excitement. "Let me see you flash your light."

The Fae light burns brighter then dims.

She smiles. "Okay, I'm going to ask you some questions. To answer me, you flash your light once for yes and twice for no. Do you understand?"

Ziggy flashes once.

"Good." Rachel reaches up and tickles Ziggy's surface. "First question: Was there a Fae in the house when Mrs. Crenshaw fell?"

Ziggy flies off toward the side of the house. He flits back, rushes around the staircase's bannister, and shoots up the stairs.

"Ziggy?" she calls.

Ziggy returns to his original position and flashes once, a clear answer to her question. Rachel releases a breath through her nose.

"Is the Fae still here?"

Almost instantly Ziggy flashes twice. No.

"All right. Last question: Is this the work of another Miser Fae?"

Ziggy hesitates, before finally flashing once.

Rachel pulls her lips into a straight, thin line. "Are you sure?"

Another hesitation before Ziggy's flash answers *yes*.

"Crap."

"Your grandmother's shattered hip needs to be replaced," Rachel's mother, Jenny Cleary, says softly to Dougal as she takes his hand across the table. "She'll be fine, though. It's to be expected when someone reaches that age, so it's just going to be a routine surgery."

Rachel watches Dougal while absently picking at her dinner. The mashed potatoes tastes mealy for some reason and the peas are grayish. The steak is edible, even if Rachel would've liked it to not be quite as bloody. The meal tastes as an unappetizing as it looks. Nevertheless, she's relatively sure everything on her plate is fit for human consumption.

When Dougal doesn't respond, her mother continues, "Nancy Crenshaw always bounces back. In the meantime, you're staying with us. I've already notified your parents that they can reach you here."

Dougal stares at his untouched meal, a forlorn expression on display. There's an uncharacteristic weariness to him. His shoulders are slumped, curved inward. His perpetual frown is accompanied by his downturned mouth, like he's trying to search for answers to an unsolvable question. Why now? Why his grandmother? He's definitely not the happy-go-lucky Scot Ridge Crest High's come to know and love, and with good reason.

"This weekend, the three of us are going to move your grandmother's stuff into the downstairs bedroom. I'm not sure when she'll be released from the hospital, but the last thing we need is to have her struggling up and down the stairs."

"Mrs. Crenshaw won't like it if we mess with her setup,"

Rachel says, chasing a gray pea into the pink-tinted mashed potatoes.

"Well, Mrs. Crenshaw doesn't have a say in the matter anymore." Jenny spears the overdone steak on her own plate, grimacing. "Stop playing with your food, Rachel."

"I'd hardly call this food," Rachel mumbles to herself.

"Mrs. Cleary, will ye mind if I— May I turn in early?" Dougal asks. Rachel has noticed, as has Dougal, that her mother doesn't understand him at all when he goes full Scottish.

"Sure," she says, turning her attention back to Rachel. "Honey, will you show Dougal to the guestroom and give him an extra blanket? I think there's a phantom breeze in there."

Rachel excuses herself, grateful to escape her plate, and gestures for Dougal to follow her. She leads him to the second story, down the long, winding hall, and toward the back of the house, where three guestrooms are located. The Silver Room, an airy bedroom with silver accents to break the otherwise clinical white décor, is the only room suitable for anyone to stay in.

"Are you okay?" she asks.

"Aye," Dougal mutters, dejected.

Rachel opens the built-in wardrobe and pulls out a white-and-gray striped blanket from the top shelf.

"The bathroom's through there." Rachel points to a closed door on the opposite side of the room with her free hand, before she places the blanket on the bed. "Extra towels are under the sink."

"Do ye really think Nan'll be all right?" he asks. Dougal takes a seat on the edge of the bed, the springs squealing in protest. Fear becomes apparent in his eyes.

"I do," she says. "Knowing your grandmother, I think she'll

come out stronger just to get on peoples' nerves."

He responds by giving her an incredulous look, before he shrugs. "Prob'ly."

Rachel takes out the figurine she's kept in her pocket. "I found this next to her chair," she says, handing it over as she sits beside him.

Dougal looks the totem over. "What's it?"

"I don't know, but it's the second one I've seen today, and both times were unpleasant."

His eyes move to meet her gaze. "Are ye thinkin'—?" He glances back to the figurine in his hand, studying the carving's delicate details. It must've taken the artist a ridiculous amount of time to make. "I don't know of any fair folk that leaves gifts for their victims."

"It could've been a warning?" she says, though deep down she doesn't believe this. There's something too ominous about the figurines—something she can't quite put her finger on—that makes it malignant. Rachel stands again, and says, "Do you want Ziggy to keep you company tonight?"

Dougal shakes his head.

"Okay." Rachel heads back to the doorway. "Goodnight."

"Night," he says.

She closes the door behind her and takes a moment to clear her mind. The last thing either of them need is another wild goose chase around town in search of Fae. Rachel walks back to the staircase and descends slowly.

"Nancy made me swear not to call Matthew, and Sophie lives in Scotland. What else could I do?" Jenny says to the unknown caller. There's a long silence, before she continues in a whisper, "I really don't have the strength to babysit two teenagers

23

and a geriatric tyrant."

Rachel grinds her teeth as she slips into the dining room to clear the table. Cutlery clatter into plates and glasses tinkle together as she makes her way into the kitchen to wash the dishes.

"Have you done your homework?" her mother shouts from the living room.

"Yes," she growls, plugging the drain and running the faucet to fill the sink. Rachel grabs the dishwashing soap, squirts a generous amount into the water, and watches the white bubbles grow beneath the steady downpour.

"Did you give Dougal an extra blanket?" her mother asks, now standing somewhere close behind her.

Still seething, the most she can get out is a grunt.

"Okay, good."

Rachel looks over her shoulder, ready to argue.

Her mother leans against the kitchen counter, scratching her brow.

"What's wrong?" Rachel asks, shutting off the water.

"I have to drive to Bangor soon and look after your cousins for a while," she says, before looking up. "Your aunt decided she needs a holiday. Can you believe it?"

"How convenient." Rachel waits until she's turned back to the sink before she rolls her eyes. Somehow her mother always finds an excuse to run off when things at home aren't to her liking. Her cousins, both older than Rachel, can't live by themselves without constant supervision. "When are you going?"

"I'll probably have to drive through tomorrow morning."

Rachel scrubs the dishes hard beneath the water. "And when will you be back?"

"In a week or so," her mother says. A few beats of silence

stretch between them before she blurts out an exasperated, "I can't very well say no, Rachel. She's my sister."

"I didn't say anything to the contrary."

Her mother huffs in response. "I can feel you judging me from over there."

Rachel pulls her lips into a tight line as she focuses her anger on cleaning the dirty dishes, cutlery, and glasses. It's not like she can do anything else. Her mom's going to leave whether she wants her to or not, so what's the point in even trying to get her to stay?

"You'll keep an eye on things, right?"

"Don't I always?" Rachel says, setting the dish on the drying rack.

Another awkward extended silence, before her mother says, "Will you get Mrs. Crenshaw's room ready for her? I'll be back before she comes home, I'm sure, but—"

"I will. Don't worry."

The frustrated sigh is followed by a simple, "Thanks."

Rachel listens to the retreating footsteps. Her mother first moves back toward the living room, before she changes direction and makes her way upstairs. Rachel halts her relentless scrubbing of the dishes. There's no use fighting against Jenny Cleary when her mind's already been made up. She's, after all, as stubborn as she is beautiful. Ask anyone in town.

This time she's not coming back. The thought pops into Rachel's head from nowhere.

After everything Jenny's endured—becoming a widow at such a young age, having a mental breakdown and then keeping it from her only child, struggling to get by as a single parent, and the whole situation with the Night Weaver—Rachel doesn't hold the need to distance herself from this godforsaken town against her mother. Heck, no one will even bat an eyelash if she hits the road and never looks back. The Night Weaver's manipulation and influence over the summer is just the proverbial cherry on the cake.

"Don't be absurd," she whispers to herself, finishing up with the dishes.

She pulls the plug and watches the water swirl down the drain. Drying her hands with a dishtowel, she looks out of the kitchen window where the moonlight brightens up the otherwise dark backyard. It's quiet out there—not creepy quiet, just nighttime quiet. Peaceful.

It's the calm before the storm.

Chapter Three
Chilled to the Marrow

Long before the sun is up, Rachel awakens from an unseasonal chill. Still half-asleep and shivering, she wraps a blanket around her shoulders and stumbles out of bed. She exhales puffs of air, her extremities numb. With Ziggy bouncing along by her side, Rachel crosses her bedroom and opens the door. She exits into the hallway, tiptoeing to where the thermostat is located, and turns up the heat without paying close attention to her actions. She quickly retreats to her bedroom with Ziggy in tow, closes her bedroom door again, and dashes back to bed.

"What are the chances of you being able to warm me up?" she whispers. The golden sphere bobs in place, before it slips back to its preferred locale—snuggled up beneath the covers next to her feet. "Thought so," she says through chattering teeth.

Rachel pulls the duvet up to her ears. She inhales cool air through her nostrils and exhales warm air into the space between her body and the blanket, hoping to get cozy that way. A few minutes pass, but the cold lingers. Groaning, she gets out of bed a second time to check on the window, figuring she might have forgotten to close it properly before she turned in.

As Rachel pulls the curtains aside, Ziggy rolls out from

underneath the covers and illuminates the interior of the bedroom. The golden glow confirms the window is shut fast. Not even a trickle of a breeze can get inside. She blinks a few times, lifting the fog in her mind so she can figure out why her bedroom is freezing.

Ice forms on the edges of the glass and quickly freezes over the entire windowpane. Her heart thumps faster, while she moves her hand to the umbrella pendant.

"Ziggy?" her voice quivers.

The golden orb rushes to her side just as an unseen finger traces a line through the ice. The accompanying squeak as a second line is traced makes her forget all about the cold. A third line is traced, forming an *H*. She watches on, her palms sweating. Soon, the word HELP comes into existence. Rachel's legs thaw enough for her to take a step closer, one hand still wrapped firmly around the pendant.

Orion's face suddenly flashes in the windowpane, mouth opening into a scream, eyes pleading.

The alarm on her nightstand blares, startling her out of the inexplicably realistic nightmare. Her eyelids shoot open, and she stares at the white ceiling, heart still pounding. Rachel's hair clings to her skin, while her body is tangled in the bedsheets. She brushes the hair out of her eyes, focusing on getting her breathing under control.

"Rachel, you're going to be late for school," her mother shouts from the other side of the bedroom door. "Get up, get ready. This is not a drill."

"I'm up." Rachel reaches over to hit the OFF switch on her alarm. When the clock stops its incessant noise, Ziggy rolls up from her feet and comes to rest on her pillow. "You should've woken me when you realized I was having a nightmare."

She pets the golden sphere, which glows brighter.

"It's too late to suck up to me now."

She shifts one leg off the edge of the bed and places a bare foot onto the purple-and-black geometric carpet. Rachel groans as she remembers her abysmal performance with the SATs, wonders if she'll be able to broach the subject with her mother before she travels to Bangor. She pulls herself up and throws her other leg off the bed. It's probably best to rip the Band-Aid off quickly, as painful as it may be.

She rubs her temples and shifts her gaze toward the window. The curtains are drawn, unmoving. The image Orion in peril is still fresh in her mind, renewing her fear of what might have befallen the missing Fae prince.

"It was only a nightmare," she whispers. "He's probably living it up in the palace. Right, Ziggy?"

Ziggy rolls onto her lap, before dimming ever so slightly.

Her heart sinks. "One flash for yes, two flashes for no. Is he in trouble?"

Ziggy doesn't answer her—maybe because he doesn't know either.

Her fingers move to the umbrella pendant. She turns the pendant around between her fingers, and says, "Will you be able to find him if we cross into the Fae Realm?"

This time there is no warm golden light to answer her question.

"Rachel," her mother cries out again.

"I'm up, Mom," Rachel barks back. She returns her attention to the sphere on her lap, whispering, "I need to get ready for school—"

Two flashes signals the *no*. Ziggy floats up and weaves through the air, still flashing gold in timed intervals.

Rachel gets out of bed and walks to her wardrobe. "I'm not going into the forest without a plan, Zigs. Besides, Orion made me promise not to follow him and you can't take me to him even if I did."

The Fae light zips through the air like an aggravated wasp, weaving in and out of her line of vision. It flashes once, dims. Flashes once more.

"Settle down."

Rachel pulls out a tank top, a cute sweater, and a pair of jeans to wear for the day. She inadvertently scans the interior of her wardrobe, taking inventory of what lies on the shelves and hangs from the railing. She has no idea what Orthega's fashions are like. Surely nothing she has lying around in her closet will be suitable. Maybe last year's Halloween costume can be repurposed for a journey into the Fae Realm? She touches the red cloak with the silky black lining. She could wear her Little Red Riding Hood costume inside-out if need be, and hide whatever clothes she wears underneath. Aside from the cloak, though, she's at a loss.

When Rachel's done dressing, she grabs her sling bag and opens her bedroom door.

Dougal comes down the hallway, but he doesn't look like he's in the mood for school. The bags under his eyes are pronounced, his hair is tousled, and he keeps yawning.

"Ye look like ye've seen better days," Dougal says as they meet at the staircase landing.

"Ditto," she says. Together, they descend the stairs. "Are you sure you should go to school today?"

"I'm not goin' to sit around here and count my toes the

whole day," he says.

"It's better than listening to lectures on things we'll probably never use in the future, though."

"Aye, but I don't like being alone all the time, either."

When they reach the bottom of the staircase, Rachel notices her mother rushing for the front door, holding her eyeliner pencil and lipstick in one hand and grabbing her coat with the other. She looks up to see them standing near the staircase and sighs in relief.

"There's lunch money on the kitchen counter, pizza money is on the microwave, and I'll pay some extra cash into your account so you can buy groceries for the week." Her mother sounds out of breath. It's like she can't get out of Shadow Grove fast enough. "Don't let me hear about you two holding parties while I'm gone."

"Yer leavin', Mrs. Cleary?" Dougal asks with a hint of surprise.

"Yes, dear." She looks at her wristwatch. "My sister called me last night—"

"I'll fill Dougal in on the way to school," Rachel cuts her off. "Bye, Mom. Love you."

"Remember to get Mrs. Crenshaw's room ready tomorrow." She rushes out of the front door, leaving an annoyed Rachel and dumbfounded Dougal behind.

"I hope nothin's wrong with yer aunt." Dougal finally breaks his silence as they walk to the kitchen to find something to eat.

"Nothing's wrong. My mom just looks for reasons to bail when things get inconvenient at home." Rachel grabs a couple of bananas from the fruit bowl on the kitchen counter and finds some travel-sized yogurt tubs in the fridge. She hands the breakfast-to-go to Dougal, who stares at the banana and yogurt. "It's the breakfast of champions in this house."

"Ye sure we shouldn't go through the drive-thru on the way to school?"

"And risk being tardy?"

Dougal scoffs at her reason.

"Sure, fine. Whatever." Rachel leads him into the living room.

"Do ye wanna skip school today?" he asks, stuffing his breakfast into his backpack.

"Can't," Rachel says. "Fridays are Mr. Davenport's weekly test days, because clearly he has nothing better to do with his time."

She opens the front door and exits the house with Dougal following close behind. They don't speak on their way to her car, but he does raise an eyebrow as he peers across the roof of her Hyundai i10.

"I had a nightmare last night," she says, opening the driver's door.

"About?"

"Orion." Rachel climbs into the car and Dougal slips into the passenger seat. She continues with a vague retelling of the nightmare, telling him about how real it felt. "I think he's in trouble."

Dougal sighs heavily.

She glances at him from underneath her eyelashes and clicks her seatbelt into place. "What?"

"Rach, he explicitly told ye not to go after him. Remember?"

"I remember." Rachel turns the key in the ignition, and the engine whirrs to life.

"I can't go with ye. At least, not while Nan's in the hospital," he says.

She reverses out of the driveway. "I know," she says.

"And ye still wanna go into the Fae Realm? By yerself?" Dougal's frustration leeches into his voice. When she doesn't contradict him, he says, "Yer a damn fool, Rachel Cleary."

Rachel bites back a cutting remark of her own. "Are you done mothering me yet?"

"No. I have a few choice words left on the matter," he retorts.

"Have at it then. Get it *all* off your chest now, because once I get out of this car, we're not getting into this again," she says. When Dougal doesn't respond, she shifts her gaze away from the road to look at him. "Well? I'm waiting."

Dougal crosses his arms and shakes his head. "What's the point? Ye have already made up yer mind."

Rachel turns her attention back to the road. "Actually, I *never* said I'm going. You just assumed I am."

When they near the Eerie Creek Bridge, Dougal rolls his eyes. "Do ye even know where Orion is?"

"I'm sure Ziggy will figure it out *if* we were to go, which I haven't decided on yet."

"Yer gonna get yerself killed because of that oversized lightbulb, and I will become the Sheriff's prime suspect." Dougal pushes his hand through his hair, his usually pale complexion already reddening as his blood pressure spikes.

"*If* I go, which I doubt I'll be doing, I'm already coming up with a way to explain my disappearance in case I don't return. Stop worrying," Rachel says.

"I don't like this one bit." Dougal continues grumbling in

Gaelic, much to Rachel's dismay.

When he's let off enough steam, he sulks for the remainder of the journey to Ridge Crest High, situated on the other side of the moderately sized New England town. She takes the backroads today, driving through the suburban areas in order to avoid the traffic on Main Road, but the scenic route doesn't improve his sour mood. Even his takeout breakfast isn't enough to turn him amicable.

Rachel expects him to jump out of the car as soon as she pulls into a parking space in front of the school, but Dougal surprises her by staying put.

He calmly gets out after she's pulled the key from the ignition, waits until she's retrieved her bag and locked the doors with the fob key, and walks her up to the entrance. Still, his annoyance doesn't dissipate. It rolls off him in waves, crashing into her—and anyone else who dares to get close to the Scotsman—with a tsunami's strength.

"Can you, like, relax or something? You're scaring the freshmen worse than usual," she hisses as they walk through the crowded hallway.

"No," he grumbles, pulling his backpack higher up on his shoulders.

"Dougal, my man," Vinesh calls his greeting as he and a few other footballers approach from the other end of the hallway.

Dougal scoffs, murmurs something unintelligible, and gives Vinesh a halfhearted high-five.

"I heard about your grandmother," Joe Jr. says. "Is she okay?"

"I s'pose. It could've been worse," Dougal answers.

Rachel heads to her locker, just a few feet away from the

gathering of teenage boys, and listens as the football jocks bestow platitudes and sympathies on Dougal. They mean well, of course, but Dougal is clearly not in the right mind for this. She unlocks her locker, exchanges the textbooks in her bag for her purple ledger, and checks her hair in the mirror affixed inside the door.

"They're rowdier than usual," Cam says beside her. "Reason?"

"Not that it's any of your business, but Dougal's grandmother took a bad fall yesterday."

"Is she all right?" Cam asks.

"The better question is whether the doctors and nurses are okay." Rachel closes her locker.

Cam snickers.

"You're earlier than usual."

"English test," he says. "Thought I'd try and study for it in between my extracurricular activities."

"Which includes?" Rachel leans her shoulder against the locker, giving him a once-over, unable to keep her suspicion at bay.

Cam shrugs. "A little of this, a bit of that. Obviously it's nothing good."

"Obviously," she says. "So, what's your deal, Cameron Mayer? According to Holland Keith, you're a gay drifter who skins cats beneath the full moon." Rachel earns herself an incredulous look. "Nobody believes a word that comes out of her mouth, though. Don't worry."

"Jeez, remind me not to get on her bad side," Cam mumbles.

Rachel flashes him a smile. "The worst thing that'll happen to you *if* you get on her bad side is you'll end up like me."

"Breathtakingly beautiful?" he says.

She feels her cheeks warm. "You're a smooth talker, but no. I was thinking more along the lines of becoming a pariah."

"What's that?" Dougal's voice reaches her ears.

"Oh, this? I dunno, man. I found it in my locker this morning. Vinesh got one too," Brandon answers.

"Can I see?" Dougal asks.

Curious, Rachel looks over as Dougal inspects something in his large hands. She can't make out exactly what it is, but when the blood drains from Dougal's face, her concern intensifies.

"Vin, can I see yers?" He glances up to meet Rachel's gaze. The worry seems to have changed into something else, something close to pure dread. She halfheartedly excuses herself and walks up to his side.

"Sure," Vinesh says. He hands over a bone white carving to Dougal. "They're kinda creepy, but sorta cool. We don't know who sent them or how they got into our lockers, but we're not the only ones who got one."

Her blood turns to ice as she looks at the two carvings. The one is a figurine of Brandon in his practice gear—lying face-down, sprawled out. The other totem depicts Vinesh dressed in much the same manner, lying flat on his back, his neck twisted at an awkward angle.

"Ye're seein' this?" he asks her in a whisper, so nobody nearby can overhear them.

"Yes."

"Who else got one?" Dougal asks the others.

"I overheard Bianca Novak calling hers disgusting, and then there's Rebecca Franklin," Brandon answers.

"Don't forget Ashley Benson," Vinesh says.

"Oh, yeah. She got one, too."

"All right." He hands their totems back. "I'll see ye in a wee bit then," Dougal says to his friends. He turns to face Rachel. "We have History first period?"

She stares at him blankly. "Yes, but—"

"Let's go."

Rachel waves halfheartedly to Cam as she turns on her heels. They walk quietly through the crowded hallway, side-by-side. Most of the students make way for Dougal, who towers above everyone at school—staff included. The freshmen give him wide-eyed looks of wonder. Girls flutter their eyelashes at him, lick their lips, giggle together and whisper about his good looks.

Yes, he's easy on the eyes, but wow. Have some dignity already.

"The warning bell is about to ring."

"Ye can skip the class today. This is more important than learnin' about Napoleon's defeat at the Battle of Waterloo."

"We're not even studying that, Dougal," she says in a higher than normal pitch.

"Fine, Nixon's Watergate thin'. Same diffs." He waves his mistake off as inconsequential.

Technically, the history curriculum is trivial in comparison to the looming horrors awaiting Ridge Crest High's students, especially if those totems *are*, in fact, signifiers of their imminent future. There's no question about what matter takes precedence, but it's difficult for Rachel to get her head out of school mode when she's physically at school. Besides, who in their right minds can get mixed up with Napoleon and Nixon? They're in the same class, for heaven's sake! She doesn't have the energy to call him out on his ignorance—or laziness—this time, though. Not with everything that's going on.

Rachel leads him through the labyrinth of corridors, past the lockers and classes and dawdling students. The first bell rings and students scurry, hoping to avoid a detention slip for tardiness. The hallway slowly clears. By the time the second bell rings, they're heading into the old school's wing, where hardly anyone wanders at any time of day.

"Here," she says, indicating to the girls' bathroom. Rachel looks over her shoulder to make sure nobody's spying on them before she turns her attention back to him. "Do you want to go inside?"

His eyes pin on the door leading to the girls' bathroom. "No," Dougal says. "And ye found th' second one on Nan's side-table?"

"Yes."

His gaze shifts to study the hallway, which ends in a T-junction. Dougal points ahead and says, "Where does this go?"

"Old schoolhouse," she says.

He walks past her without another word, heading into the seldom-explored bowels of Ridge Crest High. Rachel follows. What else can she do?

"If you want to hunt for ghosts, perhaps we should come back tonight when they're active?"

"Ye and I both know this ain't no wraith's doin'." He slows his pace so she can catch up. "There's another Fae in town, Rach, and the bastard's gone and hurt my Nan. This is personal, yeah?"

"I get it, Dougal, I really do. But what do you expect us to find by wandering into the old schoolhouse? We are defenseless, and wholly unprepared to take on another Miser Fae by ourselves," Rachel says. "Your grandmother and Orion both insinuated that the Night Weaver is one of the weaker Miser Fae.

We don't know what else is out there and we definitely don't know how strong they are."

"Go back then," he says. "I don't need yer help."

Rachel stops in her tracks, her eyes wide and forehead creasing. "Real mature."

When he doesn't respond, she hurries back to his side and continues down the corridor. There's no way she's going to let him go after a Miser Fae alone. She'll never forgive herself if he winds up dead all because she didn't want to miss a class.

The hallway branches off. The old bell tower is to the right. To the left lie some classrooms, which'd fallen into disuse decades earlier.

"Let's start at the old classrooms and work our way back here," she suggests. Rachel gestures to the left, indicating where they should begin.

Dougal nods, turns left, and continues forward.

After a while, she says, "I know you're angry with me because you think I want to go into the Fae Realm and find Orion."

He exhales through his nose. "Why couldn't ye have preoccupied yer time with Greg, huh? Greg's a bahookie, aye, but at least I could've kept him in line. I can't keep a Fae prince from hurtin' ye, Rach."

"Damn it, I don't *need* you protecting me," she says, unable to keep the frustration from her tone. "Also, what in heaven's name is a *bahookie*?"

He crosses his arms, closing himself off. "Somethin' ye're too good for anyways."

Asking him to change his nature, to disregard one of the fundamental elements of who he is, isn't fair. Still, it's exasperating to have a part-time bodyguard, watching her every move so he can keep her safe, especially when she'd been doing perfectly fine on her own for the majority of her life. Besides, he can't just show up and play the big brother when it suits him.

Her thoughts come to an abrupt halt halfway to the end of the hallway. The white paint is yellowed, cracked and peeling away from the walls. The doors are located closer together and scratched-up from years of neglect. All the windows are boarded up and the air is stuffy with dust and disuse. Rachel's attention shifts to a specific door, green instead of the usual red, with a faded sign fixed at eye level. BOILER ROOM, it states.

"What's the matter?" Dougal asks when she stops in front of the door.

She studies the thin wooden partition from top to bottom.

"Rach?"

The weirdly shaped object sticking out of the lock seems to call out to her. Not like the forest. Simply because it's so out of place. The hair at the back of her neck stands at attention as she reaches out to touch it. She recoils, shudders for reasons she can't explain, and looks to Dougal.

"Are you sure you want us to do this now?" she asks. "Because I have a really bad feeling about what's waiting behind this door."

Chapter Four
The Skeleton Key

Dougal pulls the strange object—long, pale, and gnarled, like a twisted twig—from the keyhole. Rachel is reminded of the ghost boy who's said to walk these halls, leaving destruction in his wake, playing tricks on anyone who dares to enter the old school building. After all, if Fae are real, why can't ghosts be?

"It's a key," Dougal says, frowning. "A key made from bone by the look of it."

Her nose pulls up in disgust. "This is a bad idea."

Dougal reaches to the doorknob, twists it and pushes the door open. The hinges don't squeak or creak or whine, as if they've recently been oiled. It's almost creepier this way. Almost. A gush of warm air hits them head-on, along with a cloying smell that churns her stomach.

He pulls his shirt over his mouth and nose. "It smells pure rancid down there."

Rachel uses her sweater's collar to clamp over her own mouth and nose, unable to respond lest she vomits up the nothingness in her stomach.

Dougal reaches inside the dark interior and pulls down on a rope. A lightbulb flickers on, swinging to and fro from the ceiling. Shadows elongate in the yellow light, dance in staccato against the boxy walls. A small landing with a staircase, leading down into the depths of the school, appears ominous in the half-light.

Rachel wants to beg Dougal not to let her go into the bowels of the school, but her pride keeps her silent.

"I bet ye there's nothin' to be scared of at the bottom of this staircase." His words are muffled behind his shirt, but the unconvinced tone is clear.

Ignoring his fake bravado, afraid she'll sound snide if she addresses it, she simply says, "Let's just get this over with."

Dougal carefully descends, the darkness swallowing him whole. She follows, although her footing is uncertain on the narrow concrete steps while her eyes adjust to the lighting. With her free hand, she searches for a bannister to keep herself steady. She finds the cool, thick metal railing, which feels awkward beneath her hand. It's like no care was taken when the bannister was painted. Her breathing sounds loud in her own ears, panicked, but it's the best she can do considering the smell.

This is the epitome of stupidity.

Dougal stops at the bottom of the stairs, his hand moving across the wall, as if he's blindly searching for a light switch.

"I doubt there are any other—" Before Rachel can say more, phosphorous lights flicker on, a mechanical buzz resonating from the long, white bulbs lining the ceiling. She groans from the sudden brightness and blinks to clear her sight. "I stand corrected."

She dares to take the sweater away from her mouth and nose, only to be assaulted by the smell of rot. Rachel gags. The disgusting odor coats her tongue, esophagus, and stomach lining.

She rushes to the corner of the basement area and heaves, spilling mostly digestive juices onto the concrete floor. The undeniable stench of decay is everywhere, clinging to every part of the basement, to her clothes and hair. She retches again.

"All right?" Dougal asks, rubbing one palm across her back while he tries to keep her hair out of her face.

"No. This is the second time I'm throwing up in as many days."

"Are ye up th' duff?"

"Huh?"

"Are ye pregnant then?" he says without humor.

"*No*. For heaven's sake, Dougal, what do you take me for?"

He shrugs. "Jist wonderin'."

"Well, stop wondering about stupid things and start thinking about why it smells like something's died down here," Rachel says.

"Aye."

She wipes her mouth with the back of her hand and slowly straightens to look around the basement area. Colorful pipes run the length of the space, ending now and then in large metallic containers. Dust and grit layers the floor, seemingly undisturbed for months—maybe years—until now. When her gaze falls on Dougal, he no longer wears the mask of annoyance. There's concern in his expression, and an obvious hint of fear glimmering in his eyes.

"Are ye ready tae continue?" he asks.

Something crunches nearby, like a foot accidentally sliding across the filthy floor. They both look in the direction of the sound, searching for a nonexistent lurker. Ice runs through Rachel's veins. She grabs Dougal's arm and stares at the unidentifiable heap lying near the bottom of a metallic container.

"What?" he hisses.

Rachel points to the crumpled heap—*Please let it be fabric.*

Dougal's gaze drifts over to the area. His frown becomes more pronounced as he places a hand on her shoulder. She can't figure out if the gesture is to hold her back or if he wants to use her as a shield. At this point, anything's possible. She drops her hand to her side and they slowly move together toward the metallic container, hesitant to find out what exactly they're dealing with.

The closer they dare to move, the more intense the repugnant smell grows. A persistent buzzing becomes louder. Rachel swats a fat fly away from her face. The heap stirs slightly, making a sickly, squelching sound, disturbing the swarm of insects ever so slightly.

She and Dougal halt and wait for any other sudden movements. When nothing else occurs in the brief reprieve, they take another step closer.

Eyes stare up at Rachel from a flat, unrecognizable face that's haphazardly folded into a neck and torso. Boneless limbs lie every which way, stretched out beyond recognition. A swollen tongue hangs from the mouth, lips pulled into an awkward, ugly gape. It looks like a film prop or a twisted Halloween decoration that'd been left out in the sun. The heap twitches again and a bulge appears in the neck. A thick, serpentine thing slips out of the mouth, protruding from between the lips, slinks across the flattened nose, and whips the chubby cheek. It quickly disappears before a bloody snout becomes visible. Whiskers move and beady eyes stares out from the jawless face, cradled between broken teeth.

Rachel steps back and suppresses a scream, which comes out

as a squeak. She stares in abject horror at the scene. Her stomach flips in revulsion. The damage is done, though. The image will forever haunt her nightmares.

"In the name of the Wee Man," Dougal whispers, aghast.

"I told you," she says. Anger takes over as she opens her eyes again. She averts her gaze to look directly at Dougal, his face now the shade of ash. "I freaking told you we shouldn't come down here, didn't I?"

His eyes fix on the boneless body, his jaw works as if he's speaking under his breath, but he can't find his voice.

"Dougal, c'mon." She nudges his shoulder, pushing his immense form backward so he can snap out of his stupor.

"He's boneless. Utterly boneless," he finally utters, unable to prize his gaze away from the heap of human remains. Dougal raises his hand, wipes his palm over his forehead and eyes, and shakes his head. "How's it even possible?"

"If we stick around here for much longer, I'm pretty sure we'll find out. Let's go." Rachel tugs at his sleeve, but he doesn't budge. "We need to report it."

"Aye," he concedes.

"We need to report this *now*."

He nods, but doesn't move his feet. The shock seems to have gotten the best of him. It's understandable, but considering the killer could still be lurking somewhere nearby, watching them, waiting to strike—

Rachel tries again. Unable to keep the quiver from her voice, she hisses, "Dougal, damn it."

"I heard ye the first time," he barks, snapping away his gaze from the wretched soul. "Unlike ye, I have to process my emotions when I come across murdered folks. Not everyone can go on unaltered like a bloody robot."

Surprised by his outburst, she says in a low, threatening tone, "What's *that* supposed to mean?"

Dougal breathes loudly through his nose, and marches past her. "Ye know full well what I mean."

"I actually don't." She balls her hands into fists, exasperation and confusion stiffening her muscles. "No, what are you going on about?"

"Och, please," Dougal mutters. He spins around to face her, cutting off access to the exit. His face is still red, but his ice blue eyes have grown even colder. "Ye're so calm, ye barely blinked right now." He gestures in the general direction of the corpse. "Normal people don't react like that. And don't even get me started on yer pompousness."

"Now I'm pompous?" Rachel tries making sense of the warped puzzle pieces in her mind. "Sorry, but I'm struggling to understand how I got to be the bad guy here. It's not like I killed the guy."

"The way ye talk. It's like ye're always talkin' down to me, to Nan, to everyone," he interrupts her. "Ye never show who ye are underneath the fakeness, and Lord help me, ye always know what's best. Even when ye don't know *anythin'*, ye're somehow always right. It's annoyin' to say the least. No wonder ye don't have any friends."

In her peripheral, she notices something lingering nearby. Rachel turns away from Dougal, searching for the lurker. There's nothing there, though—it's probably just her mind playing tricks on her as it processes that traumatizing image.

Ready to stand up for herself, she turns to Dougal, when suddenly she notices it again. The hair on the back of her neck stands on end. Her heart picks up speed as she tries discerning the ghostlike figure from the corner of her eye.

"We need to go," she says.

"I don't know who ye are, Rachel. It's like ye have no depth as a person." When she doesn't respond, he says, "Freak out, for God's sake!"

The figure takes a clipped step toward them, limbs bending unnaturally. It makes a staccato movement with its shoulders, before taking another step forward. The creature's head jerks to the side, fingers twitch revealing talon-like nails. The rest of the strange creature's body is obscured as it flickers in and out of existence, as if it's stuck between two worlds.

Rachel's heart pounds harder with her growing anxiety. She's about to make a run for it when Dougal presses his balled hand against his head. His fingers move into his hair, violently tugging clumps from his scalp. A deafening roar rips from his throat. The sound rebounds.

"What's happenin' to me?" He goes down onto one knee.

"Fae Influence, I suspect." Rachel grabs hold of him by snaking her arm around his waist, and helps get back to his feet.

Dougal drapes an arm across her shoulders for support, leaning on her with much of his immense weight. He drags his feet as she half-carries him the way they'd come. He's not the easiest person to maneuver, but she manages to get him up the stairs regardless of the approaching flickering creature. Rachel kicks the door shut behind them and hears the lock click into place. Whether the barrier would provide a modicum of protection, however, is debatable.

"It feels like there's a swarm of bees buzzin' round in my head," he explains through labored breaths.

"Hold on," Rachel says. She comes to a stop halfway up the

hallway, leans Dougal against the wall and makes sure he's steady before reaching to the back of her neck. With deft hands, Rachel unclips the umbrella necklace, and, holding one side of the pendant with her index finger and thumb, presses part of the smooth stone against his hand.

Dougal blinks rapidly, the redness of his skin fading away in an instant.

"Better?" she asks.

"Aye," he says, sounding relieved.

"Good."

They remain quiet for a moment, frozen in the main, deserted hallway of the old schoolhouse, before Dougal says, "We can't report this."

Rachel's eyes widen. "Our fingerprints and shoeprints and possibly some of my DNA are down there. We *need* to report it, unless you want us to become murder suspects when the body starts to stink up the whole school."

"There's a real mean Fae down there, too."

"Yeah." Rachel sighs. "So, what do we do?"

"I don't know how to put a proper outfit together half the time and now ye want me to come up with a plan to deal with this?"

"Contrary to popular belief, I don't have *all* the answers." She fixes her free hand on her hip and taps her foot, waiting for him to continue his earlier tirade. Fae Influence or not, the insults he'd thrown at her had still burrowed into her mind. He'd hurt her, more than she would ever admit out loud, because he isn't wrong.

Dougal pushes his tongue against the inside of his cheek as he ponders their next move. With a hefty sigh, he says, "Seems like yer gonna 'ave to go find Orion."

Chapter Five
Rickety Old Things

"What happened to the whole 'I can't protect ye from a Fae prince' thing?" Rachel raises an eyebrow.

Dougal gives her a mildly infuriated glare, but at the same time she can see the ice in his gaze thawing.

She lifts her free hand up in mock surrender. "Hey, I'm just paraphrasing you."

"Now is not the time to grow a sense of humor," he mutters. "How do we get outta here without bein' seen?"

Rachel points straight ahead, where an emergency exit is situated down the hallway. "Are you good to walk on your own yet?"

"Aye, but we'll have to walk fast. I'm not keen on gettin' a repeat performance of whatever that Fae did," he says, releasing the pendant.

She fastens the necklace around her neck. "I don't know, you seem to have gotten everything off your chest."

"Yer pokin' at the bear, Rach."

"I'm just having a little fun," she says.

Ready to leave this unsavory part of Ridge Crest High still in one piece, they head briskly for the faded green double doors.

Dougal glances over his shoulder. His eyes widen as he lengthens his strides, moving faster ahead of her. She instinctively follows his gaze. The boiler room's door swings open behind them, slamming hard against the wall, wood splintering as a result. Nothing seems to exit the boiler room and there's no obvious sign of anyone following them, but that's not saying much.

She turns back to the front, where Dougal is struggling to open the emergency door.

"Push down and forward." She races to catch up with him.

"I know how to open a bloody door." He grunts from the effort.

"Push harder."

She uses her momentum to slam her shoulder into the door, hands grappling for the bar. She pushes along with him.

Dougal cusses in Gaelic as he also repeatedly rams his shoulder into the door. The wooden barrier shakes beneath the assault, threatening to crack from their combined, desperate force.

Gradually, the brass bar gives way underneath. Flecks of rust fall onto the floor, turning her hand brown. The door stops short a hairsbreadth from opening.

"Stand back," Dougal commands in a gruff voice.

Rachel releases her grip and takes a step away. She surveys the area behind them in the hopes of pinpointing the Fae's exact location. It's like searching for a hungry leopard in the African plains. By the time you see a leopard, it's already too late.

"C'mon, c'mon, c'mon," she says, looking back to Dougal as he struggles.

"I'm doin' my—"

A grinding screech is followed by a burst of sunlight as the doors open behind her.

"Ye happy?"

She pivots.

Dougal stands in the doorway, his frightened eyes studying the hallway behind her.

After a beat, he focuses on Rachel again. "Are ye waitin' for a written invitation? Move it," he says, gesturing to freedom.

They exit the old schoolhouse, jog around the corner of the building, and move through the parking lot. Rachel releases a sigh of relief when she spots her white Hyundai i10 amongst the other parked cars, whereas Dougal keeps casting concerned glances over his shoulder. His paranoia would've been infuriating under normal circumstances, but being hunted by creatures from another realm isn't exactly a common occurrence.

As they run, she rummages around in her sling bag for her keys and feels the cool metallic keychain lodged beneath one of her textbooks.

"Anything?" she asks, tugging at the keychain.

"Aye, and comin' up fast behind ye."

Rachel frees her keys from the textbook's hold and pulls them from her bag. With practiced movements, she finds the fob key by touch alone. A beep signals as the doors unlock. In unison, Rachel and Dougal fling their doors open and throw themselves into the Hyundai's front seats. The little car is not much in the way of safety, but it'll hinder the invisible predator's advances. At least, that's what Rachel hopes.

As she tries fitting the key into the ignition, Rachel notices the staccato creature approaching the driver's side, its awkward movements picking up speed. The key slips out of her fingers, dropping onto the mat.

"Move yer arse, Rach," Dougal says, slapping the dashboard

as he stares past her.

She reaches down, frantically searching for the key between her feet. "Hold on a sec." Her fingertips brush the metal before she swipes up the keychain.

Fitting the key into the ignition takes her longer than necessary.

"Rach—"

The car's engine starts and the radio blares to life, cutting Dougal off mid-panic. She shifts into first gear and presses her foot on the gas pedal, burning rubber as she races out of the parking space. A loud bang rattles her window. Both of them duck in response.

Rachel doesn't let up on the gas.

She dodges a couple of other parked vehicles in the lot as her car swerves toward the exit, and narrowly avoids clipping Greg's Mercedes Benz in the process. "Learn to park, Greg," she screams.

As the car nears Ridge Street, Rachel looks around to make sure there isn't any oncoming traffic, before she skips the stop sign and speeds away from the school. "Is it following us?" Her hands shake despite her grip on the steering wheel.

"Doesn't look it," Dougal says.

Rachel doesn't slack off until they reach the next crossing, and then it's only to rid herself of her sling bag and to secure the seatbelt across her body. She sits back in her seat, takes a deep breath to calm down, and slowly pulls away. Beside her, Dougal also settles into the passenger seat.

"That was a close call," she says.

"Aye, too close for my likin'."

Rachel turns to look behind them again, and finds the road clear of the Miser Fae. There is, however, an oncoming motorcycle—Cam's motorcycle. When she rights herself, her heart is still pounding with adrenaline and fear. She pushes her emotions away, forcing the muscles in her face to remain neutral.

"Act normal," she says to Dougal as she lowers the driver's side window.

Cam comes to a halt beside her car, lifts his helmet shield and leans forward to look inside. "You guys all right?" he asks.

"Are you stalking me now?" Rachel asks, not a hint of humor in the question.

He grins, shrugs, and sits upright on his seat. "Maybe. Come find me at Pine Hill when you're ready to have some real fun." Cam closes his shield and revs the motorcycle, before speeding away.

"I have a bad feelin' about that guy," Dougal mumbles.

"You have a bad feeling about everyone." Rachel shifts into first gear and pulls away, heading in the same direction as Cam. "But the feeling is mutual."

Dougal grumbles something unintelligible, before saying, "What now? Are ye goin' to the Fae Realm to get Orion?"

"I don't even know how to begin planning for a trip into the Fae Realm," Rachel says, cruising down the quiet street. "What's the weather like over there? What's the fashion? I'll stick out like a sore thumb and probably get myself killed long before I ever lay eyes on Orion."

"Well, we can't leave that thin' at the school." Dougal's voice hitches. "What about everyone who'd gotten one of those weird figurines? Are we gonna just stand by and watch them get hurt?"

"No, but we need to be smart about this. I mean, how long will it take me to actually find Orion in the Fae Realm? Maybe a week if I'm lucky? It's impractical," Rachel says. "Everything we need to fight this Miser Fae should be right here in Shadow Grove, but …"

When she doesn't continue, Dougal says, "But?"

Rachel's strength dulls even more as she wracks her mind for answers. "I don't know."

Dougal shifts in his seat. "Then we better get our funeral outfits ready."

As grim as it sounds, Dougal makes sense. There's a pencil-thin line between an accident and certain death.

They remain silent for a while, before Dougal breaks the silence. "Where are we goin'?"

"Before I do anything absurd, I want to hear your grandmother's thoughts on what we're up against. I don't recall reading about that particular Miser Fae in my father's journals, but I expect it's been holed up at the school for years. Maybe since Mrs. Crenshaw's days at Ridge Crest High," Rachel explains. "It's probably what inspired the tale of the ghost."

"What ghost?"

"The one who supposedly roams the halls and haunts the old schoolhouse," she says. "Seriously, Dougal, what do you guys even talk about?"

"Mostly just girls and cars," he answers, shrugging. "Sometimes football."

Rachel shakes her head as she flicks on the indicator and turns onto Main Road, driving past the colonial buildings of the historical sector. Those milling about the thriving small businesses have no idea what types of danger prowls around this town. They don't *want* to know. The locals believe what the Sheriff and town council want them to know. Anything else is simply nonsense—fake news.

She drives toward the edge of Shadow Grove, where a four-story building sits at the bottom of a grassy hilltop. Metal lettering is fixed across the entrance, proclaiming it to be Shadow Grove Hospital. The windows sparkle in the morning sunlight, the well-kept lawns and flower gardens give it a professional vibe without losing too much of the small town charm. On the surface, Shadow Grove Hospital almost looks like a world-class medical facility.

Such a pity it's all for show.

Rachel waves to the uninterested security guard standing at the entrance and drives into the parking lot. She searches for a vacant spot between all the stationary vehicles. There are *always* too many cars here. Some cars have literally rusted from weathering the elements over the years. Layers upon layers of dust and grime cover other vehicles. They just stand here to make it look like the hospital is always busy, when it rarely has any patients.

"It's so freaking weird," Rachel whispers as she finds a space near the entrance.

"Huh?"

"The cars," she says, absently nodding to a nearby vehicle. "The town council misjudged the size needed for the hospital's parking lot, so their brilliant plan to fool the tourists was to fill it up with second-hand cars."

"Are any of 'em for sale then?"

Frowning, Rachel parks her Hyundai i10. "I guess you should ask Mr. Farrow if he's willing to sell, seeing as some of these cars belong to him. His spare parts need to come from somewhere."

Dougal purses his lips together and nods. "I'll do that."

"Tired of me being your chauffeur?"

"Aye." He opens the car door. "Ye're a menace on the road."

Rachel grins, shrugs one shoulder, and switches off the engine. She looks at the parking lot, at the cars in their various stages of disrepair. Some are salvageable, though. If Dougal uses some elbow grease and puts some money into the project, he can build up a stunning vehicle.

"What type of car are you in the market for?" she asks as Dougal makes his way around the Hyundai and they walk together to the hospital's entrance. "Something macho, I presume?"

"I'll take anythin' I can afford." Dougal pulls the glass door open and gestures for her to enter first. "It ain't near visitin' hours, so how're we gonna see Nan?"

"You forget where we live," Rachel says, walking into the hospital.

The lobby is too quiet for a hospital. The receptionist has her back to the door, a pair of earbuds firmly fixed into her ears. The short-haired woman bobs her head to an unheard beat, her shoulders moving along. Rachel bypasses the desk and head straight for the elevators around the bend. She presses the button and folds her arms across her chest, looking at the digital screen atop the doorway as it counts down.

L3 … L2 … L1 …

The elevator pings, and the doors slide open.

Rachel steps inside. Her hand hovers over the panel on the wall. "What floor's your grandmother on?" she asks, glimpsing his way.

"Third." Dougal looks over his shoulder, frown deepening, before he enters.

She presses the button and the doors close on them. As Rachel turns around, she catches Dougal shaking his head, scratching his chin.

"What?"

His eyes flick down to meet her gaze. "Nuffin'." Dougal grimaces and shakes his head again. "It's prob'ly just my imagination, but I sweat that receptionist's eyes were red. Not like cryin' red, but scarlet. Don't worry." He drops his hands to his side, leans back against the elevator wall. "I mean—" He stops talking as the elevator announces their arrival on the third floor with another ping. The doors slide open. Dougal casts a glance at the desolate lobby before he pushes away from the wall and exits the elevator.

Rachel follows him out, unsure if she should press the matter, and takes her place at his side. The tiled hallway stretch on before them, undecorated and empty of wanderers awaiting news of their ill or dying loved ones. There are no nurses rushing about, no doctors walking around, no patients searching for the bathroom or some other amenity.

Dougal leads them around a corner and through a set of double doors, where a familiar voice echoes through the otherwise quiet ward.

"You call *this* food?" The distinctive tone is full of disapproval, even disgust. "It's an inedible pile of slush, and that's me being generous. Get it out of my sight this instant."

A nurse backs out of a room, tray in hand.

"Your grandmother seems—"

"By all means, take your time, Mandy. Perhaps I'll starve to death before one of those quacks has the chance to hack me open."

"—in good spirits," Rachel finishes.

The nurse rushes down the corridor, toward the bustling station, too rattled to notice anyone who doesn't belong there.

"Now ye know where I get it from." Dougal clicks his tongue, and heads for the room the nurse had exited. "Mornin', Nan," he says, disappearing inside. "Ye look fit as a fiddle, broken hip aside. How're ye feelin'?"

"I feel like I've fallen down the stairs, thank you very much," Mrs. Crenshaw answers tersely. "Why aren't you in school?" There's a pause. "It doesn't matter, we have pressing matters to discuss." The old woman calls out, "Rachel, stop skulking around and come in where I can see you."

Rachel takes a hesitant step forward and stops in the hospital room's doorway. From her position, Nancy Crenshaw looks both childish and ancient, huddling underneath the thin hospital blankets. With her hair down and disheveled in the morning sunlight, which filters through the horizontal blinds, there's something almost unrecognizable about her. Something profoundly mortal. Rachel doesn't care for it in the least.

"Honestly, Rachel. I'm not dead yet," Mrs. Crenshaw says in a softer, more sympathetic voice. "Wipe your tears away, unless you want this one to turn on his waterworks." She sticks out a thumb and juts it to her side, where Dougal sits hunched over beside the bed.

Embarrassed, Rachel uses the back of her hand to wipe away some stray tears and walks toward the empty seat on Mrs. Crenshaw's other side.

"Nan, we know what did this to ye," Dougal whispers. He looks up at his grandmother through his eyelashes. "It's another Miser Fae."

"Indeed," Mrs. Crenshaw answers. She inhales deeply. "Rachel's grandfather called this one a Death Omen. I foolishly nicknamed it The Bone Carver after our first run-in during my youth, and I guess it must've taken offense. It probably bided its time until I least expected it to show up." She rubs her brow. "Have there been any other incidents?"

"Aye, one we know about, and a few warnin's have been sent to others."

Mrs. Crenshaw nods and slowly turns her attention to Rachel. "Any sign of the Fae prince yet?"

"No."

After a heavy, thoughtful silence, Mrs. Crenshaw says, "Right, so, I'm going to need you two to sit tight and not go chasing after this Fae until I get out of the hospital. Whatever happens, well, it needs to happen. We'll sort it out later."

Rachel grimaces, glances across the bed to find Dougal wearing a similar guilty expression, and quickly looks to her hands, nervously picking at her thumb cuticle.

"Please tell me you two didn't do anything stupid. Rachel?" When Mrs. Crenshaw doesn't get an answer, she says, "Dougal?"

"I didn't think we'd find anythin'—"

"I leave you alone for one night. *One night*," Mrs. Crenshaw cuts off his weak explanation as she throws the blankets off her body. "Mandy! *Mandy*," she shouts, working her way to the side of the bed.

"Nan, ye can't leave. Yer hip— Nan, stop." Dougal's voice grows thicker with worry.

"Mrs. Crenshaw, please, you'll aggravate ..." The nurse's voice drifts off.

The world falls into a gradual hush. The argument between

Mrs. Crenshaw, Dougal, and the nervous nurse go on unabated. Their body language and hand gestures speak volumes, but she cannot discern a single word coming out of their mouths.

She grasps the umbrella pendant resting against her skin, making sure she hadn't lost it. The stone is cool against her palm, but it reassures her nonetheless. She turns away from the disorder and stares at the door, waiting for the threat to show itself. She bristles in anticipation, while her heart thumps harder, faster.

Then the music of the Fae realm starts. The melody is unmistakable as it surrounds her, consumes her. A beautiful call that forces her to her feet. She searches the room for a sign of an unwelcome presence—whether corporeal or ethereal, it doesn't matter—but there is nothing. Nobody else seems to hear the music; they hardly notice her anymore as Mrs. Crenshaw attempts her escape from the hospital bed.

The music grows louder, more desperate.

"Orion," she exhales his name, looking toward the closed window. Blue, cloudless skies lie beyond the horizontal blinds, nothing more.

An elbow shoves her out of the way and the real world spills back into the quiet. She catches herself before she can fall into her seat, unable to discern individual words amongst the argument. Rachel blinks a few times, clearing the fog from her mind, and realizes an oversized orderly has joined them. He's the least of her concerns, though. Her attention moves to the nurse who stands at the foot of the bed—an older woman dressed in navy scrubs. She points to the open door. The nurse's hawkish eyes pin Rachel in place for a few tense seconds, before she moves her gaze to the other side of the room.

"Out. Now," the woman's voice booms over the rest of the

commotion, the no-nonsense attitude commanding enough to make Rachel's feet move without her permission.

Still dazed, Rachel find herself exiting the hospital room with Dougal in tow. The door slams shut behind them, the heated argument dissolving into a mere whisper. She turns to stare at the closed door before taking a solemn step back.

"Ye need to find Orion. Nan isn't gonna be any help right now," Dougal says. He wipes the sweat from his brow. "I'll make sure Nan doesn't bolt the first chance she get, and try to keep people from gettin' killed as much as I can."

"I can stay with you. We can figure this out together."

Dougal's shoulders slump, the energy seeming to drain out of him. "Rach, we need help. If Nan didn't see this Fae comin', what chance do we have by ourselves? Ye need to go find him. Find any help." He slides down the wall to the floor and pushes his hands into his hair.

Rachel must've missed a lot of what had transpired in the hospital room when she'd zoned out, which is probably for the best, judging by Dougal's expression.

She leaves him there, in front of his grandmother's room. Whether this decision is the right one—the most *humane* one— she can't be certain, but she has a bone to pick with a Miser Fae, and that can't wait.

Chapter Six
A Real Pain in the Patella

Rachel sneaks into the old schoolhouse the way she and Dougal had left, through the double doors that have been left ajar. Her footsteps echo as she cautiously makes her way back to the boiler room, her heart pounding like a drum in her chest. Every creak from the rotting wood makes her jump; every rattle from the rusting pipes gives her pause. She surveys the area, takes a step forward, listens.

The skeleton key that had been left in the boiler room's door earlier is now missing. Maybe Dougal had pocketed it? She doesn't know. Rachel takes a deep, shaky breath, looks around a final time to ensure she's alone, before she drudges up the courage to open the door. She waits for the smell of death to assault her senses, but—

Rachel sniffs tentatively.

How is the stench inexplicably gone?

This doesn't make sense.

She walks down the stairs, careful not to make a sound, and ventures to where she and Dougal had seen the boneless corpse.

Nothing.

It's not like a corpse can stand up and walk away. What the hell?

She studies the undisturbed dust where the body had lain no more than an hour ago, searching for a sign of the Miser Fae, *anything* that could possibly explain what she's seeing—or not seeing. There isn't even a drag mark to indicate a direction someone or something could've gone. And the boneless corpse can't be hidden with a glamour, because she would've tripped over it. Fae influence was also impossible thanks to the Ronamy stone she wears around her neck.

Rachel places her palm against her forehead as she tries to come up with logical explanation. Nothing makes sense when it comes to Miser Fae, though. She can't begin to explain their motives for doing half of the things they do. But this is a whole new level of weird.

Her arm drops to her side and she retreats to the stairs, glancing over her shoulder to make sure the corpse didn't magically reappear.

Nada. Zilch. Nothing.

Once she's back in the hallway, she closes the door and leans with her back against the wooden partition. Rachel allows her mind to wander, hoping to find answers in the crevices of her subconscious—perhaps something her father or Mrs. Crenshaw or Orion had said could lead her to a solution.

"Miss Cleary, why aren't you in class?" the authoritative voice says.

Rachel opens her eyes, only to find Mr. Davenport, her English teacher, standing in the hallway with his arms crossed. He reaches up to push his black-rimmed spectacles higher onto the bridge of his nose, before he snaps his fingers and gestures for her to move.

She drags herself away from the door and walks in the

direction he'd indicated.

When she passes him by, he says, "You've been acting odd lately."

"It's an odd town," Rachel answers.

Mr. Davenport doesn't respond.

They walk together through the hallways of the old schoolhouse, toward the newer additions.

"What were you doing there?" Rachel asks.

Everything about Mr. Davenport's face looks sharp—straight nose, pointy chin, pronounced cheekbones, hawkish gaze. And he always wears black turtlenecks and chino pants, contrasting against his pale skin.

"I saw you sneaking in there earlier," Mr. Davenport says, raising a thin, severely arched eyebrow. "Not exactly the type of thing a formerly top student would do, is it?"

Rachel blinks slowly, averting her gaze, and stares down the hallway. Leave it to Davenport to kick her when she's down.

"Shall I ask what is wrong with you or would it be for naught?"

There has been some speculation as to who Mr. Davenport was before he came to Shadow Grove two years earlier—failed poet, disgraced academic, vampire, serial killer. She's personally always leaned toward the *serial killer* idea, mostly because he comes across as a narcissist.

Holland Keith had discovered Mr. Davenport's Instagram account last December, and shared the link with literally every person on her contact list—*Merry Christmas, Maggots. Don't say I never gave you anything.* Rachel had made the mistake of clicking on the link and had subsequently been bombarded with selfie after selfie of the man—always dressed in his usual black-on-black ensemble, always in the same thoughtful pose, only the background ever changing. The descriptions on his pictures weren't any better—*True genius goes unappreciated by the masses.*

Yeah, keep telling yourself that, Mr. Davenport.

"Aside from my splendid failure yesterday, I can confirm that my grades aren't slipping in any of my other classes, just yours, and I doubt it's because I'm doing subpar work."

Mr. Davenport stops in his tracks. "Are you suggesting that I am not treating you fairly? That I am incompetent?"

"Incompetent?" Rachel stops and turns to look up at the man, his glasses muting the severe glare. "Oh no, you're by far one of the most qualified teachers in this dump. I find it curious, however, how all the top students at Ridge Crest High are struggling to keep their grades up in your class. Greg Pearson, for example, has always been at the top of the class, but even his English grades have mysteriously fallen below Georgia Cramer's. Care to explain why?"

He stares at her, the seconds feeling like hours, his eyes narrowing and thin lips pulling into a straight line. "You certainly have grown bolder since last year, Miss Cleary. Trouble at home?"

"I'll have that particular conversation with the guidance counselor if it ever becomes necessary."

Rachel turns on her heels and continues her trek. Mr. Davenport's footsteps close in on her once more. They cross into the main building, making their way through the clear hallways. Mr. Davenport steps ahead of her and opens the administration office's door, gesturing for her to enter. Rachel gives him a courteous nod and walks inside where she finds Cam sitting on one of the metal chairs with the red plastic-covered seats and armrests.

"Take a seat, Miss Cleary. I'll gladly book your little chat with Principal Hodgins," Mr. Davenport says.

Cam looks up as she walks toward the open seat beside him, pursing his lips together to hide a smile.

"Fancy meeting you here," Rachel says, taking her seat.

"I'm in here so often Gail has taken it upon herself to start giving me free coffee." Cam holds up his Styrofoam cup for her to see.

"So, you're on a first-name basis with the school's receptionist now?"

"Jealous?"

Rachel reaches over and takes the cup from his hand. "Should I be?" She lifts the cup to her lips and takes a sip—too sweet and milky for her liking, but it does the trick. She hands back his coffee.

"I thought you and Dougal would be miles away by now, probably Thelma and Louise-ing it for some heartbreaking reason," he says, before resting the Styrofoam against his lips. He doesn't drink his coffee, though, simply watches her for a while.

Rachel raises an eyebrow.

"You did get the reference, though, right?" When she doesn't respond either way, he says, "Never mind." Cam takes a sip of his coffee. "What are you in for?"

"Cutting class, being caught in the old schoolhouse, giving a teacher grief," Rachel says, shrugging. "I'm a bad influence, ask anyone."

He snickers. "Well, it's a good thing I'm not exactly a saint."

She smiles, sits back in her seat, and says, "You remind me of someone."

"Oh?" Cam's eyes widen. "Someone you like?"

"Perhaps," she says. "Perhaps not."

"Cameron Mayer," Principal Hodgins' perpetually bored voice enters their conversation. "What did you do this time?"

Cam winks at her as he stands. He turns his attention to the principal, and crosses the distance to the stout man with the beady rat eyes. They speak in hushed tones in the open, the principal nodding now and then, glancing over to her, before whispering further.

Cam reaches into his pocket. Something exchanges hands. The principal tucks away whatever it was and his face turns a deep scarlet. It is not a subtle transaction.

"Yeah, well, it saves me paperwork, so do as you please." Principal Hodgins retreats into his office, and slams the door shut behind him, the matter apparently having been dealt with.

Cam returns to where Rachel sits.

"What was that?" she asks.

"Exactly what it looked like." He picks up his backpack and helmet from another chair. "You coming or not?"

She reluctantly stands.

"Good. Let's skip this joint." Cam jerks his chin to the door and takes the lead, waving to the receptionist as he opens the door.

Rachel follows him, even though she's unsure if it's the right decision.

On one hand, Rachel's happy she's off the hook—she did kind of dig her own grave by calling Mr. Davenport out on his egotistical power trip. If he had his way, she would be suspended or worse. On the other hand, she's unsure if this is any better. Some kind of deal had been struck to get them both out of trouble, but what would it cost her in the long run? People don't do nice things out of the kindness of their heart, at least not in Shadow Grove.

"I just got you out of detention. A thank you would be nice," Cam says as they walk down the empty hallway.

She rushes ahead and quickly moves in front of him, forcing him to stop. "What did you give the principal?"

"It's a secret," Cam whispers, looking at her from beneath his eyelashes.

Rachel frowns, studying him closely for a hint of deceit. Finding none, surprisingly enough, she steps aside and allows him to pass.

"Where are you going?"

"You ask *way* too many questions," he calls back. Cam raises his fist and punches the air, like some heartthrob in a 1980s teen movie.

He's so weird.

The bell rings and the classes file out into the hallway, allowing Cam to disappear within the throngs of kids. Rachel inhales deeply and shakes her head. She turns in place and spots Greg in the main corridor. Determined to get the answers she so desperately needs to put this Miser Fae out of business, Rachel marches down the crowded hallway. Her peers give her a wide berth, parting like the Red Sea, their whispers reach her ears. She can't care less what they think about her anymore. Not now, when any one of them could be next.

Ahead, she sees Greg turning down the hallway, another girl hanging on his arm.

Rachel picks up speed to catch up to him, turns the corner, and grabs Greg by his shoulders before he can get out of her reach. As he spins around, she slams him back into the lockers lining the wall. Pressing her forearm against his chest to keep him in place, she glares up at him.

Greg stares back, a sheepish grin playing in the corner of his mouth.

"Get off him! Let g—" Greg's companion shrieks, making the scene much more interesting than Rachel had intended. The school bell rings, signaling the start of the next class, and saving them from curious onlookers.

"Get to class, Carla," Greg says in a calm, diplomatic tone that doesn't betray the mischief twinkling in his gray eyes.

"But, but, but—"

He forces his gaze away from Rachel to the short girl standing behind her. His expression hardens. "Rachel and I have private matters to discuss."

Carla huffs. "I *so* didn't sign up for this kind of humiliation."

From the corner of Rachel's eye, she spies the girl stalk off, while the rest of the crowd disperses. Classroom doors shut, the hallway grows silent.

He turns his attention back to Rachel, the mischief returning. "I never can tell if you want to kill me or kiss me."

"I don't have time to play your twisted games, Pearson," Rachel hisses. "But I do need your help." She reluctantly releases her hold on him.

The playfulness dissipates. "What's up?"

She looks over her shoulder to the janitor's closet, and motions for him to follow her inside. Once they're there, he closes the door behind him, shutting them in darkness. A breath later, there's a click, and the hanging bulb drenches them in artificial light. Every wall in the small closet is lined with shelves, some full of cleaning chemicals, others are left bare.

"I need access to the town council's archi—"

"No," he interrupts her before she can finish her sentence, let alone try to explain why she needs his help. "Last time, I almost got grounded just for showing you that stuff. If I sneak you in there, and word gets back to my dad, he'll probably kill me."

"Don't be so melodramatic. Your dad won't kill you," Rachel says, crossing her arms. "Maim you, maybe, but he definitely won't kill you. Someone needs to inherit the great Pearson fortune."

"Hilarious," Greg replies in monotone. "If you'll excuse me, I still have to study for the English test later on."

"Screw the test," Rachel retorts. "Mrs. Crenshaw is in the hospital, Dougal is in no condition to help, and my mom ran off to Bangor again. I need to get inside that archive right now before people end up dead."

His jawline tenses as he bites back a response.

Rachel considers closing the distance between them. She deliberates standing on the tips of her toes, caressing his cheek ever so gently, before she presses her lips against his. It's what Greg's counting on, too. She can actually see him fantasizing about this exact scenario. He wants to go back to what they had shared this past summer.

It'd been good. They spent every available moment together over the summer, holding hands, kissing in public, covering all the metaphorical bases. There were also interesting discussions, things they both enjoyed reading about but never had anyone to talk with before—scientific discoveries they've read about, conspiracy theories they couldn't rationalize, historical facts that seemed so unreal but weren't. The fling was fun, memorable even, but that's all it would ever be—a fling.

She hates herself for even contemplating using his feelings to get what she wants, and she hates him for wanting whatever little piece of herself she's willing to give, when he *knows* they aren't compatible.

He's a Pearson, for heaven's sake.

Being a Pearson means your life isn't just yours. It belongs to your family, the community, and the town council. A Pearson is expected to study at an Ivy League college, graduate at the top of the class, and go into the family business. Somewhere in between all of those tasks, they'll have to find someone nice to marry—preferably someone who also comes from money—and have some kids. Usually, the significant other won't need any training in being the epitome of elegance, but if they do, the new Pearson will embrace their role without hemming or hawing.

And while most people probably believe love can conquer all, Rachel isn't that naïve. Fairy tale endings don't exist for girls like her, even when there's a starry-eyed Prince Charming involved.

Still, if his feelings were all she has to bargain with—

Rachel unfolds her arms. "I can't do this," she whispers, her courage fading. "I'm sorry, Greg, I just can't do this."

Had it been anyone other than Greg, she'd have thought nothing of using their weaknesses for personal gain. It would've been meaningless, easily forgotten. But this *is* Greg. They share a lifetime's worth of history. They share Luke—Greg's deceased twin brother and Rachel's best friend. Whatever happens between them won't be meaningless, won't be forgotten. It would set the tone between them for the rest of their lives, and she can't bear the idea of losing his friendship due to selfishness.

Rachel takes a step toward the door, ready to leave the claustrophobic closet and come up with another plan to get rid of the Miser Fae prowling around town.

"I know about Orion," Greg says, not even a hint of bitterness in his voice. Rachel halts in her tracks. "If I hadn't intercepted the rumor, the whole school would know that you spent the night with him, too."

She slowly turns to face Greg, feeling uncomfortably close in the confined space.

"Your reputation wouldn't have survived that type of gossip, Rachel," he says. She watches him, unsure if he's threatening to spread the information or not. "Guys like Orion *love* to take advantage of girls like you."

"Girls like me?" Rachel narrows her eyes, daring him to say something sexist.

Greg closes the infinitesimal distance between them. "You know," he whispers as he moves his other hand around her waist. "Easily manipulated girls."

She tilts her chin up just in time to see a red flash in his pupils. It could've been a trick of the light, or maybe her imagination playing tricks on her. On the other hand, it could be something far more sinister. Considering the latter, Rachel decides it might not be in her best interest to get on Greg's bad side while she's stuck with him in the confines of the janitor's closet.

Greg raises a hand to brush a strand of hair out of her face. "I don't expect us to pick up where we left off, Rach, but maybe—"

"We can start fresh?" she whispers. Rachel forces herself to give him the sweetest smile she can muster and searches his eyes for another tell. There's nothing perceptible, though. "Do you think it's possible?"

He releases his hold on her and leans back against the

shelves, smiling one of his genuine smiles—the ones he reserves for her alone. "Hi, I'm Greg Pearson, and you are?"

This is so twisted.

Rachel manages to relax every muscle in her body, keeping her face neutral. "It's a pleasure to meet you. I'm Rachel Cleary," she says.

They carry on the conversation for a good five minutes, acting like they've only just met. From Greg's expression, he seems pleased. If he suspects anything untoward, he certainly doesn't show it. Then, when Rachel thinks the situation can't become any weirder, Greg looks at his wristwatch.

"I need to stop by at the library to clock some study time before English." he says. "See you after school?"

"Mrs. Crenshaw—"

"Of course," he interrupts, blinking a few times. "I forgot. Sorry." Greg shakes his head, as if clearing his mind. "You should leave."

Not wanting to delay his departure with questions like *what is wrong with you?*, Rachel touches his wrist and smiles. "You first. I'll go after a few minutes, so it doesn't look too suspicious."

"Yeah, that'll probably be for the best," Greg chuckles. He stretches back to rub the back of his neck. "See you when I see you."

He shifts around until he can reach the knob. Greg looks over his shoulder one last time, flashes a half-grin at her as slips out of the closet.

The door closes behind him, and she releases a shaky breath she didn't know she's been holding. She stares at the door, counting off every second that passes. The adrenaline, which kept her upright throughout the exchange, evaporates out of her system. She doubles over, her legs growing weak as the reality of how close she had come to—

Dying? Influence or not, Greg won't ever physically harm you.

Rachel pushes away the tears stinging the corners of her eyes, and rests her trembling hands on her knees, struggling to catch her breath through the sobs making their way up her throat.

Is he even under influence?

Unsure what to make of the red flash she'd spied in his pupils, she asks herself, "What else can it be?"

It could be nothing. You could be paranoid for no reason.

The soft knock on the door causes Rachel to jerk upright. A head of blonde curls appears as Mercia pops inside the closet, concern etched into her forehead, her lips turned down.

"Rachel?" Mercia says, keeping her voice soft. Her gaze flits to Rachel's hand, now pressed against the shelf. "You're bleeding."

Rachel glances at her hand to see a deep, self-inflicted wound in the corner of her thumb's cuticle.

Mercia rummages in her bag and holds out a tissue. "He's gone. You can come out now."

Rachel purses her lips together to keep her feelings hidden, and takes the offered tissue.

A heavy silence settles over them before Mercia whispers, "You saw it too, didn't you? The thing inside Greg?"

Taken aback, Rachel can do little more than stare at Mercia as she opens the door wide and steps out of the way. Rachel exits the closet, but keeps her eyes on the girl who'd most probably eavesdropped on the entire exchange in the janitor's closet.

"I'm like you," she says.

"What are you talking about?"

Mercia shrugs, a conspirator's smile now taking residence on her face. "Walk with me." She juts her chin toward the main hallway.

As Mercia rounds the corner, Rachel grabs her by her wrist, forcing her to stop in her tracks.

"Mercia?" Rachel hisses. "What do you mean?"

Mercia shakes off Rachel's hand and snaps her fingers. A flame ignites out of nowhere, before sizzling out just as fast. A thin trail of smoke wafts into the air, obscuring their view of each other. A scorched note is pinched between her index finger and thumb.

"Take it," Mercia says, holding the piece of paper out toward her.

Rachel hesitates.

"It won't bite you. Take it."

She takes the note with her uninjured hand and carefully unfolds the singed paper, keeping her gaze on Mercia. Her attention drops to the single word, written in cursive: *Munich*. She looks back at Mercia, not comprehending.

"If you want to know what it means, I suggest we go somewhere else. These walls have ears," she says.

Rachel follows Mercia's beat-up green Volvo all the way to the Eerie Creek Bridge. She watches as the car pulls to the side of the road, parking on the creek's bank, before she follows. Rachel inhales deeply before climbing out of the driver's seat and slamming the car door shut.

Mercia, who's already waiting for her beneath the old willow tree, crosses her arms as she nears. "Took you long enough."

"Some of us actually adhere to the speed limits," Rachel says.

Mercia snorts, shakes her head.

"So, what's up? Why did you drag me all the way out here?"

"My family fled Europe after witnessing the Pappenheimer family's torture and executions for witchcraft in Munich." She pitches her voice loud enough to be heard over the rushing water of the creek. "The Pappenheimer family were forced to endure heinous medieval persecution. I can't even bring myself to repeat the story." Her voice broke.

A breeze kicked up and ruffled the leaves of the willow while Mercia gathered her nerve to continue.

"So, my ancestors fled to England before they suffered a similar fate and eventual execution. Originally, they settled in Lancashire, England, which was a huge mistake, because in 1612, the Pendle Hill witch trials started. Again, they fled for their lives, and this time they had to cross an ocean to survive." Mercia brushes her hair out of her face and hooks the windswept strands behind her ear. "In 1692, they uprooted from Salem, Massachusetts, and roamed New England until they finally settled here, in Shadow Grove."

"Okay, but you could have told me all of this at the school," Rachel says. "Also, *why* tell me any of this?"

"If someone other than you should figure out I'm a real witch, I'm dead. Don't think this town is above building a pyre." Mercia looks to the water, an array of emotions crossing her face. "As for your second question— Look, I didn't mean to eavesdrop on you and Greg, but I was truly worried about you. Ever since he paid me to act like his girlfriend, I sensed something off about him. It's not the regular Greg-Pearson-is-just-being-a-jerk off, it's more along the lines of something-is-seriously-wrong off."

"Yeah, I figured that out the hard way." Rachel sighs. Later. She'll help him later. "What do you want?"

"It's not about what I want—it's about what I need." Mercia holds herself tighter. "I need goldmint to stop the damn seizures before they ruin my life."

Rachel grimaces. "I don't—"

"Cut the crap, Cleary. We both know that thing in Greg wouldn't have thrown such a temper tantrum if it wasn't obsessed with something it clearly can't have. And *I* am not stupid enough to believe you and the Fae prince haven't cozied up to one another." Mercia releases her hold on herself and steps closer to Rachel. "For twenty goldmint pills, I get you into the town council's archives for as long as you need. For fifty, I help you find Orion *and* keep Dougal alive while he's running around here like a headless chicken."

"Thirty," Rachel blurts, though she doesn't know how she feels about this. "Thirty goldmint pills and you help Dougal keep everyone safe from the Fae terrorizing the school."

"Forty, and then I'll help."

"Thirty-five is my best offer. Take it or leave it."

Mercia sneers, grits her teeth. "Damn it," she says, putting her hand out. "This doesn't make us friends."

Rachel takes her hand and they shake.

Mercia brushes past Rachel as she walks back to her Volvo. "I'll come to your house after school. You better have the goldmint pills by then."

"Or what?"

Mercia snickers. "Fae are like mosquitos, a nuisance at best.

Cross me and I'll conjure up something much, much worse."

Rachel sighs, watching the dainty girl walk away. "Fine," she calls back.

Only when Mercia's car is driving down Eerie Street does Rachel return to her Hyundai, keys in hand.

"Sorry, Orion, but I need all the help I can get," she whispers, already feeling guilty for what she's about to do next.

Chapter Seven
Fractured Sense of Self

There are so many things occupying Rachel's thoughts that when she comes back to herself she's already on the other side of Shadow Grove, driving past the abandoned train station, the steelworks, and closed down factories. Soon, she sees the sun-bleached sign hanging askew across the entrance to Pine Hill Trailer Park, where small houses and mobile homes stand alongside each other, stacked too closely together to be comfortable. A dog barks madly somewhere along the fence, while a few indignant shouts fill the otherwise quiet day.

The neglected, solitary apartment building—located at the very edge of Shadow Grove—rises out of the earth. Ashfall Heights is an eyesore the town council simply can't get rid of—it's a mistake made two generations earlier, when a promising baby boom had been interrupted by the Great Depression and World War II. Wilderness surrounds the unsightly H-shaped building, which has been left to crumble for close to two decades. Yet, for reasons she can't begin to explain or understand, the more she visits, the fonder she grows of the place.

Rachel steers into the oversized abandoned parking lot, avoiding the deep potholes scarring the asphalt and construction debris littering the area. She parks at the entrance, across two spaces, and unclicks her seatbelt.

She reaches around the seat to find her bag. She slings her bag over her shoulder, climbs out of her car, closes the door behind her, and crosses the distance between the parking lot and the graffiti-riddled entrance of Ashfall Heights. She barely notices the grimy interior of the foyer anymore, hardly thinks twice about entering the elevator that sounds like it'll crash back to earth if she breathes too loudly. The doors close and the gears feebly grind as the elevator ascends. She searches for Orion's apartment keys on her keychain.

Six weeks earlier, Rachel had found the keys and a hastily written note in Orion's handwriting lying on her pillow. The note simply read: *Please check on my greenhouse.* How it had gotten into her bedroom, she doesn't know, but ever since then she's spent most Saturdays in the quiet apartment—making sure the watering system is functioning, reading through the various handwritten journals in the greenhouse to familiarize herself with the exotic plants, and trying not to kill any of them before he gets back from wherever he is in the Fae Realm.

The elevator slowly opens and Rachel marches down the ninth floor's corridor, passing the faded red doors with their black numbers. She ignores the smells and sounds, the yellowing walls and worn linoleum flooring underfoot. At apartment 9-M, Rachel unlocks the door and enters. It's stuffy and dark inside, and she blindly feels around for the light switch, which she flips on. The artificial light brightens the sparsely decorated living room with its few pieces of furniture and the posters hanging on the walls.

The closet door sits on the left side of the entryway, across from the kitchen. She opens the closet and walks up Ashwell

Heights' forgotten stairwell to the tenth floor. The entire tenth floor has been commandeered by Orion to become an indoor greenhouse. It was full of foreign and beautiful Fae plants, most of which Orion uses to manufacture his signature designer drugs.

The medicinal plants section is in the center of the greenhouse, surrounded by hundreds of other plants she hasn't had a chance to study yet. She heads directly to the desk, which is littered with numerous mason jars and handwritten journals. Each mason jar is marked with its contents—harvested Stardust, Nacht-Lilies, Ocean Roses, and Droom Leaves, among a variety of other unpronounceable names. Rachel ignores the unprocessed herbs and reaches into the top desk where Orion keeps his stash.

She rifles through the plastic baggies, searching for the goldmint. Though it's not the most popular drug Orion produces—that honor goes to the various sexual enhancement drugs—goldmint is still plentiful. The thirty-five pills, which Rachel will need to pay Orion for, are already likely to cost a small fortune. She carefully counts out the pills, grabs another unused Ziploc bag from the desk, and seals them up. Next, she writes an IOU and slips the note into the goldmint folder, which she returns to Orion's desk.

Rachel pulls off the blood-soaked tissue she'd wrapped around her thumb and looks at the angry, red wound. With her free hand, she searches through the mason jars for the Stardust and loosens the lid. She sprinkles the Stardust onto the raw, jagged gouge on her thumb, and bites back a yelp of pain. A pinch of the Fae herb is all she needs to allow the wound to heal at inhuman speed. It's a small injury compared to the one she'd received when the Night Weaver impaled Orion with her darkness, but it's still remarkably tender as the magic goes to

81

work. She feels her flesh slowly knit together, the skin growing taught as it stretches across the wound.

Rachel grabs her sling bag and heads down the stairs. A minute later, she's locking up the apartment and making her way back to the elevator.

By the time she climbs inside her car, pulls on her the seatbelt, and starts the engine, Rachel is already worrying about the consequences of borrowing drugs from a powerful Fae prince, of being caught with the pills, of handing them over to Mercia. So many things can go wrong. Still, she can't go toe-to-toe with a Miser Fae without some magical back-up, and she doubts Mercia is a narc.

Rachel makes a wide U-turn in the parking lot and begins the drive back to the road, her heart racing and palms sweating. Not fear due to having to face a dangerous Fae in the not so distant future, but because the sheriff's deputies love to camp out, waiting to pull over anyone who looks even a bit suspicious.

She passes the trailer park, the closed down factories and steelworks, and the train station without seeing any official cruisers lingering about. Even as she heads straight to Main Road, Rachel can't find a way to relax.

When she arrives back at school, she's a nervous wreck. There's no way of knowing if she'll even be able to spell her name correctly on the test, let alone get a decent grade. If she doesn't show up for the test, though, Mr. Davenport will make her wish for death.

Can today just end already? She gets out of the car and keeps her hand pressed against the sling bag. As she makes her way back into the school, she sees Cam walking ahead. *What is* your *deal?*

He glances over his shoulder and flashes a smile before

coming to a stop.

"You came back?" she says, walking up to him.

"I actually studied for the English test." Cam shrugs. "You heading that way?"

"Mhmmm."

They fall into step along the main hallway to get to Mr. Davenport's class. "You look concerned," Cam says.

"I'm having a terrible day," Rachel mumbles.

"Want to talk about it?"

"Nope. Not unless you start spilling your secrets."

"Touché." Cam pushes his hands into his jacket pockets. "Well, if you're really having a bad day, I can always get you out of this test. Just say the word and I'll make it happen."

She raises an eyebrow. "I'll be fine, thanks."

"Yeah, keep telling yourself that." He reaches out to open the door and allows Rachel to enter the empty classroom first.

The action irks her for some reason. Usually, she doesn't mind when Dougal does it, but with Cam, it's a whole other matter. A tiny voice inside her warns her not to trust him. Why, though? He's just a regular guy, isn't he? Yeah, he has his quirks as most people do, but something about him gives her pause.

She walks to the middle of the classroom and takes her seat, keeping her sling bag firmly gripped between her ankles. Rachel plants her elbow on the table and rests her forehead in her palm, mentally readying herself for the test.

She feels eyes on her, making her uncomfortable.

It's nothing, she thinks, but glances to the side, anyway.

Cam sits across the room at his own desk, grinning at her.

Why do I always attract the creeps?

Mr. Davenport's accident takes the form of another fall—a misstep that has him slipping as he enters the class with the English tests clutched in his hands. He hit his head so hard against the tiles, Rachel's certain she hears the back of his skull crack. The test papers fly into the air as a flurry of activity commences. Students either panic or take action to help the most despised teacher at Ridge Crest High.

Faculty members arrive in droves, trying and failing to regain order.

The class is eventually dismissed, the English test postponed until a later date, and the ambulance is called.

Rachel passes Mr. Davenport's desk and sees a figurine lying in the open top drawer.

"Yup," she pops the 'p', her theory proven right. This time, Rachel doesn't pick up the totem, simply exits the classroom along with the rest of the students.

Cam stands across the hallway, seemingly waiting for her.

"Was that your doing?" She eyes him suspiciously.

"Sorry?" Cam looks genuinely surprised by the question, but that's not saying much.

Rachel stares at him, not sure if she believes him or not. She takes her place beside him, watching the EMTs rolling the gurney out of the classroom with Mr. Davenport strapped in tight.

"It's surprising how easily our peers are traumatized. There wasn't even a drop of blood and look at them." He juts his chin in Bianca Novak's direction, who's bawling her eyes out on Ronald Steven's shoulder.

There are others in a similar state of despair, either crying or in complete shock. Best friends, Tammy Richards and Valeska Howes—for example—are several shades paler than they had been when they'd first entered the classroom. Tammy is crying in a pretty kind of way, a single teardrop trickling down her cheek. Her response is very subdued, almost ladylike. Valeska, on the other hand, catches flies with her 'O'-shaped mouth, gaping as she looks between the gurney and the classroom.

"I've always said they don't watch enough horror movies," Rachel says.

Cam snorts, but manages to suppress his laughter before he can draw attention from the others.

As Rachel takes a step forward, ready to follow the EMTs out of the building, he says, "You don't really think I'm responsible for Mr. Davenport's fall, do you?"

Rachel studies him for a long moment, before she says, "Weirder things have happened."

Instead of arguing with her, Cam simply shrugs and walks down the hallway.

Chapter Eight
Bones Don't Scry

Should I get Ziggy, just in case things get out of control?

Rachel immediately dismisses the idea. She wouldn't put the Fae light in harm's way, regardless of the fact that it's nothing more than a ball of energy with a personality.

Maybe I need to notify Dougal?

Again, she instantly decides against it. He has enough to deal with, and there's no telling if Mercia's part of the bargain will pan out.

This is my problem to handle.

"This will do," Mercia says, setting a large wooden chest on the basement floor in front of the bare north-facing wall. She opens it and takes out several flat, rounded objects, covered in red velvet fabric. "I wouldn't normally do this outside of a protection barrier, but desperate times call for—" She fumbles one of the objects, catching it before it falls. "Whoa. That was close."

"Do you need help?" Rachel steps closer.

"Thanks, but if I break one, I just get grounded. If you break one, you literally die." Mercia carefully places the last rounded object on the floor before reaching back into the wooden chest.

Rachel perches on an upturned crate, whatever it had once held long since gone.

Mercia lifts a large, oddly shaped object from the chest with both hands.

"Okay, let's see if I remember how this works." Mercia rights herself and squares her shoulders, staring at the wall. She says a weird word, and the object flies out of her hands and fixes against the wall. Mercia grins as she steps closer and pulls the velvet fabric off from the object, revealing an obsidian disk in an ornate, black frame. Eight crescents are carved into it, just large enough to hold whatever else Mercia's unpacked from the crate. She returns to the stack of velvet-covered objects and picks one up. She closes her eyes as she unwraps a smaller one, whispering something Rachel can't hear before the disk flies to the large black mirror and slips into a crescent bracket.

"You're going to have to tell me what we're doing," Rachel says. She crosses her legs. "I can't figure it out."

"I'm putting together an interdimensional scrying mirror," Mercia answers, eyes still closed as she reaches for the second disk.

"Oh."

Mercia whispers to the object in her hands, which follows its brother into another empty crescent in the mainframe. One after another, the disks fly to the wall, until all eight smaller obsidian mirrors are in place. Mercia opens her eyes and smiles at her handiwork, pushing the empty chest aside with her foot.

"There."

"Now what?" Rachel asks.

"Now," Mercia begins, glancing over her shoulder to Rachel, "I need something personal of Orion to focus on. Something he's touched or—" Her gaze falls to Rachel's neck. "That'll do."

Rachel reaches up to the umbrella pendant and holds it firmly.

"I'm not going to break it."

"See that you don't." Rachel reluctantly takes off the Ronamy Stone. She crosses the basement and hands the necklace over.

Mercia takes the necklace in both hands as she steps up to the black mirror, closing her eyes again. Her words are mere breaths, spoken so.

As Mercia opens her eyes, the pendant glows in purples and blues, with hues of green sometimes flashing intermittently. She raises her hand. The golden chain swings forward and backward, the umbrella pendant almost touching the mirror. Her blonde hair blows wildly around her face as the enchantment becomes louder, more insistent.

An impossible wind rushes through the basement, blowing around loose paper and dust.

Rachel pushes her hair out of her face, staring at the strange frame as it turns counterclockwise. Faster and faster, the frame moves, the smaller obsidian surfaces reflecting extraordinary landscapes. Images take shape, impossible worlds are revealed. There's a realm where black peaks stab at cerulean skies and rough cliffs disappear beneath angry purple waters. Another realm shows darkness and fire and cities built into mountainsides. Another mirror reflects a world of glass, where people are ruled by technology and machines are worshipped like gods. There are castles built in the sky, societies that live underwater, and unimaginable creatures.

Mercia's voice crescendos across the phantom wind's howling.

Suddenly, the frame halts its movement and the large oval mirror shows Orion standing beside a black stallion, dressed in an unfamiliar uniform. Black armor gleams beneath the red insignia emblazoned over his chest. Twin deer, on their hind legs—the same one she saw on Mercia's goldmint pills. And hanging on his belt is a sheathed broadsword, the silver hilt depicting a stag's head—antlers and all.

Mercia stops chanting and lowers the glowing pendant. She tilts her head as she gazes at the mirror.

"He's in the Fae Realm," Mercia says. She places her free hand against the surface, the image rippling like water. "It'll take about three days on foot to reach his camp, but the journey is not without danger." She pulls her hand back and fishes a brass compact from her jean pocket. Mercia whispers a few words, and the glow of the pendant fades. A moment later, the wind hushes and the images on the mirror vanish. "That's sorted." She pivots and holds out the necklace to Rachel. "Once you give me the goldmint, I'll give you the map."

Rachel replaces the necklace around her neck as she moves to the old armchair where she'd set her sling bag, then rummages until she finds the plastic baggie. As she turns around, Mercia's relief is almost tangible. Her shoulders relax as she exhales. Rachel returns to hand over the baggie.

"Okay." Mercia pockets the goldmint. She takes a step closer and opens the brass compact to reveal yet another set of obsidian mirrors. "I transferred the map into this travel-sized mirror." An image of the ACCESS PROHIBITED sign takes shape in the reflective area. "The top mirror shows Orion at any given moment. The bottom one will show you the next landmark to look for on your way to him. So, basically, it's your map. Once you go past the signpost, the image changes. Simple yet effective, don't you agree?"

Rachel grumbles an affirmative as she stares at the mirror. "You said something about danger?"

"I don't exactly know what made me say it. The terrain isn't friendly, sure, but it's something else. I think what I sensed relates more to the people Orion's hanging around with … They're giving off iffy vibes," Mercia explains, handing over the compact mirror. "Just keep an eye out for trouble and you'll be fine."

"That's it?"

Mercia shrugs. "That's it."

Dubious, Rachel studies Mercia's expression, searching for something insincere. Surely there's more to this trip than simply walking for a few days. The Fae Realm is, after all, a whole other dimension, with unknown dangers and whatnot.

"Don't look at me like I've just signed your death warrant." Mercia steps toward the wooden chest. "Seriously, there are simpler ways to kill you *if* ending your life was my intention. Besides, why would I, when you're one of the few people I, like, don't entirely hate?"

Rachel pockets the compact mirror. "Yesterday—"

"I wasn't thinking clearly," Mercia cuts her off. "I'm so used to everyone making fun of me and my condition that I sometimes forget there are actually a few decent people in this town. Don't think I didn't notice you slapping Eddie Roberts' phone out of his hand sophomore year when I—" She stops talking as she hunches down and opens the lid on the chest, averting her gaze. Mercia clears her throat. "Females typically wear pants and tunics when they travel long distances in the Fae Realm. You should also braid your hair, that way you won't stand out too much when you come across any locals."

"Okay, but what if I don't find Orion and I need to get back to the Harrowsgate? Will this thing show me the way?" Rachel bites the inside of her lip.

"Even magic has its limits," Mercia says. "Go, get ready." She looks up. "You're burning valuable daylight."

"You'll help Dougal, right?" Rachel asks.

"I give you my word as a Holstein witch. I'll help keep everyone semi-safe."

"Semi-safe?"

"Well, it's not like I'm all-powerful. If I were, don't you think I'd have this situation under control by now?" Mercia snorts. "Now go. I need to pack up the mirrors."

"Yeah, yeah." Rachel takes her leave, heading for her bedroom to pack the essentials. A *lot* can go wrong in three days, especially in an unknown realm where she cannot distinguish between friend and foe. If something goes wrong, she's on her own. Nobody will come looking for her. There's no cell phone signal, no Wi-Fi, no emergency services.

Rachel settles on taking only the bare minimum. This includes: a thick rolled-up blanket, her toiletries, a lighter, extra underwear and socks, enough food to last her a week, and a water bottle. She decides on a pair of black jeans, a white winter's shirt that laces up in the fronts and looks medieval to the untrained eye, as well as a pair of black hiking boots. At the last minute, she adds a heavy-duty torch and extra batteries, as well as a second outfit into her backpack—black leggings and a thick winter jacket with a faux fur hoodie and cuffs. That's the best she can do on such short notice.

"Rachel," Mercia shouts from downstairs as Rachel braids her thick, red hair. "If you take any longer, you might as well wait until morning."

Rachel ties the ends of her hair and picks up the faux leather backpack she plans on taking along. "Come on, Ziggy. Let's go find Orion and bring him home."

The Fae light flies ahead of her as Rachel exits her room and makes her way back downstairs, where Mercia stands in the foyer, the chest of mirrors waiting outside the front door.

"Took you long enough," Mercia mumbles. "You have the compact mirror?"

Rachel touches her front pocket. "Yes."

"A first-aid kit for emergencies?"

"Yup."

"Water, food, and—"

"I can open the bag for you to check if you want?"

"Sorry, it's not every day I send someone off into the unknown." Mercia crosses her arms. "The Fae light I saw flying past is going with you, right?"

Rachel nods.

"And that's your sleeping bag?"

"It's a blanket," Rachel corrected her. "I couldn't find my sleeping bag."

"Don't you think it's kind of important to have a sleeping bag when you're going out into an unknown wilderness?"

"Yes, but the sleeping bags are probably somewhere in the attic, and time is running out."

"Okay." Mercia grimaces. "Good luck then, I guess."

"Your enthusiasm is infectious," Rachel says in a deadpan tone as she walks toward the open front door. "I sent Dougal a text telling him you'll be helping, along with your number."

"And?"

"You should explain the witchy business to him," Rachel

says. She locks the front door behind them. "He's a little close-minded on some things, but eventually he'll come around to the idea of you having magic."

"Close-minded in what way?"

"Well, Dougal isn't the type of person who'll divulge your secret unless it is a threat to someone he cares for, but he won't be too happy about having to work with a witch either." Rachel descends the porch steps and walks across the lawn. "Truth be told, it's likely he'll be speaking in Gaelic every time you go near him, which isn't half as bad as it sounds."

"I'll keep that in mind," Mercia says. "Don't get yourself killed, okay?"

"It's definitely not on my to-do list," Rachel calls back. She steps onto Griswold Road.

"Oh." Mercia's voice halts her. "When you go through the gate, just think about Orion, otherwise you may end up somewhere completely different. The Harrowsgate sometimes has a mind of its own."

That explains why Dougal and I ended up in Telfore. We had no idea where we wanted to go.

"Thanks." Rachel waves her goodbye, and continues walking up the road.

Ziggy flies ahead, dipping toward a dense shrub. The Fae light circles the foliage as Rachel nears the sign. Ziggy flies back to her side before returning to the shrub. She turns her attention to the greenery.

"Please tell me I don't have to talk to a bush," Rachel says.

Ziggy flashes once.

She throws her head back to look at the sky, where the sun is already plunging toward the horizon. With a frustrated groan, she rights herself.

In case there are any hidden faeries, pixies, and knockers present, she knows it's only appropriate to ask permission to enter the forest, but there's something about talking to plants that just screams *crazy*.

"Hi," she says, grimacing at the tremble in her voice. "Yesterday, Mrs. Crenshaw was attacked by a Miser Fae, as I'm sure you know, but Dougal and I can't defeat the creep without help. So, I need to go to Orthega, find Orion, and bring him back here." Rachel looks back at Ziggy. "How was that?"

Ziggy answers by dimming, as if to say, "Meh".

"Please?" she adds, directing the word to the bush, while keeping an eye on Ziggy.

The Fae light flashes once, apparently approving of her manners.

"Can we go now?"

Another single flash answers. Ziggy flies off, moving beyond the invisible barrier without slowing.

Rachel steps up to the ACCESS PROHIBITED sign.

The magical barrier, which surrounds the entire forest, sent electrical tingles across her skin the last time she'd entered. Those ripples hadn't been entirely unpleasant, but Rachel's fairly positive that when she and Dougal passed through without permission, they'd inadvertently set off the forest's defense mechanism.

She takes a moment to gather her courage, and fills her lungs with the crisp autumn air, then takes a cautious step forward. Nothing hinders her advancement. Rachel takes a second step forward. No tingling sensation. With an exhale of relief, she walks deeper into the forest, calling out her thanks for being granted permission.

Ziggy glides past the first tree, weaves around the second, and circles the third.

"Hey, wait up." Rachel ducks beneath a low branch. She climbs across raised roots, and manages to keep a few paces behind the seemingly jubilant golden sphere.

Ziggy bounces in midair as if to tell her to hurry, before rushing back to her side.

"I'm saving my energy," she says when the Fae light circles her. "Think of it as a marathon, not a sprint."

Ziggy rushes forward and back several times, urging her to move faster.

"Dude, you're getting on my nerves. Cut it out or I'm turning back."

In response, Ziggy loses some of his vibrancy, grows a shade darker. He hovers a few steps ahead of her, only moving forward when she does.

"Now you're taunting me?"

One flash from Ziggy confirms her assumption.

Rachel shakes her head and picks up the pace. "You're a real pain sometimes."

She always anticipates birdsong or hopes to see a squirrel or hare scrambling for cover, but the trek through the dense forest is devoid of life. There's an unbearable hush, a nothingness that seems to burrow into her very being. Apart from her footfalls on the fallen leaves, aside from her rhythmic breathing, only—

The melody picks up from somewhere deep within the forest. She's willing to give into the temptation of following the sweet sound if it leads her closer to where she needs to be. If it leads her to Orion …

Meanwhile, her thoughts and a sulking magical lightbulb are her only company. Strange questions she can't begin to answer pop randomly into her mind. How long until she gets to the portal? Is it even considered a portal? Who built it? Why did they build it? Is Stonehenge actually another one of these Fae portals?

"You still angry with me?" Her soft spoken words sound like a shout into the void, but it's better than the countless weird questions wracking havoc on her psyche.

Ziggy answers with two flashes. *No.*

"Are we relatively close to where we need to be?"

Ziggy hesitates, but eventually a single flash comes. He slacks off and sidles up to her, glows a bit brighter, before wandering ahead again. She follows, wordless, until she steps over a vaguely familiar rotting tree trunk. Ziggy disappears around a red maple, moss covering the northern side of the bark. She weaves around the red maple tree and faces her immediate future. Four white birch trees are twisted together to create a natural, living arch, and carved at the top is its name—Harrowsgate.

"Finally," she breathes the word, staring at the gateway to Orthega.

A mixture of excitement and anxiety floods her system as she nears the faerie circle. Emerald green grass is accompanied by a variety of wildflowers, which continue to bloom even in the cooling months. Mushrooms encircle the strange formation—the "faerie circle" as Dougal had claimed. Her heart beats faster, not in fear but in anticipation. She *wants* to cross the mushrooms. An inherent need pulls her toward the Harrowsgate. Rachel battles against the urge and instead makes her way around the faerie circle, studying every inch of the birch tree arch. There's no telling where she'll end up once she crosses through—hopefully she'll avoid Telfore this time—and she has no idea if she'll find Orion. She has to try, though. For Shadow Grove and all the people who calls it home.

Rachel completes the circle and repositions the backpack on her shoulder.

Ziggy moves closer to her, now a vibrant gold that swirls like liquid.

"You ready?" she asks.

One flash answers her question.

Rachel nods, holds out her hand in front of her, and unfurls her fingers.

Ziggy inches closer until he's hovering over her palm.

The sunrays penetrating the canopy of leaves catch his surface and rebound, creating a magical lightshow that brightens the arch.

The world as she knows it becomes an insignificant memory as she crosses the mushroom border with Ziggy in hand. There is no resistance this time, no crackling energy running across her skin. This time, the only things that matter are the arch and the immeasurable possibilities lying beyond it. It's as if all the problems she's ever faced, all the good memories she's made in her lifetime, are inconsequential.

She reaches out with her free hand to touch the gateway and exhales through her nose as the something indescribable ripples against her skin. The melody stops and Rachel recoils, snapping out of her trance.

"Tricky little thing," she whispers, grinning.

A soft, almost imperceptible humming resonates from the Harrowsgate, the sound intensifying the temptation. She lifts Ziggy higher and moves him into the gateway, watching her hand disappear into the rippling void. With a deep breath, she squeezes her eyes shut and takes another step closer. The humming grows louder, more distinct. Suddenly, it feels like she's moving through air. It's nothing like falling. No. It's more like she's drifting on a slight breeze. The air grows denser around her and cools her skin. The Harrowsgate wants her, and deep inside her, she feels like she needs to answer its call.

The sensations of moving through space and time, of literally crossing into another universe, comes to an abrupt end.

Rachel opens her eyes and finds herself standing inside another circle, where rounded stones protrude from yellowing grass. She looks around, finds an angry sky overhead and a dirt road at the bottom of the hill.

Ziggy flashes in her hand.

"Okay, where to now?" she asks.

Ziggy moves away and hovers at eye-level, not flashing.

"Oh, yeah, Mercia's mirror." Rachel fishes the compact mirror out of her front pocket and opens it with her thumb. The obsidian surface ripples as an image takes shape—a grassy hilltop. She looks around, notices a road surrounded by small rolling hills, all covered in grass. "Well, that narrows it down."

Ziggy flies out of the stone circle, heading in the opposite direction of the road.

"You sure?"

One flash.

She mumbles an unconvinced, "Okay," and follows the Fae light toward the rolling hills, where long, yellow blades of grass wither in silence. Rachel glances up at the darkening sky, expecting lightning to flash or thunder to roll before rain pelts the dehydrated earth. There's no sign of lightning, though. And those clouds, regardless of their threatening appearance, don't look like rain is coming anytime soon. If anything, there's a snowstorm approaching, which will make her search for Orion so much harder.

"I think it'll be wise if we start moving faster now. We'll make camp when it gets too dark to see, okay?"

This time Ziggy doesn't answer her with a flash. The Fae light simply picks up speed, apparently knowing exactly which way they need to go. She hastens after the ball of light, repositioning one of the backpack's straps over her shoulder as she goes.

Chapter Nine
Badlands

The journey is long and monotonous across the unchanging scenery.

Rachel walks up and down rolling hills until the tediousness becomes almost unbearable. The mirror shows her which markers to look for as she makes her way across the foreign landscape, but they are so mundane, she can easily miss them. The mirror also reflects Orion sitting at the head of a table, talking and sometimes arguing. Sometimes the sign is a strange rock peeking through the wilting grass, other times a patch of wildflowers pop against the rocky face of a hill.

Now and then she takes five minute breaks to drink some water and rest her legs, but she doesn't waste time. People are counting on her—efficiency is key.

After what feels like eons, the yellowing landscape turns gray and barren. The soil becomes rockier, less stable underfoot. She listens to the crunching beneath her soles, tries to ignore the aches in her thighs and calves and ankles. A bird braves the strange weather, silently gliding through the air. Rolling hills give way to seemingly endless rocky terrain and on the horizon, the silhouette of a mountain range stretch against the ever-darkening sky.

A stream trickles nearby, drawing her attention away from

the horizon. She ventures toward the tiny creek to fill her bottle.

Hopefully there isn't some weird Fae disease contaminating the water.

The water looks clear enough and is cool to the touch. Desperation to quell her thirst wins out in the end, and she takes a tentative sip. There is no odd taste.

Oh well, what happens will happen.

Rachel takes a larger sip and drinks deeply before refilling her bottle.

She spends a few minutes evaluating her surroundings for the umpteenth time, wondering whether this would make a good camping site. The ground is too uneven to get a comfortable night's rest, though, and there's nothing to make a fire with anywhere in the vicinity. It's just rocks, boulders, and gravel. Pressing on in the hopes of finding a more hospitable site is her only option.

Rachel takes the time to put on her jacket, covering her head with the faux fur hood to protect her ears from the raging wind and the blistering cold. Then, she takes a last look at the mirror— the image of a white boulder with an insignia carved into its surface—and shakes her head. There's no telling if she'll find the next marker in the dark, but she has to try. Rachel repositions her backpack, stuffs her hands into the deep pockets for warmth, and continues the long walk toward the mountains.

The temperature plummets significantly as night draws closer.

As tired as she is after the long and mildly disturbing day, moving keeps her blood pumping, keeps her warm to some extent. And the faster she gets to the boulder, the quicker she'll find Orion.

Night falls and Ziggy closes the gap between them so she can see where her feet land. The wind picks up, the whistling she's grown accustomed to turns into a deafening howl. Shivers run down her spine and up her arms. Rachel keeps her tired eyes on the ground, hunching over as she battles the elements.

"Let me know if you find it," she calls.

Ziggy, who's no more than a dot of light in the intense darkness, flashes.

Not even a star is visible in the overcast sky—no moonlight shines the way.

Her legs are sluggish from the cold, muscles scream for mercy, joints beckon for rest. Rachel stops and shakes her head, unable to take another step forward.

"I need to make camp, Ziggy."

The Fae light flashes once in understanding and flies back to her side.

Rachel sets her backpack on the ground. "I'm sorry. I wanted to go on, but I can't."

Ziggy flashes again, slowly floats to the ground, and settles between a few rocks.

Rachel unhooks her blanket from the backpack and shakes it out before taking a seat on top of a rock. She pulls the blanket over her lap with her numb fingers.

"This isn't going to be the most comfortable night's rest, so if I'm grumpy tomorrow, you can't hold it against me," she says.

Ziggy flashes once.

"I'm probably going to be sore from head to toe, too."

Another flash.

"Look at you being all understanding and stuff." Rachel takes a bite of a granola bar and chews slowly, watching Ziggy from the corner of her eye. She swallows and takes a sip of water to wash it down. After her meager meal, she wiggles around to find a comfortable position to sleep in. The problem is that there's nothing comfortable about sleeping on a pile of rocks.

"Are you going to keep watch for me?"

Ziggy answers with a single flash, before dimming down to a dull gold.

Rachel smiles. "Night-night, bright light."

Ziggy's surface ripples in response.

She closes her eyes, half wondering how long it'll take her to fall asleep with the rock jutting into her hip, before she unexpectedly drifts off into a deep, dreamless slumber.

When Rachel awakens a few hours later, it's still dark out. The bitter cold penetrates through the blanket and her clothes, and seeps into her skin. She spots Ziggy floating nearby in calculated zigzags, probably doing a perimeter check. Rachel groans as she sits upright, stiff after the previous day's walk and awkward sleeping position.

How many miles had she walked yesterday? Surely more than five. Ten, maybe? Hopefully more than ten. She wipes the sleep from her eyes, yawns, and stretches her sore muscles as best she can.

Rachel sighs as she stands.

Worse things have happened than starting a day without coffee. She rolls up the blanket.

It's a bit of a hassle to maneuver the blanket back into its original size, but she gets it done and zips the blanket shut. Before she fixes it to her backpack, she has another granola bar, finds her toiletries, and goes about her morning routine as usual—sans the luxury of running water.

"Zigs." Her voice is still husky with sleep.

Ziggy floats back to her side, brightening as she pulls the compact mirror into the open.

The top mirror shows Orion, fast asleep, whereas the bottom mirror shows the next marker. It looks like a weird tree, where the branches are bare and growing horizontally.

"Let's see if we can find this tree by the time the sun rises."

One flash.

Ziggy leads the way through the impenetrable darkness, shining brightly so Rachel can see where she's stepping.

"Are we far from Amaris?"

There's an obvious hesitation before the Fae light responds with two successive flashes. Rachel's brow creases. The last thing she needs now is to run into Orion's older brother, King Nova.

The sun crests behind the silhouetted mountains in the distance and the darkness slowly dissipates around her, revealing the bleak landscape once more. Light gray stones, in every imaginable shape and size, cover the ground. No matter where she looks, it's dreary, lifeless, and alien. It's not exactly what she'd imagined the Fae Realm to look like.

Granted, her fantasies had been more along the line of lush, dense forests for as far as the eye can see, alive with birdsong. Colorful flowers blooming all over valleys, where robust herds of deer grazed near crystal clear rivers. The Fae, she'd imagined, lived in treehouses of some kind, while faeries flew around and pixies played with children. This landscape was nothing near as beautiful as the picture in her head.

The temperature climbs as the sun continues its ascension.

By midmorning, Rachel sees the lonesome, bare tree standing in the distance, its branches growing off to one side. The tree is as gray as the rocks surrounding the trunk, yet it appears so out of place in this depressing world. She stops beside it, presses her hand against the smooth bark, and looks at the mountains in the distance. Judging by how the mountain range has grown since daybreak, she's made good progress. There's no telling if the mountains are even where she needs to be, but it sure looks like the obvious route. Rachel takes out the compact mirror and opens it.

Her shoulders drop as the mirror's black surface reveals her next landmark—a strange rock formation.

"Oh, goody. More rocks," she mumbles. Rachel searches the area for the next landmark—a needle in a haystack.

The expanse is mostly flat, but in the distance—near the mountain range—three white peaks jut from the earth and reach high into the sky. Rachel double checks the image to make sure those are the rocks she should pass before returning the compact mirror to her pocket. She takes off her jacket, wraps it around her waist. "Five minutes, then we move."

Rachel takes a seat beneath the tree. She has a drink, eats a granola bar, and gathers her strength for the long journey ahead.

"No rest for the wicked," she says as she gets to her feet again.

Then, Rachel sets off toward the next marker.

At some point, she catches herself humming a song she can't place. The song sounded like something her dad used to listen to, something you wouldn't know you're acutely familiar with until you hear it again.

"Na-na-nuh-huh.   Something-something-something   …" Rachel hummed the rest. "What is that song?"

Unable to figure out the title or any of the lyrics, she gives up and puts it out of her mind.

Her boredom prevails.

"I should've brought my phone along," she says.

Rachel barks a laugh. The absurdity of wanting her phone to amuse herself with catches her off guard. Surely there are more important things she could've dragged along. Perhaps a camping stove. A damn pot, so she could boil water. She grimaces as she lowers her hands to her sides, suddenly livid with herself for not planning this trip better before setting off.

Yes, she likes the outdoors. She's gone camping in the past, had gone on fishing trips with Greg and Luke when they were kids—when Luke was still alive. She knows the basics of camping, yet she'd dived headfirst into a possible suicide mission in a whole other world without giving it a second thought.

"I am *such* an idiot."

She runs through the implications of having not brought along the bare necessities of survival, coming up with bizarre worst-case-scenarios if she doesn't find Orion soon. Even *if* she finds him, there's a good chance that he won't want to come back. What then?

Rachel stares ahead, toward the growing mountain range, where snowcapped peaks reach to the heavens. Even from her position, she's able to make out the steep inclines and treacherous cliffs. There's also some vegetation visible, but the meager selection of bare trees are separated by large, rocky terrains.

There are no obvious cave entries or outcroppings that could act as protection against the elements, though.

Her thoughts turn to wild animals, predators that may roam the mountainous region, prowling in search of their next meal. What types of exotic Fae creatures might try to kill her there? A three-headed beast with glowing red eyes, perhaps? Or maybe she'll be murdered by something more sinister, something akin to the Night Weaver. She could very well end up like that poor person in the school's boiler room, completely deboned.

She stops in her tracks, closes her eyes, and takes a deep breath.

This negativity won't help anyone. Get your head straight.

Rachel exhales slowly, opens her eyes again.

Ziggy hovers a few feet away, waiting for her to continue across the desolate landscape.

"Just give me a second." Inhale, exhale, inhale. "Okay." She starts walking again, catching up to Ziggy in no time.

When midday arrives, Rachel reaches the three-peaked rock formation. She sits at its base, and takes off her shoes, removes her socks to air her feet, and evaluates the damage. Blisters are already forming from the friction of her socks against her tender heels.

Rachel wrestles her backpack onto her lap and finds another pair of socks and some Band-Aids. It's the best she can do.

Next, she pulls out some food into the open—an apple and some beef jerky—as she chats with Ziggy about whatever pops into her head. Talking keeps her from dwelling, keeps her sane.

"My water is running out fast," she says.

One flash.

Rachel only takes a couple of small sips. "Are we near a water source?"

Two flashes.

She sighs and reluctantly closes her water bottle.

As her break comes to an end, Rachel puts on the pair of fresh socks, pulls on her hiking boots, and finds a handful of trail mix to nibble on while she walks.

Rachel continues talking, and Ziggy periodically responds with flashes.

It remains a one-sided conversation for the most part, but it's better than eerie silence.

The weather changes sometime during the afternoon, revealing a cobalt sky hidden beneath fluffy white dioramic clouds. As the sun's rays warm the world, the temperature becomes balmy, comfortable even.

"Let's play a game," she says. "I spy with my little eye something beginning with an R."

Ziggy quickly sinks to the ground and lands on a rock.

"Too easy, huh?" Rachel laughs out loud.

The sphere flashes once as it gains altitude again and flies ahead.

"Okay, I spy with my little eye something beginning with a—" Rachel cuts herself off. In the distance, moving parallel to the mountain range at a quick pace, several riders come into view. Surrounded by billowing dust, they seem to be outriding the devil himself as they push their horses to their limits. One of the riders pulls ahead from the rest.

Perhaps those are Nova's scouts? Maybe he knows she's in the Fae Realm?

"Hey, Ziggy, should I be worried about those particular Fae?"

The Fae light slows down, as if evaluating the riders moving around the base of the mountain range, before flashing twice.

"Good to know," Rachel says. "It would've sucked if we came all this way just to get stopped by a few male Fae and their pretty ponies."

Ziggy flashes once. His usual mirth is missing, though. There's no zigzagging across her path anymore, no playfulness whatsoever. It's all business.

"I'll shut up now."

She's answered by another single flash.

Rachel watches as the riders disappear in the distance before she relaxes again.

In the silence, her body makes its aches known again. The backpack's straps cut into her shoulders, the weight she carries settling in her lower back. She reaches up to rub the tension out of her neck and shoulders, groans as she touches the knots in her muscles.

An hour before nightfall, Rachel and Ziggy reach the footfalls of the mountain.

"I think we should get to higher ground, in case those Fae return," Rachel says, pulling her bottle of water from her backpack. There's a mouthful left, nothing more. "And we should search for water."

One flash.

Rachel pulls the compact mirror out of her pocket and studies the image reflecting on the surface. Another rock with an insignia carved into its face. She looks around, but finds nothing that resembles the image.

"Ziggy, come look here," she says. The Fae light bobs closer. "Can you go ahead and see if this marker is up there somewhere?"

A single flash.

"Don't go too far, okay? Just do a quick scan and come back."

Without answering, Ziggy flies off, bypassing the mountain's treacherous slopes.

Rachel conserves her energy by half-sitting, half-leaning against the rock formation, afraid that if she relaxes too much, she won't be able to move for the next week. Without water, this is not an option.

Approximately ten minutes pass before Ziggy returns, flashing gold repeatedly.

"Calm down. Did you find the rock?"

One flash.

"Water?"

Another single flash.

"Is it far?" Rachel studies the steep slope she'll have to take up the mountain.

Ziggy hesitates and grows dimmer. One flash answers her question.

Rachel inhales deeply through her nose, her body begging her to stop for the day. She can't, though. Her thirst is already becoming unbearable, and she only has a few drops of water left. She *needs* to move, whether she wants to or not.

"Lead the way."

She pushes away from the rock formation, and heads to the winding path up the mountains. Her progress is slow, especially with the precarious shifting of loose rocks underneath her feet. Finding any type of traction is nearly impossible in the daylight— risking the ascension at night would be foolish.

They're able to clear the first flattop mountain, which leads directly into a higher, steeper mountain. She's ready to stop for the night, but Ziggy is adamant in continuing.

"Really?" Rachel drags her feet as she follows the Fae light. "I'm not going to climb that thing *now*. We can wait until morning."

Ziggy flashes brightly, and swerves dangerously close to her head, before shooting ahead. Just as the golden sphere reaches the mountain's side, Ziggy vanishes into thin air.

"Ziggy?" Rachel walks closer, forgetting her qualms. Losing Ziggy now ... She doesn't even want to think about it. "This isn't funny."

Ziggy half-reappears from the mountain's side, flashes brightly several times, before slipping into obscurity again.

Rachel exhales in relief and follows Ziggy through the glamor—a carefully constructed image of a roughhewn wall—and into a narrow serpentine passage behind it.

The Fae light bounces in midair a few steps ahead.

"You could've been less dramatic about it."

Ziggy keeps heading down the path, shining brighter as the world grows darker. The passage still has abrupt inclines and treacherous slopes, but at least she doesn't have to navigate her way across loose rocks. This helps. Not a lot, considering every part of her is in revolt, but the packed ground does make things easier. The darkness is an overpowering force of nature, though, and it threatens to suffocate her in the confined space. The wind moves through the passage, screaming as it erodes the rocks on either side. A gust thrusts her forward, the force of it pushing her onward.

"This wasn't the best idea," Rachel says. She squints to see past Ziggy's glow. The passage is too narrow and twists too often to set up a camp. It would be murder on her already aching body to sleep here. Also, she doubts she'll get any sleep with the furious wind coming through this place. "You better get me somewhere relatively safe soon, because I'm about to drop dead from exhaustion."

Ziggy flashes once.

Not long thereafter, her eyelids become lead. She actively works on blinking less frequently, afraid if she shuts her eyes too long she'll fall asleep while walking. The passage grows narrower, as if the mountains themselves have decided to move closer together to make the journey more difficult. Around one bend, her backpack gets stuck, forcing her to take it off and carry it sideways in her already-weary arms. The farther they walk, the more impatient she becomes. Then, to make matters worse, the passage becomes an even tighter squeeze. The backpack doesn't fit through anymore. She takes her bag off and leaves it dangling between the rocks, hoping to return to it as soon as she gets to wherever Ziggy needs her to be.

Rachel turns sideways to inch through the opening, praying all the while that she won't get stuck. Just as she's ready to throw the fit of a lifetime, the passage suddenly opens up into a large cavern, brightened by moonlight reflecting off the surface of a moderately sized pond. There is vegetation here, too. Green grass surrounds the pond, along with some flowers she's seen in Orion's greenhouse. And there, just to the side of the cavern, the rock with the insignia stands.

"Thank goodness."

She's about to step forward, towards the semi-subterranean oasis, a slice of heaven after trudging two days through a wasteland, when Ziggy blocks her way. Rachel motions around the ball of light, but Ziggy doesn't let her pass.

"What the actual—?" her outburst is cut off when the pretty picture suddenly shimmers at the edges.

She pauses, confusion causing her to reevaluate the image. The picture flickers, as if she's reached the glitch in a looped video recording, and reveals what truly lies beneath the scenic view. Instead of a clear, inviting pond, a pool of yellowish water bubble in the center of the cavern, emitting a distinctive smell of rotting eggs. She suspects the fluid to be sulfur, or a similar Fae chemical. Instead of vegetation surrounding the pond, there are jagged rocks with dangerously sharp edges waiting.

"It's a security glamor, isn't it?"

Ziggy flashes once in answer.

Without a word, Rachel inches back through the narrow passage, intent on retrieving her backpack. She's ready to make several trips if she has to, prepared to carry every individual item through if she must.

When she arrives at her destination, she quickly unhooks the blanket and tosses it over her shoulder, and pulls out her toiletry bag.

Rachel holds it in one hand and makes her way back to the cavern's opening, where she sets her belongings in a heap beside the entrance. She makes a second trip to retrieve the food she's brought along. The third trip is easier. After Rachel repositions the remaining contents, she's able to fold the bag in half and squeeze it through the tunnel.

Rachel rushes to stuff everything back into the backpack and somehow closes the bulging thing without issue. She straightens, breathless after the exercise.

"I need water, Ziggy," Rachel says.

Ziggy floats around the side of the cavern, no more than a foot away, and keeping close to the wall.

"If I die here, you tell Mercia I'll see her in her nightmares."

Rachel presses her back against the wall, holding her backpack in her hand, and follows Ziggy around the cavern. She tests the surface with the tip of her hiking boot before putting her full weight on the ground. Now and then, the glamor shimmers or flickers around her, giving her an idea of where the most treacherous parts of the cavern are located. Still, she doesn't want to take any unnecessary chances by rushing.

At the opposite side of the cavern, Ziggy ascends diagonally, as if signaling a rise in the floor. She takes baby steps behind the Fae light. Rachel feels, rather than see, the gradual rise beneath her feet, thighs, and calves. Her muscles strain as she climbs the slope. Subtle changes in the cavern walls become visible as she makes her way higher.

She glances down.

"Oh. Bad idea. *Bad freaking idea.*"

Rachel swiftly averts her gaze from staring at the ground, which seems miles beneath her feet. Her pulse races. Flashbacks of how the Akrah Cloak dropped her to distract Orion fill her thoughts. Her stomach does a few somersaults. Overcome with a bout of vertigo, she squeezes her eyes shut and forces herself to take the next step forward, even if her mind screams for her to stop. The first step is the hardest. The second step is better.

"Just keep moving forward." Rachel takes a chance to open her eyes again and focuses on Ziggy.

A few feet higher, Ziggy disappears into the cavern wall, before he reappears a heartbeat later to reveal another glamor.

"Overkill much?"

She presses her hand against the wall to feel the actual opening. Rachel steps closer to the half-visible Fae light, and the cavern wall gives way beneath her palm, vanishing behind the glamor.

Disregarding the illusion completely, she turns on her heels and walks through.

Ziggy's soft glow illuminates the tunnel, zigging ahead.

"Hold up," Rachel hisses. She hunches to avoid hitting the low ceiling. Soon, the tunnel opens into a wide chamber, the ceiling now high enough for her to stand upright without worrying about hitting her head. "Thanks for waiting," she mumbles.

Only then does she see Ziggy bobbing above a dark pool, his light revealing a shimmering trickle of water running down the roughly hewed wall.

Rachel falls to her knees in front of the pool, eyes stinging with gratitude as she submerges her hand.

Ziggy dips lower.

Her haggard reflection stares back, emotion and exhaustion clear beneath the dirt embedded in her skin. She leans down and splashes the cool water on her face and neck, washing away the accumulated grime and sweat. She cups her hand and bows closer to the pool, lapping up the water in a desperate attempt to sooth her dry throat.

Once her thirst has been quenched, Rachel removes her backpack, unhooks the blanket, and rummages around inside for her bottle. Rachel fills the bottle, and places it on the uneven floor beside her before she pulls out her toiletries bag.

"One more day, then we'll hopefully find Orion."

Ziggy flashes once, and moves toward the blanket, ready to rest for the night.

Chapter Ten
Brittle But Not Broken

Sometime the next morning, as she's packing up her belongings, a scuffle manages to catch her attention. Confused by the sound, she looks to where Ziggy is bobbing near the entrance.

"Ziggy?"

Ziggy flies back to her side, flashing golden light in her face.

"What is it?"

Something moves outside the cave, somewhere in the death trap they'd traveled through to get here.

Rachel waits, listens. How many have stumbled into this place and will she be able to fight them off if the need arise? There's no way to tell from her position. She gets to her feet and puts her backpack on.

"There's a way out, right?" she whispers.

One flash.

"Okay, stay close."

Ziggy leads her deeper into the narrowing cave, where the ceiling lowers drastically. Soon, she needs to go on her hands and knees to crawl through the passage.

She doesn't know if she's on the right path anymore, having neglected to check Mercia's mirror for the next landmark. If

Ziggy's haste is anything to go on, getting to Orion is the least of her concern.

Her knees and palms ache as she moves as fast as she can through the winding cave.

The passage opens up a smidge, just enough for her to get back on her feet.

A frustrated shriek rebounds off the walls, originating from somewhere behind her.

Panicking, she presses her hand against the wall to navigate the twisting passage through the mountain. The ceiling becomes higher again, but the walls close in on her, making it difficult to put distance between herself and the owner of the scream.

Every squeeze through the passage, every inch forward, brings her closer to an escape from the mountain and the pursuer.

"Is it far?" Rachel asks.

Ziggy doesn't answer.

Rachel looks back into the darkness, unable to make out much of anything, but her imagination is more than willing to create monstrous creatures rushing after her.

Her slow progress pays off when the passage opens and sunlight become visible from the cave's entrance.

Relief. She's overcome with gratitude from getting out of the claustrophobic situation in one piece.

"Thank heavens." Rachel steps into the early morning sunlight, raising her head and closing her eyes. She basks in the warmth shining down on her.

A large hand suddenly clamps down over her mouth, muffling her scream. An arm wraps around her waist, pulling her back against a large body. Thick fingers dig into her prone flesh and tired muscles.

"Apologies, but if that prissy Fae allowed us to have our spoils, he would have spared you this dishonor," the man says behind her.

She thrashes wildly against her assailant.

"Now, now," he purrs, one hand roving across her body. "You wouldn't have been my first choice either. Settle down and I'll make this quick."

He roughly forces her around and pushes her face-first into the mountainside, slamming the air out of her lungs. He leans hard into her back, trapping her against the wall, that one hand kneading her breast all the while.

She breathes hard through her nose, the fear of what's to come sending waves of panic through her body.

No.

Rachel kicks back with her heel into his shin with as much force as she can, disregarding the painful blisters bursting from the impact. The male's shout of pain is enough to encourage her to fight with more vigor.

She twists out of his hold and looks down at the man.

The burly soldier with beady black eyes is somewhere in his twenties, she guesses, and his dark-brown hair is sheared short against his scalp. He's dressed in a black uniform with twin red deer embroidered on his lapels. So, that probably meant Orion was the "prissy Fae." His ears are pointed, but not as elongated. And there's a nasty scar running across his throat, like he'd either been cut or survived a hanging.

He roars as he stomps closer to her, arms outspread.

Ziggy appears, and crashes straight into her assailant's face, effectively blinding him.

His face turns red as he battles against Ziggy's assault, the

Fae light weaving in and out of the man's reach in expert, choppy movements. Wherever Ziggy touches him, angry red welts form on his skin. Blisters pop up, encircling the burns.

Yeah, her Fae light doesn't take nonsense from anyone.

As Ziggy keeps her attacker busy, Rachel scans the area, searching for an escape.

The vegetation of the vast plateau within the mountain range mainly consists of grass and trees, but from the look of things, there isn't much in the way of hiding places. There is a saddled horse grazing nearby, which is enough of a sign to get her to move again. She runs to the horse and, thanking her stars that she's had some lessons when it came to riding the animals, finds the stirrup. Rachel quickly gets on top of the steed and grabs hold of the reins.

With a click of her tongue, the horse trots forward, before gradually moving into a gallop.

"Ziggy, we're leaving," Rachel shouts over her shoulder as the horse picks up speed. She's still reeling over the close call. If he'd been stronger, if Ziggy hadn't been there to help her … "Ziggy!"

A few worried beats later, the Fae light flits past her, crisscrossing ahead.

Rachel chances a glance to the Fae they'd left behind, her assailant reduced to a heap in the dirt, face burned and hands scorched. She swiftly averts her gaze, grimacing, almost feeling guilty.

"Is he dead?"

Ziggy flashes twice.

"Pity."

She steers the horse well away from both the unknown threat

119

in the mountain, as well as the man who'd assaulted her, before slowing to an easy trot.

Ziggy floats closer to her side.

"Was that guy human?" Rachel asks, although she doubts it. "His ears were pointy, but short, so—"

Two flashes.

Rachel frowns. "Halfling?"

Ziggy flickers once.

"Stupid Halfling," she whispers, stifling a sob. She fishes the brass compact mirror out of her pocket and opens it in her palm. Rachel studies the obsidian surface closely, discerning an arch-like feature, seemingly looming over a thinning forest. "This one won't be too difficult to find." She pushes herself up on the stirrups and scans the region again.

Rachel points in the direction of a smooth peak above tall trees, merely a tip visible, but the surface gleams wherever the sun touches it.

They change direction. Ziggy takes the lead, while Rachel steers the horse behind him.

"I should probably give you a name," she says to the horse, brushing the white and brown mane. It's the best she can do to keep her mind from wandering to the assault. "Something neutral, yes?"

Up front, Ziggy flashes once.

"What about Blair?"

The horse whinnies, as if saying, "I'd rather visit a glue factory," while Ziggy flashes twice in disagreement.

"Tough crowd. Okay, let's try something more cultured. How about Tolstoy?"

Ziggy immediately flickers twice, dims, and then flashes

twice again.

"There's just no pleasing you."

Rachel passes the time by running through a list of names, all of which Ziggy hates. At times, the horse would make its thoughts known with either a neigh or a snort, but generally didn't seem too invested in the conversation.

"Journey?"

Ziggy doesn't immediately answer her proposal. Then, just when she thinks the Fae light's grown bored with the game, it flashes once.

"I've got one nod of approval. What say you?" Rachel leans forward in the saddle and brushes the horse's muscular neck. "Do you like the name Journey?" An ear twitches. She sits upright again, grinning. "It's a unanimous vote then, and fitting, if I may say so myself."

They reach the arch-like peak long after the sun has set, but even in the dark, she notices that the bases of each pillar is riddled with strange symbols, half-hidden behind strategically placed rocks.

"We should make camp somewhere, give Journey a break."

Ziggy flashes once.

She searches around for a well-hidden site, close enough to the arch-like structure but far enough to give her a semblance of security. There's a trickle of water running past the area she chooses. Some grass, too. It's better than nothing.

She dismounts, walks through the thick foliage, and leads Journey to graze nearby.

"Keep your light dim," she whispers as Ziggy reaches her side.

One dim flash answers.

Rachel takes off her backpack and drops it at the base of a tree before stretching her legs and back. Her thighs ache from being on Journey the whole day, while lower back screams for a soft bed. She walks around a while, fills her water bottle, and moves back to where she left her backpack.

No way will she sleep tonight. Not with that Halfling still alive and relatively well. He's probably already looking for her and his horse. He's probably contemplating his revenge. That's what she would have been doing if he'd—

"Could you do a perimeter check?" she asks Ziggy.

The Fae light bobs away and circles the area she's chosen for the night.

"Relax. You're fine," she whispers. "Hopefully tomorrow, you'll find Orion. Then you can go home."

Time ticks on and night closes in. A laugh echoes through the forest, distant but undoubtedly male. A command is shouted somewhere else. Rachel listens, anticipating the sounds will grow louder and more volatile. Nothing of the sort happens. There's smoke in the air, notes of food drift along on a breeze. Her stomach rumbles, wanting a proper meal. A bird sings. Soon, the darkness deepens, grows silent.

Ziggy settles at her side and she tickles the top of the sphere with her fingertips, unable to shut her eyes even for a minute.

Long before dawn, Rachel mounts Journey and heads back to the arch, following Ziggy's bobs and weaves.

"Please don't be a gateway. Please don't be a gateway. Please don't be a gateway," she whispers her mantra, squeezing her eyes shut as they move through the opening.

When no weird sensation comes, she opens her eyes. Hundreds of white tents lie at the bottom of the road, circles placed within circles, stretching as far as the eye can see. Smoke trails up from the settlement, but there is no movement in the spaces between.

Rachel looks up the side of the arch, spying a vacant watchtower carved from the mountain itself. She scans the area for clues as to what type of settlement she's venturing in to. It's early enough to go unnoticed, but there's no telling what they'll do when they see her.

She finds the compact mirror and opens it, waits for an image of a tent to materialize on the smooth surface, an indecipherable flag fixed above the entrance. The image of Orion is obscured by pre-dawn darkness.

Rachel shuts the mirror and replaces it in her pocket as Journey trots toward the quiet, sleeping campsite. She searches for a tent with a flag above its entrance, for anything remotely official. Maybe she'll get lucky.

Are humans even tolerated around here?

Her growing anxiety makes her feel like she's swallowed a rock as she approaches the settlement.

Journey slows her advance as the first tent comes up.

A couple of horses graze in a small clearing. Embers burn in a nearby fire pit. Journey moves expertly through the open space, sliding between tents as if having done so a million times.

Rachel continues searching for a flag. When she sees none, she maneuvers Journey deeper into the settlement, where she instead finds a wooden weapon rack, full of swords and spears and axes.

Journey travels through to another inner-circle, where a sleeping, uniformed man occupies a chair near an extinguished fire. She veers away from the soldier, earning herself a bump from Ziggy. The Fae light rushes in between two tents, the space too small for a horse.

Gritting her teeth, she halts Journey and dismounts.

First I fail the SATs, then I steal a horse—although technically it's not the first time I've done that—and now I'm sneaking around a military camp. What's next?

She carefully follows Ziggy deeper into the camp, ducks behind white canvasses, sprints through open spaces, all while scanning the entrances for the nondescript flag.

The morning grows brighter as the sun crests the horizon, and people began rustling inside the tents.

Rachel's heart beats faster and terror pushes to the forefront of her thoughts. What if Orion isn't here anymore? With her sneaking around a military encampment, the only logical conclusion anyone can make is she's an enemy spy, and there's a good chance the enemy is King Nova. They might very well execute her.

Ziggy bobs in midair before bouncing off the sides of the stretched fabric.

Get down, you suicidal lightbulb.

Rachel peers around the tent just as a soldier walks into the open. She jerks back into the shadows, praying he didn't see her, and makes herself as small as possible in the shadows. Footsteps approach.

"Wake up, scoundrels," comes a commanding voice from somewhere behind her. "The general wants three scouts to head out within the hour. I volunteered you sorry lot for the mission. Get dressed."

Footsteps pass her hiding place and fade into the distance. Groans and yawns come from within the tent she's using as cover.

Rachel sucks in a breath through her gritted teeth, and risks taking another look. The area clear, she sprints to where she last saw Ziggy and hides behind a stack of wooden crates labeled: BUMBLEBERRY WINERIES.

"Ziggy," she whispers. Rachel inches around the crates, careful not to bump into anything and alert the entire army to her presence. "Zigs?"

Ziggy glides into view before rounding the tent again.

Her jaw stiffens with irritation.

Rachel follows Ziggy around the tent and is greeted by a black flag, twin red deer silhouettes stand on their hind legs in the center. The flag hangs limply above the entrance, the tattered edges hardly shifting in the slight breeze moving through the camp. Shouldn't this have been harder? Yes, getting here wasn't the easiest thing, but this feels a bit anticlimactic.

She pulls the white canvas aside and steps into the gloomy interior where a large table is covered with maps, scrolls are stacked into high piles on the single chair. Rachel walks inside, the thick carpet muting her footsteps. On one side of the tent is a curtained-off area, large enough to hide a bed. Across from the gauzy fabric, a metal tub—lined with swaths of cotton—sits on a brazier, in order to heat the water within.

Keeping her breathing steady, Rachel reaches up to push the curtain out of the way, but freezes as a blade cuts through the fabric, stopping short before it can embed itself in her throat.

She swallows hard, the tip of the dagger tickling her skin in the process.

"Give me one good reason not to kill you right here and now." Orion's voice is calm, too calm.

The tip of the dagger presses harder into her skin by the unmistakable silhouette behind the curtain.

Rachel says the first thing that pops into her head. "Mrs. Crenshaw will be über-pissed."

Whether it's a good reason not to be killed, though, is unclear.

The curtain slides out of the way. Fabric flutter to the floor as the dagger cuts the curtain in two. With the dagger still pointing at her throat, the dark-haired Fae prince studies her with his galaxy eyes, forming a Fae light in his free hand. It floats into the air, joining Ziggy against the tent's ceiling.

Orion's brow furrows as the silence between them stretches on.

"Miss me, Faerie Boy?" Rachel raises her finger and pushes the blade away from her throat, ignoring the clean slice against her fingertip. She'd rather lose a finger than have a severed artery.

Orion moves the dagger back to its original position, the suspicion in his glare intensifying.

"Well, this is awkward," she says.

Rachel purses her lips together, her gaze moving to his left forearm, where the tattoo curls all the way up his arm, around his biceps, and moves over his shoulder. The black lines coil and twist around his bare chest, ending on his right waist. The tattoo is one thing—the faded scars marring his skin is a whole other matter.

"*How* did you even get in here?" Orion asks.

"I walked most of the way, but I procured a horse from one

of your men yesterday, after he tried to sexually assault me."
Rachel senses something *off* about Orion. "I called the horse
Journey. Pretty thing, a docile mare, has loads of personality."

"But how did you get into the camp?" Orion asks, dropping
the dagger from her neck.

Rachel shrugs. "My womanly wiles, of course."

Orion rolls his eyes.

Rachel slips the backpack's straps off her shoulders and
places it on the floor. She moves to a round table situated next to
his bed, and picks up the brass pitcher standing on a dented tray.
Rachel fills the matching goblet with what she hopes is just red
wine.

"What's the legal drinking age around here?"

"We don't have liquor restriction laws in Amaris." Orion
takes a seat on the edge of the bed.

"Good to know." Rachel lifts the goblet to her lips and takes
a swig of the heavily spiced wine. Cinnamon and citrus notes play
on her tongue.

"What are you doing here, Clarré?"

"I've come to take you home." She wanders toward the large
table, studying the foreign maps lining the surface. A red stag sits
atop what appears to be a county, surrounded by mountains. She
guesses that's where they are. The golden crown, however, is
positioned precariously close to where the camp is located. There
are other red and gold markers, too, signifying troops across
various territories over Orthega. "And just in the nick of time, it
seems."

Orion materializes on the opposite side of the table, and uses
his forearm to topple the red and white markers off the map. His
expression is inscrutable. Orion regards her with a stony gaze, yet

a smile plays in the corners of his mouth.

He presses his hands on the table and leans forward. "Didn't I tell you not to follow me?" Orion masks his smile with a snarl. "Nova has eyes everywhere, even in this camp, and he will stop at nothing to get his hands on you if it means he has a chance to hurt me."

Rachel raises her free hand to her heart, tilts her head. "Aw, I'm touched. To think, a poorly planned war campaign can be swayed in one brother's favor by little old me."

Bristling, Orion pushes away from the table. "Poorly planned? I'll have you know I've been doing this for centuries."

"Yeah, well, judging by your security, you've lost your touch. It's amazing Nova hasn't sent assassins yet." She turns on her heels and makes her way back to the bed, sipping on the wine as she goes.

"Who says he hasn't?"

Rachel snorts and glances over her shoulder. "I say."

Chapter Eleven
Sidetracked

Bells toll as the alarm is raised. Deep voices shout across the camp for men to ready themselves against an attack, to answer the call if they are able.

A heartbeat later, a breathless, red-faced soldier with barely a single whisker on his lip rushes into Orion's tent. The boy comes to an abrupt halt when he sees the Fae prince standing at the table. He salutes to Orion's back, his chest heaving from exertion.

"Sir," he says, hand still raised.

"What is it?" Orion barks without turning around.

"The generals *urgently* require your assistance. Nova's army is forcing its way North and there's a security breach to the West."

Orion's voice is thick with command and laced with displeasure. "I'll be there to in a few minutes."

"Yes, sir, but …" The boy's fist, firmly fixed beside his waist, trembles.

"But?" Orion turns to face the messenger.

The boy visibly shrinks under Orion's scrutiny. "Sluagh, sir. A horde of Sluagh are heading right for us."

"Why didn't you start with that?" Orion snaps. He vanishes into thin air, leaving the shaking boy alone with Rachel in his tent.

"What's a Sluagh?" she asks, taking the last sip of wine.

The Halfling's eyes widen as he finally seems to notice her. "It's the souls of the restless dead. Men who didn't receive their last rights. How——?" He snaps his attention over his shoulder. "Coming!" The boy runs off.

She sets the goblet on the empty tray and makes her way to the tent's entrance. Men run around in full body armor, armed and ready to die. Orders are barked, though they can't drown out the screams of the dying. A fire blazes nearby, the smoke and flames already visible through the canvas' opening. Horses gallop past, trampling those who aren't fast enough to get out of the way.

Rachel ducks back into the tent, only to find Orion dressing in his uniform in a hurry.

"From what direction did you come?" he asks, buttoning up his shirt as he walks over to the table with the map. "This is where we are right now." Orion points to where the red stag had been earlier.

Rachel studies the map, noticing the black strip on the western side of the mountain range. She points to it, before she drags her finger to where she guesses the Harrowsgate had opened and let her out.

"You came through The Barrens?" He eyes her with that same stony glare.

"Is that what you call the place with all the rocks?"

"Yes," Orion says.

"Then yes. Why?"

"You led the Wild Hunt right to us."

"I did nothing of the sort," she says.

Without warning, he's gone again. The shrieking increases

around the camp, screams grow louder. The world spins around her, faster and faster, until her equilibrium is so off-kilter, she doubts it'll ever recalibrate.

Breathing becomes harder as smoke fills the tent, while beads of sweat take shape on her hairline. Rachel blinks away tears, her eyes burning as the gossamer plumes surround her.

"Ziggy," she coughs, coming back to herself. Rachel backtracks to the opening of the tent, searching the ceiling for the Fae light. Smoke tickles her throat. "Ziggy, we need to go." Another coughing spell wracks her body.

Ziggy descends, blinking gold to signal his arrival.

She grabs hold of the sphere and pivots, rushes out into the open. Flames lick at the canvas, eats away at whatever is inside. Waves of heat roll through the area as a slight breeze picks up, pushing the fire through the encampment.

Rachel steps forward, ready to move east, to where the fire has not yet spread, when a horse runs past. The soldier on the animal's back raises his sword high. She ducks out of the way just in time.

"Isn't that Journey?" she says, looking down at Ziggy.

One flash.

"No …"

The soldier screams his battle cry at the top of his lungs and disappears into the shroud of smoke. Journey's loud neigh resounds through the camp. The horse's fear is unmistakable, makes the threat a reality. Another frightened neigh—cut off too soon, too unnaturally.

Rachel chokes back a sudden sob, her heart breaking for Journey.

Metal meets metal, a groan, and a yell of fury.

Ominous silence succeeds the clash.

Something heavy drops to the ground, followed by a squelch.

Thump.

A severed head rolls out of the smoke, blood still flowing from its neck.

Her heart feels like it's about to pound its way out of her chest and her mind screams at her to run. Rachel is unable to move, can't even breathe. She usually has two go-to responses in situations like these—fight-or-flight. Now, however, a third f-word has made itself known: freeze.

A ghastly humanoid creature steps out of the smoke, an apparition from the lowest levels of the eternal abyss. Shriveled skin hangs from its bones, its modesty hardly preserved by the tattered rags it wears. A white skull peeks out from thinning black hair, a chunk of flesh missing from the right side of its face. An axe, too big to wield for an ordinary being, drags behind the creature, leaving a trail of scarlet in its wake.

One large foot lifts above the soldier's amputated head before stomping down. A sickening crack resounds. The soldier's filmy eyes first bulge, before one pops out of the socket and the other squishes into oblivion. The foot lifts again. Another stomp, then the heel grinds into the remaining mess.

The Sluagh turns its red eyes on Rachel.

Snap out of it!

Parts of her brain shut down completely—specifically the part regulating pain—in preparation of the inevitable end.

The Sluagh narrows its eyes, confusion twisting its already questionable features into a heinous grimace that promises unending torment.

Hands suddenly wrap around her waist. Then, an immense

pressure quickly crushes in around her. She sucks in what could be her final breath as the scene evaporates into nothingness. Darkness replaces smoke, nausea supplants fear. Her blood feels like liquid metal, moving sluggishly through her veins, burning her from the inside. The sudden weightlessness sets in a heartbeat later, combined with the horrible sensation of being ripped apart molecule by molecule.

The world tilts and then rights itself before the nothingness dissipates into a living room. The immense pressure evaporates, leaving her feeling almost hollow.

"Are you insane?" Orion shouts. "You just stood there."

The residual dizziness after having been glissered to safety makes her feel faint. He catches her before she can crumple into a heap and gently sets her on a plush, red carpet.

"That *thing* killed Journey." Her voice warbles. "It killed the soldier ..."

"That's what Sluaghs do. They kill," Orion says. "Stay right here," he enunciates each word.

Rachel nods, still holding onto Ziggy, and Orion vanishes again.

Through blurry vision, she shifts her attention toward the granite mantle where he'd been mere seconds ago, then moves higher to the oversized white sheet covering something against the wall. She looks around. More white sheets protect pieces of large furniture.

"Where the hell am I now?" Her whisper seems to echo into the empty house. Rachel releases Ziggy from her vise-like grip, and the Fae light hovers forward. It flies toward the granite mantle, illuminating the carved words: *Vhars Bdun.* "Yeah, I don't speak Hobbit." She looks away from the mantle.

The golden sphere bobs to the side, brightening the wooden doorway.

She shakes her head. "I'm not moving."

Ziggy flashes its light, insisting she follow.

"No."

She can still hear Journey's final cry, the terror in that last, short neigh. The sound of the soldier's head being mutilated by that monstrous foot—seeing someone lose their head, like literally lose it, was not something she'd been prepared for. Worse, she led those things to the camp. She's to blame for their deaths.

This time, Rachel isn't able to compartmentalize her emotions.

"I'm responsible," she says softly. Tears run down her soot-covered cheeks. "Oh, God, what have I done?" Rachel's muffles another sob with her hand.

Ziggy comes to a rest on the carpet and rolls closer.

"I killed all those people."

Two flashes.

She shakes her head. "I just wanted Orion to come home and help us. I didn't … I never meant to …" Rachel squeezes her eyes shut, unable to rid herself of the memory of the Sluagh as it crushed the soldier's skull. How many other Sluagh had followed her? The kid had said there was a horde. How many was that? Better yet, how many more soldiers will succumb as a result of her?

All the heat in Rachel's body seeps away.

Rachel lies down on the carpet and curls herself around Ziggy, appreciating his warmth.

She has no idea how long she lies there, weeping for the

Halflings she'd condemned to death, worrying about Orion's safety.

When her tears dry up and her shoulder begins cramping, she sits upright and looks around again.

Rachel pushes the hair out of her face to mask the shudder crawling up her neck.

She scrambles to her feet and walks to where Ziggy hovers near the door. "Hopefully this place has a bathroom."

One flash.

Rachel gestures for Ziggy to go ahead before following the Fae light through a short hall where several closed doors line the walls. At the end of the hallway, moonlight spills onto the stone floor. She walks into the glass-domed stone room, blue light illuminating the bottom of a rock pool. A marble bust of a lion's head protrudes from one wall, and the water flowing from its mouth hits the stone grating inserted into the floor. Past the shower, a narrow alcove is carved from the stone and a marble bench lines its interior. A hole in its center, just large enough for—

"Oh, no. No, no, no." Rachel wrinkles her nose in disgust as she regards the primitive toilet. She searches for the toilet paper, but instead finds an ornate wooden box with a golden inlay. Curious, Rachel opens the box and finds silky fabric cut into square pieces. She takes a step back and throws up her hands in frustration. "Come on, already. There isn't even a door here."

Rachel's sleep is a fitful slumber, full of horrific visions and terrifying consequences.

When she awakens, having slept far later than her usual seven o'clock, it feels like she has run a marathon. Groggy, still exhausted, she gets out of the four-poster bed in one of the bedrooms, and grabs a pair of men's breeches and a white tunic from the wardrobe, as well as her own belt to keep from drowning in the clothes. Her mind is a hurricane of thoughts as she tries discerning which issue she needs to tackle first—Orion hasn't returned; there is no food in the kitchen; and she needs to make her way home and sort out the Miser Fae terrorizing the town.

Everything, her entire life, is spiraling out of control.

The Sluagh attack at the encampment had cost her the meager supplies she'd brought along for the trip, including her toothbrush and toothpaste. She deserves being inconvenienced, obviously. Going without oral hygiene is, after all, nothing in comparison to death. But, after rummaging around the pantry the previous evening, she'd found some dried mint and baking soda—or something similar, at least—and made herself toothpowder.

With water aplenty, and her oral hygiene sorted, food is now her main concern.

Rachel makes quick work of freshening up after her nightmare-laden night, and heads out of the cabin to explore her immediate surroundings.

The picturesque outdoors is full of vibrant emerald-greens. Bright pink and yellow wildflowers grow in abundance, withstanding the oppressing cool weather that makes its way through the valley. Birdsong in the trees and the rushing water of a nearby stream keep her company. Beyond the treetops, a white-capped mountain peak fills the view, surrounded by the bluest sky she'd ever laid eyes on.

Rachel follows an overgrown path that leads away from the cabin, searching for anything edible to satiate her hunger. She has no idea how to identify wild edible plants in the Human Realm, let alone forage for food in the Fae Realm. She spies fish in the stream, but doesn't know how to catch them without a rod. There are no birds' nests she can raid for eggs.

Ziggy tags along for the futile trip, of course, but even the Fae light has its limits.

By midday, the cold weather has become uncomfortably humid, and Rachel returns to the cabin empty-handed. A quick search of the interior confirms she's still alone. The pantry remains barren.

"I'm so over this place," Rachel says. She drags her feet as she makes her way out of the kitchen and into the living room.

She slumps into a sheet-covered armchair, dust billowing around her as her stomach grumbles in protest. She closes her eyes.

Think. Come up with a plan.

Every problem she faced seemed important, each one needed to be solved. Finding something to eat was her biggest priority. Coming in at a close second was getting back to the Harrowsgate. There's no telling when, or even *if* Orion will return.

What have you learned about the plants in Orion's greenhouse?

Most of the Fae plants in the indoor greenhouse had medicinal properties, mostly herbs for tinctures and poultices. There were edible flowers in the greenhouse, too, but she'd never seen them in bloom and wouldn't be able to identify them in the wild.

Okay. Think about the fish. You don't have a fishing rod, but you can make a spear.

It was better than nothing.

Rachel gets back to her feet and heads outside again.

Beside the path, she finds a dead branch in the foliage, and sharpens the tip into something resembling a spear. Rachel makes her way to the stream, where she takes off her shoes on the bank.

Slowly, she wades into the icy water, the rocks underfoot digging into her soles. Careful not to spook the fish, she makes her way to the center of the stream, where the water laps at her hips.

"Here goes nothing," she says.

She watches the fish, waiting for the perfect time to strike. Dinner was literally within reach, she just had to suck it up and spear one of the fish. Simple, right?

Rachel stabs down into the stream, but her target torpedoes away before the makeshift spear can hit home.

"Damn it."

She gets back into position, raises her spear, and studies the fish. One minute turns into five. This time when she stabs down, her foot shifts awkwardly and the rocks give way. Rachel slips, and falls backward with a loud splash. Ice water soaks through her clothes, seeps into her skin, and chills her to the bone.

"Holy snowballs, that's cold," she gasps.

She scrambles to her feet and looks around the stream. The fish had scattered, but her spear was luckily in one piece.

You may be cold, you may be ready to throw in the towel, but you can't. Suck it up. Try again. Otherwise, you're going to starve.

With a heavy sigh, she picks up her spear, and plants herself firmly in place. She stands absolutely still for what feels like forever, before the fish swim closer again.

As the day turns to night, Rachel gives up on her failed spear fishing. She had staved off the hunger pangs by filling up her stomach with water, but she can't go on without food for much longer, and her exhaustion is absolute. At least she won't die from hypothermia.

After a long, hot shower, Rachel goes off in search of something to wear while her clothes dry overnight. A thin, oversized shirt is the best she can find, stuffed into the back of a drawer. She pulls it on, wraps herself up in a blanket, and heads to bed.

Where the previous night's nightmares were full of skull-crushing monsters, the prospect of starving now consumes her every thought.

Rachel stares at the ceiling, the blanket pulled up to her chin. She inadvertently ponders questions like how long it will take to starve to death and when her brain functions will become impaired. Will she suffer hallucinations? Does it even matter anymore how she goes out? The guilt was still there, just hiding beneath the surface, waiting to remind her of what she'd inadvertently done.

A thud sounds, followed by a muted, "Oomph."

Rachel sits upright in the bed, her head heavy and thoughts swimming. "Orion?" she whispers, afraid of getting her hopes up.

She gets a groan in response.

She throws her legs off the edge of the bed and walks across the bedroom. There's a clatter, like pots and pans falling. A drawer opens violently. Steel rattles against steel as the contents are pushed around inside. She slinks into the shadows of the hallway, and inches her way to the modest-sized kitchen, where dim lamp light glows.

"Where is it?"

She knows *that* voice.

Memories push to the forefront of her mind. *"Let's see where my brother is hiding you."* Rachel stops in her tracks, eyes widening as a cupboard door slams shut. *"Do you think I should make him watch while I break you in for my harem, pretty thing?"*

Before she has a chance to retreat from the doorway, Nova—the King of Amaris—comes into view. His white hair is pulled out of his face into a low ponytail at the nape of his neck. The purple velvet cloak she'd first seen him wear in Amaris' gilded throne room is gone. Instead, he wears black breeches with gray side-panels, paired with black riding boots, and a black jacket hangs loosely over a white tunic.

She moves one leg backward, placing her toes gently down on the wooden floor. As Rachel puts more weight onto her foot, a creak resounds in the hallway.

Nova spins on his heels, a blue flame covering the entirety of his right hand and wrist. His quicksilver eyes narrow and lean body grows rigid.

"Is my brother here?" Nova asks. He searches the hallway behind her.

Her chest tightens. Rachel opens her mouth to speak, but no sound comes out.

A tense, pregnant pause falls over him, before Nova extinguishes the flame. He regards her from afar, inquisitive, his brow creasing in confusion.

"My spies didn't tell me he brought you along."

Despite the danger he poses, Rachel blurts out, "He didn't."

Nova raises an eyebrow. "I can't figure out if you're stupid or brave." With that, he turns back to whatever he'd been doing.

Unsure whether she should run for her life or go back to the bedroom and pray he forgets she exists, Rachel simply stands there in the dark hallway.

Nova walks out of the kitchen with a lamp in hand, his shoulder brushing a hairsbreadth from hers.

"What are you looking for?" she asks, following him into the living room.

"A worn leather folder," he mutters. He sets the lamp down on the mantle. "I could have sworn I'd forgotten it here last time I visited." Nova glances over his shoulder. "Did you see it?"

"No."

Nova returns his attention to searching the living room and pulls white sheets off the furniture, unsettling the dust. The air swirls, tickling Rachel's nose. Against all reason, she crosses the room and opens the large windows one after the other. When she turns back to Nova, he's on his hands and knees, looking beneath the armchair.

Rachel blinks, convinced she's seeing things. When the scene doesn't dissipate, she shakes her head and closes the distance between them. Whatever heinous fate awaits her, she can't bring herself to watch him struggle like this. After all, it's not the most dignified position for a king to be in, no matter what realm he hails from.

"You lift, and I'll check if it's down there." Rachel gestures for Nova to get off the carpet.

He looks up at her, unreadable in that moment.

"I insist."

Nova stands and pats the dust off his clothes, before he

141

moves behind the armchair. He tilts it back, and Rachel bends down to check if there's anything resembling the missing item. She rights herself and mumbles a, "Nope," before gesturing to the next armchair.

He gently sets the chair on its feet and follows her direction.

Nova's quicksilver gaze meets hers. "So, you traveled all the way to Amaris in the hopes of retrieving my brother?"

Rachel purses her lips together, looks beneath the armchair, and shakes her head.

Moving the wooden bookcase, he says, "Humor me." Nova strains to push the large piece of furniture away from the wall. He scans the area, before shifting the bookcase back into place.

"Yes," Rachel relents.

Nova turns his attention back to her. "And?"

"Well, I didn't really have time to talk to him, seeing as I unintentionally led a horde of Sluaghs into his camp." She crosses her arms, and breaks eye contact.

"Ah, that explains it then."

Rachel glimpses his way. "Explains what?"

"Rumor has it the Halfling army, or rather what's left of it, is moving to join their forces in the northern parts of Amaris." He opens a drawer and rummages around inside. "Swaying my brother won't be easy when he's waging a war. He's rather single-minded that way." Nova closes the drawer and heads for the writing desk. "I suppose he brought you here during the fray with the Sluaghs?" He crouches and peers beneath the desk.

"Yes. Do you know what they are? The Sluaghs, I mean."

"Nasty creatures," he mumbles.

She waits for more of an explanation, but when Nova doesn't continue, she says, "Care to elaborate?"

He stands again, scratching his chin. "We believe Sluagh are unrestful souls, specifically of people—Human, Halfling, Fae, it doesn't matter—who were exceptionally evil and cruel during their lives. They exist and gain power from souls, especially the souls of the dying." Nova shrugs. "From what I can remember of my studies about them, they group together, and are mostly active during the night. During daylight hours, Sluagh usually hide in dark, forgotten places."

"And they're just found in the Fae Realm?" Rachel asks.

"No. The Wild Hunt—that's what we call a horde of Sluagh, by the way—is found in every known realm. Sometimes there are stragglers from the horde, though, and the lone wolf abides by a different set of rules. For example, a Sluagh that's struck out on its own doesn't mind the sunlight," he says. "The bottom line is that all Sluagh sow chaos and feed off destruction." Nova looks around the room. "Where could I have put it?"

"Did you check the palace?" Rachel asks.

"Of course I checked the palace."

And he calls Orion single-minded.

Rachel walks up to the bookcase and scans the leather-bound volumes housed on the shelves.

"Finding you here has placed me in a somewhat difficult position. If I take you as my prisoner, Orion may reconsider this pointless campaign against me. On the other hand, he may not feel anything for you, which makes it an utterly impractical strategy," Nova says as he scours the desk.

She spots the leather folder in the bottom shelf of the bookcase, placed on top of a stack of books. Rachel picks it up, and says, "May I add another point for you to consider?"

Nova signals for her to continue with a curt nod.

"Imprisoning me would be both incredibly rude and an unjust reward, especially seeing as I found your folder."

With only the illumination of the lamp and the moonlight coming in through the cabin windows, he seems almost normal. Nova spins around, eyes sparkling as Rachel hands over the leather folder.

"Where did you find it?" Nova asks, unwinding the leather thong keeping the contents within safely together.

"In the bookcase."

"Thank you."

Rachel leans her shoulder against the shelves, watching as he closes the folder and smooths his face into a neutral expression.

"Coming back to our previous conversation," he says, moving the leather folder behind his back. "There is a possibility that you will become a bigger threat to me. Thus, if I imprison you now, I could save myself from future problems."

Rachel gives him a half-smile. "If you use that particular argument, your subjects may wonder why their great and powerful king fears a human. Logic suggests it will cause you much bigger issues in the long run."

Nova eyes her from afar. "Well, you've just confirmed you're not stupid." He inclines his head her way before she can respond. "I apologize for my unannounced intrusion and bid you farewell."

Rachel shrugs off his apology. "Goodnight.

Their gazes meet again briefly, curiosity flashing in his eyes, before the King of Amaris vanishes into thin air.

Chapter Twelve
Blood of my Blood

On the fifth morning of Rachel's visit to the Fae Realm, she awakens to the sweet aroma of freshly baked bread wafting throughout the cabin.

Half-crazed with hunger and willing to eat pretty much anything, she follows the delectable smell into the kitchen, where a picnic basket waits on the counter. Beside the basket, sits a package wrapped in brown paper and tied with twine. Rachel dives into the basket, her craving for anything substantial too great to be ignored. Inside of it, she finds fresh bread accompanied by jams, sweetmeats, and cheese. She breaks off a doughy morsel and places it in her mouth, savoring the yeasty goodness. Another controlled bite, before she breaks off a piece of cheese and stuffs it into her mouth.

She closes her eyes and chews the cheese slowly, moaning, "So good."

Rachel unpacks the much-needed groceries, adding milk, honey, fruit tarts, and even a smoked salmon onto the counter. And there, hidden at the bottom of the basket is a written note.

She picks up the white card and studies the cursive letters, written with such painstaking precision.

*I was born into the **Court of Light**, but;*
My world is cast in perpetual gray.
Shadows are my friends, and;
Darkness will be my legacy.

—*Nova*

Staring at the note, she rereads the poem until she can recite the words by heart. Those four lines resonate deep within her, speaking to the loneliness and defeat she battles every day. Beautiful, albeit heartbreaking, Rachel can't help but wonder if this is a premature admission of guilt. The poem may be relatable, but it is not *hers*.

"What are you up to?" she whispers. Gently, Rachel places the note on the counter as if it might explode if she isn't careful, and goes to work on fixing herself breakfast. The heavy, sinking feeling persists long after she's satiated her hunger, though. She eyes the note when she finally musters up the courage to open the package. Inside, Rachel finds a sea-green cotton muslin dress with a high empire waist. Her fingertips run across the bust, tracing the delicate golden embroidery on the organza. Curious as to how transparent the bust's fabric is, she sticks her hand into the neckline and coughs a laugh.

She pulls the almost Regency-styled dress from the package and spies the carefully folded knee-high stockings and beige leather walking boots beneath it. The shoes will undoubtedly fit, and the dress—

"What? No nipple rouge?" Rachel shakes out the dress and holds it high enough so it doesn't touch the floor. It's not horrendous, but the low-cut and see-through bust is worrisome, and it's not really her style. There is no note explaining the new attire, which is cause for concern, too. But yes, the dress will definitely fit her.

"When in Rome," she trails off with a sigh.

Rachel grabs the note off the counter as she heads back to the bedroom she occupies and places the dress on the unmade bed, careful not to crease the fabric. She returns to the kitchen for the boots, before setting off for a bath in the rock pool. The water is, as she's come to expect, always comfortably warm. Whether this is due to a hot spring somewhere or because magic is employed, Rachel doesn't know. She doesn't care. Simply having a bath, something she has taken for granted before this trip, is a blessing in itself.

After the bath, she braids her long, thick hair into a loose style, then puts on the stockings and shoes. She slips on the dress next, snorting in amusement when she notices the only thing keeping her modest is a few golden threads. As revealing as the dress may be, she doesn't dislike it completely.

It's kind of empowering. Rachel turns sideways to appreciate how the dress fits her body. *Mrs. Crenshaw will approve of the draping.* She turns to the other side, studying the impeccable sewing.

"I'm told it's the latest fashion where you're from," Nova says from the doorway, startling Rachel out of her thoughts.

She quickly covers the gauzy bust with her hands, effectively hiding her chest from his appreciative gaze.

"Showing off one's"—she clears her throat—"*assets* is not popular where I live."

"Assets?" Nova raises an eyebrow.

"Boobs," Rachel clarifies.

Nova tilts his head, a deep crease forming on his forehead.

The cog turns, but there's no sign of understanding.

"Breasts," she finally says in an exasperated tone. "We don't show off our breasts all willy-nilly like this."

"Why?" There's genuine curiosity in his voice, even a hint of naïveté.

"Well, some people find women's exposed breasts offensive. Others deem it indecent."

"I repeat, why?"

"Don't you have laws prohibiting public indecency?" Rachel asks.

"There are many subspecies of Fae who prefer not to wear clothes. It is their right. Therefore, there are no laws prohibiting exposure to any of my subjects."

"Oh." Rachel doesn't lower her hands. "As much as I like the dress, I think it's best if I don't wear it. I had a rather unpleasant run-in with a Halfling who would've had his way with me if I didn't fight back, so …"

The muscles in Nova's forehead twitch before he seems to force a neutral expression. "Did you kill him?"

"Unfortunately not, but I think the Sluaghs may have gotten him."

"Good," Nova says. "Shall I wait in the parlor for you to dress in something more comfortable?"

"Yes," she exhales the word in relief.

A ghost of a smile plays on his lips as he turns and makes his way down the hallway. Swiftly, Rachel closes the door behind him and undresses before pulling on her wrinkled black T-shirt. The boots are troublesome to get off, but soon enough she's free of them, and shimmies on her pair of black jeggings. She slips the note into her back pocket, not knowing why she doesn't want to part with it yet, and ventures out of the bedroom and toward the living room—or parlor, as Nova calls it.

Eyeing her from across the room, Nova asks, "Do authorities deem your current ensemble appropriate attire in your realm?"

"Appropriate, yes, but not quite fashionable," she says. "I didn't expect to be in the presence of a king, so I left my evening gown at home."

"Are you mocking me?" Nova perches on the ledge of the open window, crossing his arms.

Rachel gestures with her index finger and thumb set slightly apart. "Just a bit."

His silvery eyes twinkle with amusement, but his face remains unreadable.

She pushes her hands into the back pockets of her jeggings. "Thank you for the food, by the way."

Nova inclines his head, but doesn't speak.

An awkward silence stretches on between them, before Rachel says, "So, what's it like to be a king?"

"Exhausting," he answers without missing a beat. A smile tickles the corners of his lips again, as if that single word has lifted a burden off his shoulders.

"Take a vacation for a couple of weeks? Go lie on some exotic beach and order cocktails the whole day."

His smile breaks its hold, a longing glimmers in his silvery eyes. "That's a grand notion."

He's about to speak, probably to elaborate on being a king, when his body language changes. Every muscle seems to tense, his quicksilver eyes widen, and then he's gone from the window ledge.

Suddenly, there's an arm around her waist, pulling her back

against a taut, muscular body. A hand wraps around her throat, gentle but unyielding.

Orion appears in the center of the living room, looking worse for wear.

Rachel elbows back, the powerful slam hitting Nova straight in his upper abdominal muscles. He exhales a *whoosh* of air, but isn't deterred. "Get off me, you oversized firefly. Zig—" Her shout is cut short as the hand around her neck tightens.

Freaking sibling squabbles.

"Brother," Nova's voice is amicable as he greets Orion, but there's an underlying threat there, too. "We've been expecting you."

Orion's gaze moves over her, evaluating every inch of her body. His jaw tenses, hands ball into fists by his sides. His nostrils flare as his golden flames trickle up his hands. "Let go of her. She has *nothing* to do with any of this."

"Oh, I know," Nova answers. The arm around her waist disappears.

Orion's hands move to his head, where he presses against his temples, his eyes shut. "Get out of my head," he hisses. "Get out!"

In her peripheral vision, Rachel spies blue flame rippling over Nova's arm. The air grows thick with electricity as the tension between the brothers becomes palpable.

"So melodramatic," Nova says. Breathy chuckles accompany the words. "Do I have your attention?" He brings his blazing arm closer to her shoulder, singeing the fibers of her shirt and flyaway hairs in her braid. Sulfur stinks up the room.

Orion extinguishes his flame, pursing his lips together to keep his rage from getting the best of him. "What do you want?" he bites the words out through gritted teeth.

"I will meet you at the Harrowsgate in five minutes, where we will discuss the terms of Rachel Cleary's release," Nova says. "If you do anything stupid, the girl will suffer the consequences. Are we understood?"

Orion sneers, but says, "Yes."

"Good. Now go."

Orion glissers away from the cabin.

Nova loosens the hand around her neck, the blue flame winks out.

"Ziggy," Rachel finally screams, and her Fae light zigzags out of its hiding place. "Attack." The golden sphere hesitates, his light dimming slightly.

"You have a Fae light?" Nova asks, not in the least bit concerned over Ziggy's presence. "Interesting."

She turns her head sideways as much as she can, looking away from him, but opens her arms for Ziggy to come closer. The sphere rushes forward and she wraps her arms around him, holding on tightly.

"I can't believe you did that after I told you about the Halfling," Rachel says.

"It was the only way for him to listen. At least, we're both getting what we want now," Nova says. "Orion will be safely away from my kingdom and you'll have your champion back where he belongs. It's a—what is it humans call it? Ah, yes, it's a win-win."

"Your tactics leave much to be desired," she mumbles.

He snickers behind her. "Manipulation is the crowning jewel in any monarch's arsenal. My tactics may have been questionable to you, no doubt, but everything I do is done to keep my kingdom safe. Think about that on your way home."

Before Rachel can respond, the world sinks away beneath her feet. Overcome with sickening vertigo, she squeezes her eyes shut. She resists the urge to scream as her weightless body is shredded apart in the void, the unseen pressure that comes along with glissering ebbs and flows around her, inside her. A flip is succeeded by a tilt, and then gravity takes hold. She releases a gasp as her feet touch down on solid ground. Her hold on Ziggy loosens and the Fae light moves out of her arms.

She opens her eyes and finds herself staring at Orion, standing in front of a birch gate nearly identical to the one on her side of the forest. It's larger, though, and there are colorful gemstones imbedded into the twisted branches. Instead of a mushroom circle, stones surround the green space in front of the Harrowsgate.

There are several armed Fae soldiers standing far enough away from them to give them privacy, but close enough to attack if something goes awry.

It's like Nova knew what would happen and planned ahead.

Ziggy flies around Orion, before moving through the Harrowsgate.

"The terms are simple, Orion." Nova holds her upright, blue flame once again enveloping his free arm. "Leave this realm and I'll send her to you.

"It's never that simple with you," Orion retorts.

Rachel feels him shrug behind her. "Oh, but it is," Nova says. "*But* if you have the silly notion to return, and if I should find out, Rachel here will atone for your sins. And you *know* I will make her pay threefold." The hand around her neck loosens enough for a fingertip to trace her necklace, before moving to the soft skin located right beneath her décolletage. "The Ronamy

Stone protects her mind from me, but her body …" Nova buries his face into her braid, his nose touching her cheek. He makes a sound in the back of his throat as he inhales deeply. A shudder runs down Rachel's spine, but she remains perfectly still at his supposed threat. "I will break her in ways you never thought possible," Nova's whisper is almost gleeful.

Orion bares his teeth like a feral beast, the flames returning to his hands.

In a display of power, Nova runs his tongue up her cheek. This time, Rachel flinches and recoils as he licks her. She's not actually scared, though. For some reason, she doesn't fear Nova the way she knows she should. He's, as Mrs. Crenshaw would say, more bark than bite.

"I haven't had a virgin for so long—"

Threat or no, Rachel can't help herself from bursting out in laughter, which catches both brothers off-guard. Nova jerks away from her and she's almost certain Orion's flames dim.

"I'm sorry," she says through her breathy giggles. Rachel rights herself and forces her face into a more serious expression, swallowing her amusement. "Okay, I'm good. Continue." Her laughter begins anew before Nova can get back into delivering his evil monolog.

"Are you quite done yet?" All pretense of Nova's villainy is forgotten.

Rachel inhales deeply and nods, managing a, "Yup."

Nova straightens behind her, and continues with a rather lame, "Leave, brother, and she's safe."

"I have your word?"

"On my honor as King of Amaris, I solemnly swear to send her back after you've left," Nova answers.

Orion presses his lips into a thin line, diminishing his flame into nonexistence before he turns on his heel and walks through the Harrowsgate. Nova releases his hold on her. In a flash, Rachel spins around, balls her hand into a fist, and punches the Fae King in the face. He sucks in air through his teeth as the song of swords being pulled from their scabbards play around her.

"Never use me like that again," Rachel says. She hides her throbbing fist behind her back.

He holds out a hand to halt his guard from advancing on them, the shiner already blooming over his left eye.

"I am the King of Amaris," he booms over the clearing.

"I couldn't care less if you were the King of freaking Hearts. I am tired of men trying to take advantage of me." Rachel pivots and heads toward the Harrowsgate. "And take a vacation, for heaven's sake. You need a break," she calls back, before exiting the Fae Realm.

Chapter Thirteen
Charnel Melancholy

Orion's scarred hands find Rachel's face when she enters the Human Realm. "Did he hurt you?" he asks, galaxy eyes full of concern as he evaluates her from head to toe. "Are you okay?"

Rachel shoves him back and walks out of the mushroom circle. She stops in her tracks, lifts a finger into the air, and turns to face him. "You abandoned me in the middle of nowhere. There wasn't food. I had no way of reaching *anyone*. And best of all, I had no idea if you would ever come back for me. So, no, I am not okay."

"Of course I would've gone back for you," Orion says. "But I had to fix—"

"Be careful of your next words," Rachel interrupts.

He grimaces. "Three-hundred-and-twelve Halflings died when the Sluaghs attacked."

The pang of guilt gives her pause.

Three-hundred-and-twelve?

Rachel crosses her arms, her knuckles still painful after having punched Nova.

"If I hadn't gone back, the loss would've been much greater," Orion continues. "Some of those men had wives and children,

Clarré. I had to answer to them as to why their husbands and fathers won't be going home."

The forest seemed colder, icy enough to chill Rachel to the bone.

"Yes, and I'm responsible for all their deaths, because I led the Sluaghs to your military camp." She acts the exact opposite of how she feels, and wave one hand through the air. She drops her arm back to her side. "Here's the thing, though. If you'd actually come back after you dealt with the Night Weaver, I wouldn't have had to enter that infernal realm to get you." Rachel stomps toward the rotting tree trunk.

"They needed me," he says behind her.

"*I* needed you."

"You're being selfish." Orion walks up to her side.

She lifts her chin higher, but says nothing to contradict him. Yes, perhaps she was selfish. Maybe she could even be classified as heartless. So what? It's not like Orion would be the first person to think Rachel is something she's not. The truth of the matter, she cares a great deal about the dead Halfling soldiers and their families, but she also has a mission to complete. Without Orion, though, it won't be possible. Shadow Grove may not be a grand kingdom with heated rock pools and toilets that date back to the Dark Ages, but the small New England town is her home. Even if she doesn't like everyone who lives here, she'll protect them with her life. Hopefully, it won't come to dying for Shadow Grove, but she will. She would sacrifice herself for this town she both loves and loathes.

"You never answered my questions," he says after as they make the trek back to Griswold Road. "Did Nova hurt you?"

"I hurt him more," she mumbles, which earns herself an inquisitive look. "I punched him in the face after you left."

Rachel's lips tug at the corners.

"You're kidding."

Rachel shows him her bruised knuckles.

Orion guffaws as his thumb runs over the back of her hand. "You actually punched him in the face?"

She shrugs and pulls her hand away, half-hugging herself against the cold. "Nova's going to nurse a shiner for at least two weeks."

"He could have had your head," Orion says. "He still can."

"At this point, Nova needs to get in line," Rachel says. "There's a Miser who needs to be put in place, Greg's acting all kinds of weird, Mrs. Crenshaw is in hospital after shattering her hip, and I owe you money."

Orion frowns. "Why would you owe me money?"

"I had to trade goldmint for a map." Rachel pats down her pockets and groans. "Crap. I forgot Mercia's mirror in the cabin."

"The Holstein girl?" he asks, and Rachel nods. "She's a regular. Don't worry about the money."

"One less thing for me to worry about," she says. "Thanks."

"So, what's this Miser getting up to?"

Rachel tells Orion all about the situation she's left behind as they make their way out of the forest—everything from finding a boneless body in the school's boiler room to discovering the bone carvings.

As they exit the forest, he says, "You do realize my powers are inhibited in the Human Realm, right? Here, I'm only at ten percent strength."

"Your ten percent is still better than my hundred percent," Rachel answers, staring longingly at her home. "Okay, so I have your keys—"

"I don't need keys, remember?" Orion cuts her short. He gives her a half-smile, the first one she's seen since he'd gone after the Night Weaver. "I'm going home to take a shower, get some more appropriate clothing on, and order an extra-large pizza. If you need me, you know where I am."

"Cool," she says, feeling weird about parting with him so soon after the whole thing in the Fae Realm. "You're not going to run off again?"

He looks off, studying the Fraser house and avoiding her eyes. "You heard what Nova said."

Resentment. That's what he's hiding from me.

Rachel sighs. "Whatever's going on between the two of you, it's festering, and innocent people are suffering. Sort out your nonsense before the anger devours you both whole."

"Mhmmm. See you soon, Clarré."

When Orion disappears again, she rolls her eyes and walks up to her quiet, empty home, where she finds the spare key hidden beneath the wicker seat's cushion. She unlocks the door and Ziggy flies into the house, meandering up to her bedroom.

The gloomy reception is evidence enough that nobody's been in there since she left.

Rachel heads to the kitchen, where she'd left her cell phone charging, and unlocks the screen. Notifications for over a dozen messages run up the screen—most of them from Greg. She scrolls through the messages, raising an eyebrow. The first message is one asking to meet up. Then there's a *Where RU?* text. The concern continues for a while, before he seems to undergo a sudden personality change and goes off on her for ignoring him. Derogatory terms are used, some creative language, which is unlike Greg.

Rachel moves onto checking her missed calls—all of them

from Greg. Voicemails—all left by Greg.

"Take a hint, sheesh," she mumbles.

Rachel dials Dougal's number.

She counts the rings until the recorded voice tells her the number she has dialed is currently unavailable, and that she should try again later. Later is out of the question. Rachel redials, waits, before—

"Pick up the phone," Rachel ends the call as the recorded voice blathers on.

The third try is as unsuccessful as the others.

Calm down. Rachel heads for the staircase. *Mercia promised she'll take care of him, so just call her.* She scrolls through her contact list until she finds Mercia's number.

There's a knock on the front door before she can hit the dial button.

Rachel changes course, ventures back into the foyer to answer the door. Mercia, her hair a mess and the bags under her eyes obvious, sighs in relief.

"I thought it was you." Mercia steps inside the house. "Did you find Orion?"

"Hello to you, too." Rachel closes the door behind her. "Were you waiting in the hydrangeas all this time?"

"Funny," Mercia mumbles. "Look, did you find him or not?"

"Yes. He's at his place taking a shower."

"Good. That's good." She nods. "Listen, I came to give you something." She pulls a pink flash drive from her pocket and holds it out. "This Fae is stronger than I anticipated. I tried. I really, *really* tried to keep everyone safe, but it's too strong." Her eyes twinkle with unshed tears, the bags underneath prominent. "I should have given you access to the town council's archive before I sent you off to find Orion, but I didn't think it would be this bad."

"What are you talking about?" Rachel asks, taking the flash drive.

"I zapped all the information in the archives onto the flash drive. *Everything.* I thought it would help me figure out what we're dealing with, but there is so much information on there. You're better at both research and puzzles than I am, though."

"Mercia, hold up. What's going on?"

Mercia chews on her bottom lip, fear rolling off her in waves. "It's bad." She begins pacing across the foyer, her hand going back to her hair. "Seven kids at school are already hospitalized, and then the bone carvings just kept on coming. I can't be everywhere at once. I can't save *everyone* at once." She gulps loudly, tears streaming down her cheeks.

"It's okay. Don't—"

Mercia breaks down, sobs wrack her body. "Just find out what's doing this, *please.* People around town have started finding bone carvings now."

"Okay, okay." Rachel holds up her hands in surrender and heads toward the stairs. "It could take a while, though."

Mercia wipes the tears away with the back of her hand and nods. The poor girl looks like she hasn't slept since Rachel left.

"I'll wait," Mercia whispers.

Together, they head toward Rachel's bedroom, where Mercia plonks down on the bed. She stares out of the window, looking like a wilted flower, and releases a heavy sigh.

"How's Dougal? *Where* is Dougal?"

"He's at the hospital, keeping an eye on his grandmother. After everything that's happened, he didn't want to leave her by herself."

"Makes sense. Are *you* okay?" Rachel asks.

Mercia averts her gaze from the window, looking up at Rachel through half-lidded eyes. "Do I look okay?"

"Not exactly."

Mercia gives her a thumb's up and turns her attention back to the window.

Rachel nods as she opens her laptop, waits impatiently for it to come to life. She pushes the flash drive into the USB port. A program opens, which looks more like a website, filling the entirety of her laptop's screen. The headline—in white, bold letters on a pitch black background—proclaims it as: THE UNOFFICIAL HISTORY OF SHADOW GROVE. A menu is situated below the headline with a search bar and revolving images— illustrations, lost artwork, and old photographs—located directly beside it.

"Nice," Rachel murmurs. She scrolls to the search bar to type in some random terms, which yields numerous results. She plays around a bit, narrowing down the search, by typing in phrases like: *bone carving*, *omen*, *Fae*, and *influence*. The first result on the list is titled: *The Collected Stories of Renaud Dupont*. She doesn't recognize the author or the book, but the summary description is highlighted with every term she'd entered. "It's as good a place as any to start," she says, and clicks on the link.

GOLVATH THE LONELY

In a long-since forgotten kingdom, a young servant girl gave birth to her elderly master's babe. The child would be his only heir, his only legacy. Illegitimate son or not, the ruined, small kingdom would be left to the child upon his father's death. And death would come swifter than anyone had anticipated. Before the babe's first month of life, before his naming day had even arrived, the old king died in his sleep, leaving behind his ever-increasing debts and a dwindling people in the hands of the nameless babe.

Some of the dead king's people left, fearing war would reach their borders, until only a handful remained. But nobody came to collect on the king's debts. Nobody came to claim the lands or abandoned villages.

Soon, those who had stayed, either due to being unable to travel or because they felt they owed the dead king their loyalty, also perished. One after the other, the remaining villagers died from disease, illness, or old age, until eventually no one was left aside from the servant girl and her son, whom she named Golvath.

They could have left the ruined kingdom, *should* have left like the others, but lost merchants and travelers who passed through the desolate lands brought stories of sweeping illnesses, raging wars, and unyielding blights from their neighboring kingdoms. These tales, whether true or not, scared the servant girl so much she kept her son hidden in a crumbling stone tower whenever a strange face came near. Nevertheless, she ventured down to meet those passing through, hoping to restock supplies. With nothing to pay for these life-saving provisions, she offered herself to those who would not show charity to a poor, lonesome woman, stuck in a penniless and abandoned kingdom.

Golvath was spared seeing his mother bartering for the necessities that would keep them alive, but he grew up as all children do, and eventually came to grips with what his mother did to keep him fed and clothed.

He used to keep himself busy by whittling wood, carving animals and soldiers, in the hopes of creating a companion for himself.

When he was old enough to venture into the village by himself, he would slip away while his mother entertained their guests to explore the ruins at the foot of the tower.

Some of the houses had been abandoned in such a hurry after his father's death that plates and stoneware had been left on the tables. Clothes and toys were scattered amongst the debris. As a boy, he used to imagine what type of people had lived in these houses, judging solely by what they had left behind. He grew bolder with his explorations as the years wore on, and moved farther from the stone tower, until he reached houses where those occupants who had held on to the very end had perished in their beds, chairs, gardens. And with nobody there to bury the corpses, the bodies had rotted away where they lay until only bones remained.

Golvath was so desperate for companionship, and so naïve, that he didn't find the skeletal remains disconcerting. In fact, he found the sun-bleached bones nothing more than a new material on which to practice his whittling.

It took Golvath a while to get used to working

with the bones, for they were much softer than wood and their porous nature made them prone to splintering and fracturing. Some bones were too small, some were broken, some wholly impractical to work with. Still, he honed his skills as best he could. Eventually, the carvings he made from the villagers' remains became magnificent pieces of art. He kept them to himself, though, too greedy to share his new obsession with his mother for fear that she would take away his beloved carvings.

In his eighteenth year, as he was coming into his inherited powers, he sat beside his mother's bed and held her hand as she whispered her final words. *"I have protected you as much as any mother can protect her children. I have given my life so you can live yours, so you might reign as your father once did. Go out into the world and find yourself a wife, and when you return, my sweet boy, rebuild this kingdom so your children might have a better future."*

Golvath would leave the land of his birth soon after his mother's death, but he was unprepared for the world that lay beyond. So unprepared, in fact, he could not speak with a single soul who crossed his path. How would he ever fulfill his mother's dying wish if he could not even speak to the fairer sex?

The uncrowned king of a forgotten kingdom, lost amongst the various cultures of Orthega, had no other choice than to use his inherited abilities to forcibly sway a maiden's heart.

The first maiden, who had hair as white as

snow, was fortunate to be saved from Golvath's enchantment by another suitor before the day of their wedding. The enchantment of the second maiden, who had lips as red as rubies, was broken by her father, who had rallied the town against the drifter. Golvath was run out of every town and village in Orthega after his devious plans were discovered, until his only options were to either return to his decimated kingdom alone, nothing more than a failure, or to continue his search in another realm.

As fate would have it, Golvath found himself near the Grimwhorl at the time, and decided to continue his search for a bride.

So beware, young maidens, one and all. For Golvath the Lonely may be watching you, waiting to steal you to a kingdom of ruin.

Rachel frowns as she stares at the monitor, the story's ending utterly unsatisfying. Renaud Dupont was certainly not up to the Grimm Brothers' standards of storytelling, that's for sure. But was this who she's dealing with right now? Golvath the Lonely? And what was a Grimwhorl? So many questions run through her mind, and so few answers present themselves.

She clicks the return button and scans through the next few search results, most of which seems to be journal entries by a variety of authors on the horrors that the people of Shadow Grove had endured over the years.

Rachel takes a break from her research to shower and put on some clean clothes, have some lunch, and tend to her blistered feet. Afterward, she quietly makes her way back to the room, where Mercia is fast asleep, and reaches under her bed. She searches around until she finds her keepsake box, lifts the lid, and slips Nova's poem inside. With that done, she returns to her desk.

Rachel reads through an article called "The Curse of Shadow Grove" which is little more than the prattling of a 1970s housewife who tries to make sense of the countless unfortunate events that have befallen the town up until then. The article does, however, mention bone figurines, which were found at several accidents, and how Mr. Fraser—probably Mrs. Crenshaw's father—had called them omens. It also mentions a girl named Mary Wentworth, who set herself alight in the late 1950s. Around the same time Mrs. Crenshaw was in high school.

"Interesting," she whispers.

The Halloween edition of the *Ridge Crest Weekly*, which dates back to 1981, explores the various urban legends of the school—from the phantom lights seen crossing the football field before dawn to moving hallways that lead nowhere, trapping straggling students in a maze for eternity. One article, titled "The Ghost Boy." catches Rachel's attention because it's the same story she heard as a freshman during orientation week—the one where a boy fell from the bell tower, who now haunts the old schoolhouse. What makes the article stand out, however, is how the author, Harvey Peterson, explains that the supposed ghost boy has a history of haunt cycles, which are always accompanied by odd figurines that are left behind as a warning.

Rachel sits back in her chair, wiping over mouth as she rereads the last line of the article.

The last time the ghost boy haunted Ridge Crest High, seven students died.

Chapter Fourteen
Skull Cracker

Rachel starts the much-needed, possibly belated, research on the Miser Fae. Her cell phone starts ringing, vibrating like crazy in her back pocket. She reaches around, pulls the phone out, and sees a photo of Dougal filling the screen.

Mercia grumbles to awareness.

"I've got to take this." She slides her thumb across the screen. "Hello?"

"Thank the heavens. Are ye comin' to the hospital anytime soon?" Dougal is breathless on the other end of the line. There's loud knocking in the background, a hollow laughter accompanying it.

Rachel looks to Mercia, who's still waking up. "I'm sort of dealing with something here." There's more knocking, and the hollow laughter turns hysterical. "Is everything all right on your end?"

"I think Nan pushed the nurses over the edge," he says. There's an audible *oomph*, a few heavy breaths, before he continues, "They're tryin' to kill us now."

"Wait, did you just say the nurses are trying to kill you?"

"I can't blame them, though. Nan's been a right wench today."

"Hold on a sec." Rachel pulls her cell phone away from her ear and says, "Hey, Mercia. Wanna go save Dougal again?"

"I don't need savin'," his voice fills her bedroom. "Nan's in trouble, ye know?"

Mercia nods, and forces herself to stand.

"We'll be there in about ten minutes. Can you hold out for that long?"

"Just hurry, Rach," Dougal grumbles, and ends the call.

Rachel returns the cell phone to her back pocket and picks up her car keys from the desk. "Ziggy," she calls and the Fae light rushes into her room, bouncing off the walls.

Mercia stares. "You have a Fae light?"

"Orion left Ziggy here before he left," she explains. Ziggy hops toward a bag, and rolls inside, ready to leave. Rachel picks up the bag and slings it over her shoulder as she heads toward the door. She grins, and says over her shoulder, "Ten bucks says Dougal is covered in something nasty."

"There's something seriously wrong with you," Mercia whispers behind her.

"You're not the first to mention it."

They make it to the hospital in eight minutes flat, a new record for her, but it's purely thanks to the fact that the streets were near empty and every traffic light was green on the way over. As always, the hospital parking lot is devoid of activity. Full as it is with all the cars, there isn't a soul around. Rachel doesn't even see the bored security guard in the area as she climbs out of her car.

"I hate this place," Mercia says, closing the passenger door. She walks around the front and catches up with Rachel, before they make their way to the hospital entrance. "I almost hate it more than Hawthorne Memorial."

Rachel glimpses at her. "You've been there? Inside Hawthorne, I mean."

"Yes," Mercia answers. "I went to visit someone."

"Of course." She doesn't pry, because it's none of her business. Still, it is a curious admission.

They walk into the foyer, Ziggy still hidden within the bag, only to find the receptionist is missing from her post. The girls share a look, before continuing their journey to the elevator. Rachel presses the call button and looks around for any sign of life.

It feels like they're in the intro scene of a bad post-apocalyptic movie, one that features zombies just waiting to grab them when they least expect it, because obviously they should have known better than to walk around an abandoned hospital.

The elevator pings and the doors slide open. Mercia enters first, but Rachel doesn't budge.

"You coming?" Mercia asks.

"Let's take the stairs," Rachel says, glancing back to the empty reception area.

Mercia doesn't hesitate in exiting the elevator. Better still, she doesn't ask awkward questions. They quietly make their way around the corner and walk up the staircase, listening to the reigning silence. Only when they reach the third floor landing does Rachel hear a persistent knocking. She halts and listens closely, trying her best to determine what's going on from afar. Fast approaching footsteps squeak on the tiled floor, rush their way. Three distinct voices join in—giggling, laughing, a maniacal guffaw—the footsteps retreats back to wherever, quick squeaks followed by a slide of some sort.

"Little pig, little pig, let me in," a crazed female says in a singsong voice, stabbing with a scalpel at the door.

Mercia peeks around the staircase and gestures for Rachel to follow her. As quietly as they can, they cross the lobby and hide behind one of the swing-doors leading into the ward.

"Or we'll huff," another female says, giggling. "And we'll puff-f-f-f."

A third voice laughs hysterically. "Who's been sleeping in my bed?"

"That's not how the story goes," the first voice whines.

Peering through the little window set inside the door, the girls watch on as three nurses loiter in front of the first room to the left.

Mercia grimaces. "They seem to have gone on an epic pharmaceutical raid. The junkies in Pine Hill would be impressed."

One nurse looks their way and they duck down to avoid being seen.

"Wrong storrry. It's the wrong storrry." The second voice rolls her *R*s and cackles.

Rachel glances through the window again and sees the three nurses in front of Mrs. Crenshaw's hospital room, pounding on the door with their fists and feet. Mandy, the nurse Mrs. Crenshaw had admonished the morning after she'd been admitted, slides down the wall to sit on the floor, still laughing like a maniac. Scattered around her are pills of every color, in every shape and size.

"My question is, where is the rest of the staff?" Rachel whispers back to Mercia. "And who's looking after the other patients?"

"I think all of the other victims were taken to the hospital in the city, because we don't have enough doctors here." Mercia says. "In the meantime, what do we do about them?"

"We need a distraction to get them away from the door," Rachel whispers. She steals a glimpse at the three giggling nurses. Ziggy begins moving around in the bag, restless, ready to play along. "Not yet," she says to the bag.

"And then what?" Mercia asks through gritted teeth.

"Let's tackle one problem at a time."

Mercia's shoulders slump slightly, but she doesn't press for more. Instead, she leans back around the corner and whispers something under her breath before snapping her fingers. Almost instantly the giggling nurses stop their laughing. Rachel sneaks a peek and sees the scattered multi-colored pills rise off the floor and levitate at eye-level.

"Ooh. Lookey-lookey," Mandy says in a childlike voice. "Pretty little pills."

The other two nurses are similarly enchanted by the phenomena, staring with wide eyes at the hovering medication. One nurse, the oldest of the three, reaches out to catch a nearby red pill, but it flies away. Her hand moves to cover her mouth, muffling another giggle. Mandy is next in line, opening her mouth to catch a pill in midair, but it moves down the hallway slowly, taunting the three nurses.

"Let's catch them," Mandy suggests, getting to her feet. "Let's catch them all." She spins in place and grabs at the pills, missing every time. She lets loose a belly laugh before moving farther down the hall. The other nurses, in a similarly captivated state, try their best to catch the pills as they move away from the door. The one with a scalpel slash at the pills, but she's unable to reach her target. "Come here," Mandy sings and twirls.

"That'll keep them busy for a while," Mercia says.

"Thanks." Rachel looks past Mercia to see if the coast is clear before making her way to the door. She knocks twice and says, "Dougal, it's me. Open up." Something large drags across the floor on the other side of the door. More objects seem to be moved before the door finally cracks open. "They're gone. Relax."

"Relax? I almost gotta scalpel through my eye," he grumbles, opening the door wide enough for her to enter.

Rachel crinkles her nose in disgust; the sharp tang of urine emanates from Dougal damp shirt.

"I don't want to talk about it," he says in a serious tone.

"What did I tell you?" Rachel says to Mercia, grinning.

"You're twisted, Cleary." The corner of Mercia's lip lifts into a conspirator's smile.

Rachel notices the dented metallic bedpan lying near the wall, the discarded chairs and metal cupboard standing behind Dougal. She shifts her attention to the tiny figure lying beneath the thin blanket. The only sign of her being alive is the movement of her chest, a rhythmic up and down as she inhales and exhales, softly snoring.

"Nan's out cold ever since the sedative they gave her this mornin'." Dougal explains. "I don't know how we're gonna get Nan out of here."

"I can help with—" Mercia is interrupted by a mechanical chirruping sound. She fumbles with her cell phone, checks the screen, and frowns. "Sorry, it's my mom," she says, before answering with a cheerful, "Hi, Mom."

Rachel and Dougal walk a few steps away, closer to Mrs. Crenshaw, giving Mercia some privacy.

"*What?*" Mercia says loud enough to earn Rachel and Dougal's attention. She waves them over and pulls the cell phone from her ear, before placing the call on speaker.

"I said: your aunt just called to say Sheriff Carter is walking up and down Main Road in nothing more than his underwear and hat, calling out for some or other 'gosh darn gunslinger' so they can have a duel. Annabeth Garter is running around on all fours like an animal, biting people. Not to mention Johnny Markham hijacked the school bus and is acting like he's a pirate on the open seas." Ms. Holstein's voice is clear, not a hint of humor in her words. "Hawthorne is now suddenly on lockdown, so there's no telling when I'll get home, but you need to get somewhere safe as soon as possible."

"I'm nowhere near home—"

"Where are you?"

Mercia pauses, grimacing. "I'm with Rachel Cleary and her cousin." When, after a few moments, her mother doesn't respond, Mercia says, "Mom? Are you still there?"

"I'm here," Ms. Holstein says, sounding none too happy. Mercia switches off the speaker and puts the phone back to her ear, the conversation continuing in whispers.

"So, the sheriff's gone off the rails, too, eh? Like the nurses? Like everyone at school did?"

"Sounds that way," Rachel whispers back. "One problem at a time." She says this more to herself than him, but he grunts an affirmative, anyway. "I think our best bet is to move your grandmother to Saint James in the city. We'll help you get her to the car, but I can't leave while the town's lost its marbles."

"Aye, I know," Dougal says. "But I don't feel comfortable leavin' ye here by yerself either."

Rachel pats his shoulder and smiles. "I'll be fine. I've caught myself a witch, after all."

"What if she goes bonkers and turns on ye?"

"I won't," Mercia answers. "Witches have a natural immunity against outside influence. That's how I know Orion isn't human—I can see through his glamor." She flashes Dougal a bright, white smile. "My trick won't keep the nurses occupied for long so we should probably get your grandmother out of here before they come back."

Dougal nods and takes a step closer to the bed. Mercia stops him, gestures for him to stand aside, before she mutters under her breath and raises her arms beside her. In response, Mrs. Crenshaw's sleeping form rises from the bed and slowly moves forward.

Dougal's expression twists in terror. He almost lunges closer, his arms outstretched. When he realizes she's not going to fall, he mutters, "Just in case, yeah?" However, the fear in his face doesn't fade.

Rachel exits the room first, looks down the hallway, and finds it as empty as when they had entered. "All clear," she says over her shoulder, stepping out of the way.

The sleeping Mrs. Crenshaw, with the blanket still draped over her, files out of the door first. She turns gently, swaying from side-to-side, before Dougal is there, arms stretched out beneath her to catch her if she falls. Mercia follows, her brow creasing with concentration. She moves her hands to stabilize Mrs. Crenshaw and slowly walks behind her.

Rachel keeps an eye on the hallway beyond, waiting until the others are nearing the lobby, before she walks backward to join them.

"We need to take the elevator down," Mercia says, out of breath. "I won't be able to keep Mrs. Crenshaw stable on the stairs."

Dougal inches toward the wall to call the elevator.

"What d'ya got there?" an unfamiliar voice says from the other side of the lobby.

Rachel pivots to look at the door that leads to another ward only to find the missing security guard staring at Mrs. Crenshaw. His hair is disheveled, uniform shirt is half unbuttoned to reveal his vest beneath, and his finger is itching for the Taser on his belt.

"Deal with it, Rachel," Mercia says through her teeth.

Without hesitation, Rachel opens her bag and Ziggy flies out into the open.

Rachel raises her hand and points at the security guard. "Ziggy, go play with the nice man."

Ping. The elevator doors slide open and Mrs. Crenshaw floats inside, Mercia following behind.

"Dougal," Rachel says, reaching over Mercia's shoulder to hand him her car keys, "don't waste time getting out of town."

"Be careful," he says, taking the keys.

"See you in a bit," Mercia adds just before the doors slide shut on her.

Rachel watches as Ziggy zigzags in front of the security guard's face, keeping the guy preoccupied by blinking brighter and then dimming. Whenever the security guard reaches out to touch the Fae light, Ziggy zips away. Amused, the guard doesn't notice when Rachel slips away.

She rushes down the staircase, grabbing the railing and using her momentum to propel herself around the landing. Rachel whistles loudly, and a few seconds later, Ziggy is by her side, bouncing off the walls.

"Good job," she says as they make their way to the first floor's landing.

Chapter Fifteen

Step on a Crack, Break your Mother's Back

Rachel exits the hospital just in time to see Dougal reversing out of the parking space, his grandmother lying unconscious in the backseat of the Hyundai. Mercia stands at the curb, watching them go, snaking her arms around her waist to hold herself.

"Thank you," Rachel says as she walks up to Mercia's side, who's face has become wan. "I truly appreciate your stepping in to help Mrs. Crenshaw."

Mercia offers a weary smile. "It's the least I could do for her." She gestures for them to walk, and Rachel falls into step beside her. "I wasn't born with epilepsy."

"You weren't?" Rachel says.

Mercia shakes her head. "Not a lot of people know I have two older sisters. Kelsey, the eldest, is twelve years older than I am, and Laura, the middle child, is ten years older than me. Kelsey swore off magic and left Shadow Grove when she was sixteen, opting to go live with her dad in California. Laura, is a different story altogether."

Mercia tries the door of a car parked in a reserved space, which belongs to a Dr. Ramsey. Initially, the door doesn't budge, but with a snap of her fingers, Mercia springs the lock open. She pulls the driver's side door open and climbs inside. Rachel walks around the front of the car and opens the passenger door.

Ziggy flies into the car, slips in between the gap of the front seats, and hovers in the backseat as Rachel joins them.

"Anyway," Mercia continues, searching for the spare key, "when I was six-years-old, Laura was babysitting me one night while my mother and grandmother were at a coven meeting or something. I don't remember the details." She sits back in the seat and inhales deeply before snapping her finger again. The engine whirrs to life without a key in the ignition. Mercia reverses out of the parking space. "That night, I saw Laura do the type of magic we aren't allowed to do—dark, ancient stuff. Where she got the book is anyone's guess. But she saw me watching her and, well, she tried to wipe my mind, to rid me of the memory of seeing her with that infernal book. Something went wrong with her spell, though."

"I'm sorry to hear, but what does Mrs. Crenshaw have to do with it?"

Mercia drives out of the hospital's parking lot and into the street. "They couldn't risk fixing me with witch magic, not when there was a chance I'd have permanent brain damage, so my mom went to see Mrs. Crenshaw and asked her to see if there isn't anything the faeries could do for me."

"Oh," Rachel whispers. "I take it she wasn't successful."

"Mrs. Crenshaw went out of her way to help me, but no. Laura's spell had created an irreversible traumatic brain injury, and the lesions are too deeply embedded in the matter to be fixed with any type of magic," Mercia says. "All that helps to alleviate the symptoms is the goldmint."

They are quiet for a while, driving down the empty street on their way to the center of town.

Curiosity gets the better of Rachel, and she breaks the silence with a subdued, "If you don't mind me asking, what happened to Laura?"

"As punishment for dabbling in the dark arts and hurting another witch, the coven stripped her of her powers. She didn't take it well and eventually had to be committed. That's who we visit in Hawthorne Memorial." Mercia looks in the rearview mirror, to where Ziggy twirls in place. "I have never heard of a Fae separating themselves from their Fae light for so long, or of humans being able to control them."

"I don't control Ziggy," Rachel says.

"But you can, can't you?"

Rachel bows her head slightly. "If you're wondering how I'm able to do it, you're in good company. Even Orion was stumped when he realized I could control Fae light."

"Maybe you have some residual powers in your blood, some magic that was passed down to you. If I recall, your family also fled Ireland?" Mercia glances at Rachel.

"Nah, we didn't flee. There were some convictions of witchcraft and heresy way back in the 1500s, but most of the claims were unfounded, and the evidence was fabricated," Rachel says. "I don't have any magic in me."

"Just because you don't have witch blood running through your veins doesn't mean there isn't some magic in you." Mercia smiles, already looking less tired. "Manipulating someone else's magic, particularly a Fae Prince's magic, is unheard of. I doubt anyone in the coven has even attempted such a feat." Mercia turns off into Main Road, slows down by the first traffic light, and looks in all of her mirrors. When the light changes to green, she pulls away, driving past the eerily quiet Whole Foods, which stands across the street from the empty roadhouse-styled diner. "Maybe your mother's family has a bit of magic," she says, shrugging.

"You're awfully calm after stealing a car." Rachel says to change the topic.

Mercia grins. "Rachel Cleary, if I didn't know any better, I'd think you were afraid of going to juvie."

"Hardly. I simply didn't think you were capable of doing something as bold."

Her humor slowly vanishes. "Peer pressure has its advantages."

Rachel raises an eyebrow.

"Be careful what you wish for," Mercia says, as if knowing where Rachel's thoughts had traveled. "Holland likes to make people do things so she can blackmail them later on. Ashley, on the other hand, thrives on—" She slams down on the brakes, the tires screeching as the car comes to a stop. "Is that your mom?"

Rachel looks out of the window only to see her mom skipping across the road, tearing out the pages of a library book and allowing the wind to blow those torn pages away.

"I didn't think she'd be back from Bangor yet," Rachel says, undoing her seatbelt.

"Are you sure leaving the car is wise?" Mercia unclips her own seatbelt.

Rachel ignores her. "Mom," she calls. Her mother looks up from the book and smiles broadly. "What are you doing?"

Jenny glimpses at the book in her hands again, and snickers. "I'm making big confetti. Duh." She rips out another page from the book and releases it from her fingers. The page flutters across the street and comes to a rest by the gutter.

Rachel takes her mother by the arm and tugs her forward. "Come on, let's go home."

"No." Jenny shakes her off.

"Mom, come on." Rachel reaches for her again. Jenny takes a step away. "Seriously?"

Jenny leans closer and whispers, "There's a monster in that house."

Rachel frowns and shakes her head. "I got rid of the monster, remember? It's safe now. The Night Weaver is gone."

"*No,*" she yells. "That thing is still there. It's *always* there."

"Should I, you know?" Mercia makes a *poof* sound, indicating using magic.

Rachel shakes her head. "My mom's already been through a lot these past few months. I don't think it's a good idea to zap her with more magic." She takes a tentative step closer, both palms up, approaching her mother like she's a wild animal. "Mom, I promise the monster's gone. Come with me so I can show you."

Jenny shakes her head, pouting.

"We have confetti *and* glitter at home." Rachel forces herself to smile, afraid of scaring her mother off. The last thing she needs right now is having to chase her mother down to stop her from hurting herself or someone else. "Don't you want to play with sparkly glitter?"

Jenny seems to consider the question, before she nods vigorously.

"Okay, but you have to come with us then."

"The monster, though," Jenny whispers. She drops the book and allows Rachel to lead her to the car.

"If there's a monster," Mercia says, walking on Rachel's other side, "I'll make it disappear."

"Like a magic trick?" Jenny is all wide-eyed innocence at this point.

"Exactly like a magic trick," Mercia says, opening the back door of the car.

"Ooh, pretty and shiny," Jenny exclaims when she sees Ziggy, scrambling inside to try and catch the startled Fae light.

Rachel shuts the door and sighs. "Thanks."

"No problem," Mercia says, already moving toward the other side of the car. "If we have someone who's enchanted, I can maybe figure out what we're up against."

"My mom's not a lab rat, Mercia."

"Obviously I don't mean to hurt her," Mercia says. Rachel follows her into the car, strapping herself into the seat. "No magic, I promise."

"Aw," Jenny says in the backseat. "I *want* magic."

"Look at the pretty light, Mom," Rachel snaps over her shoulder, her patience already wearing thin.

"Flashy-flashy."

"Let's just get her home and figure things out there, please."

Mercia nods and pulls away, continuing down Main Road. There's some gunfire as they pass the sheriff's department. Black smoke rises up from somewhere near the town square. Doors stand open and windows are broken, things are scattered across the sidewalks and streets, but not a single soul is to be seen on their way onto Eerie Street. The townsfolk must be somewhere, though. They must be planning something. But what?

"I'm glad we didn't see the sheriff on our way back." Mercia grimaces. "I don't know about you, but that image would have scarred me for life."

"Billy Boy said we're having a party in the square tomorrow night," Jenny says behind them. "There'll be fireworks, and cake, even presents. I like presents."

Rachel twists in her seat to see Ziggy in her mother's arms, her eyes fixed on the rhythmic golden flashes. "Why are you having a party?"

Her mother shrugs.

"Mom? Did you get an invite to the party?"

Her mother nods, still staring at Ziggy, brushing her fingertips over the golden surface. "I think it's someone's birthday."

"Oh, okay then. Well, if you're good, maybe we can go."

"You're not invited," Jenny says.

Rachel rolls her eyes shifts in her seat. "You'll notice," she says to Mercia, "my mom and I don't get along."

"Been there."

The rest of the journey home is uneventful, especially since Rachel's mother is preoccupied with Ziggy. As far as Rachel knows, Jenny Cleary hadn't seen the Fae light until they'd picked her up off the street. Good thing, too, because Rachel has no idea how she would have explained Ziggy if her mother wasn't one fry short of a happy meal.

Mercia offers to lead her mother inside the house, to keep an eye on her while Rachel goes in search of glitter and confetti in the attic.

Luckily, those boxes—the boxes she's dubbed dead hobbies—were nearer to the door than her father's journals. It's just a matter of finding the right box. So Rachel rummages around through the vast amount of stuff, junk they'd gathered over the years. She pulls out old paperbacks, the covers faded with time, and pencil cases full of dried-up pens. Adult coloring books and a whole plastic container of beads her mother had wanted to string together to create a kitchen curtain or something equally ridiculous. There's a box full of yarn, tangled and discolored with age, the mismatched knitting needles and crochet hooks. Fabrics and sewing threads fill the inside of another box, the overlocker rusted with disuse.

Finally, Rachel finds the box she's been searching for.

An old, unused piñata of a unicorn's head rest atop princess paper plates and pirate paper cups. There's a plastic bag full of pink confetti, which she removes, and after more digging in between the various decorations—the *It's a Girl!* and *Happy 35th Birthday!* banners knotted together—she finds a plastic container with gold glitter.

She leaves the rest of the stuff where she'd tossed it and makes her way down the attic ladder.

Rachel is barely on the second floor when the screaming starts, her mother's wails threatening to bring the walls down. The banging comes next, rattling the windows.

She rushes to the staircase and looks down to find her mom throwing herself against the door, tears streaming down her face. To one side, Mercia stands frozen.

"What the hell happened?" Rachel rushes down the stairs with the glitter and confetti under one arm.

"She was fine a minute ago, and then—" Mercia gestures to her mother, who's gone back to slamming her fists against the door.

"Mom," Rachel says, and places her hand on Jenny's shoulder. "Mommy?" She gently rubs the woman's back. "I found glitter. Do you want to see? It's sparkly."

"Please let me out," Jenny cried, turning to look at Rachel. "Please?"

"This is your home," Rachel says gently. "There's no monster here, I promise."

Jenny wails again, the sound desperate and haunting.

"Mommy, look," she says, pulling the bottle of glitter from underneath her arm. The golden sparkles glimmer in the container. "Pretty, huh?"

Her mother sniffles, the sobs turning into hiccups. She holds out her hand and Rachel places the glitter container in her open palm.

"And look what else I got," Rachel says, opening the plastic bag of confetti. She takes a fistful of confetti and throws it up in the air. Pink paper floats down over both her and Jenny. "Now we're princesses."

Jenny smiles as she studies the falling confetti, seemingly in a dreamlike trance.

Rachel hands over the confetti and places an arm over her mother's shoulder to lead her away from the door. She settles her down on the sofa and pulls the coffee table closer, just in time for Jenny to dump all the confetti out on the table.

"This is whack," Mercia says, her voice a mere whisper.

"Ziggy." Annoyance and worry edge her tone.

"The Fae light slipped out the window," Mercia says, gesturing to the open living room window. "I didn't think it mattered?"

"Why would he—?" Rachel shakes her head and heads back to the front door, Mercia close on her heels. "Today doesn't make any sense. Everyone's out of sorts," she mumbles as she opens the front door and takes a step outside. Rachel looks around, searching for the golden orb. "Ziggy, I am in no mood for y—" She cuts herself off midsentence as her gaze meet's Orion's. "Orion?"

"The townsfolk are acting really weird," he says.

"So, you've noticed?" Rachel walks down the porch steps and onto the path.

"Bit difficult to miss it when your neighbors barbeque a deputy's car in the parking lot," Orion says. "Do you know what we're up against yet?"

"Ever hear of Golvath the Lonely?"

Orion blinks slowly, shock filling his eyes. "He's just a bedtime story."

"Well, it's all I've got." Rachel shrugs, and plants her hands on her hips. "Do *you* still think I was overreacting about needing your help?"

He grimaces.

"Thought so."

"You're still angry with me, aren't you?" Orion says.

"Uh, yeah, but I have bigger problems than petty squabbles. My mom's kinda affected by all of this, and she's a handful." Rachel's words are barely cold when something shatters inside the house. There's a scream.

"No, Mrs. Cleary—stop."

Rachel gestures with a thumb over her shoulder, saying, "Cue the madness."

"Okay, I'll see what I can find out while you handle that," Orion says. "I'll be back soon."

"*Rachel.*"

Chapter Sixteen
Jaw Dropper

Rachel glimpses at Mercia as she runs down the porch steps, "Where's my mom?"

"Exactly where we left her," she says, breathless. "I confined her to the living room. So, yes, I did technically use magic, but not on her personally. It's just a barrier spell, the same one witches use to keep toddlers from sticking their fingers in electric outlets and away from stairs."

Rachel sighs and nods. "Thanks."

"It's not going to hold." Mercia turns around to walk back to the house. "We both need rest and something to eat."

"Yup."

"I mean it, Rach. We can't save the town when we're running on fumes," Mercia says.

"I know." Rachel sighs. "Why are you suddenly being so nice to me? Not to mention, you're helping my mom. What happened to the whole 'this doesn't make us friends' thing?"

Mercia shrugs. "Your mom's gone cray-cray, the guy you're crushing on is being super weird, your only friend and his grandmother have basically been run out of town, and I'm pretty sure you have a serious stalker problem."

Rachel closes her eyes and shakes her head. "What?"

"Isn't that Greg's car?"

Rachel opens her eyes and directs her attention to where Mercia is pointing down Griswold Road as Greg's Mercedes appears on the horizon. Every alarm bell in her body goes off in unison, her fight-or-flight responses readying themselves.

"Can this day get any worse?" she mutters, not in the mood to deal with him right now.

"That's a polite way of looking at things," Mercia grumbles. "What do you want to do?"

"Play dumb?" Rachel says and Mercia nods, both coming to a stop in the driveway.

They watch as Greg slows down and turns off the road, the passenger side window lowering. He sits forward in his seat, tilting his head to see them properly. Greg frowns, before he says, "Mercia Holstein, whatever are you doing *here*?"

"Well, sometimes even I like to drive down backroads and see how losers live," Mercia says. "You?"

"Where's your car, Rachel?" Greg asks, ignoring Mercia.

"It's not here, obviously," Mercia answers for Rachel, then quickly adds, "I'm glad you've not gone blind yet, you know, from using your right hand excessively." She makes a crude gesture, fluttering her eyelashes all the while.

It takes every ounce of strength to keep Rachel from laughing out loud, especially when Greg turns a deep shade of red.

He narrows his eyes at Mercia, but turns his attention on Rachel.

"I just wanted to make sure you're okay out here by yourself," Greg continues. "With Mrs. Crenshaw not around, I became concerned for your safety. The town's gone completely nuts. On my way over, Mr. Morris chased my car on all fours, barking like a dog."

Rachel shapes her mouth into an 'O', acting surprised. He must buy it, because his eyes soften as he regards her.

I should've taken drama class instead, she thinks.

"Well," Mercia says, flipping her hair over her shoulder, "Rachel is *not* by herself, as you can see, and we have work to do."

"What work?" Greg asks. "School's been closed for days or haven't you noticed?"

"Art project," Rachel lies quickly. "The theme is 'the world as we perceive it'," she continues. Luckily Greg doesn't have art as an elective. "I was thinking we should put a Freudian twist to it."

"Ooh, that's actually not a bad idea," Mercia says, playing along. "Nothing says art like wanting to sleep with your mother."

Even Rachel can't help herself from frowning.

"Or your daughter, whatever." She waves it off, unperturbed. "Anywho, we should probably get on with it if we actually want to do the project, so buh-bye, Greg."

He glances at Rachel, who shrugs.

"Sorry, but this is due soon," she says.

Greg's expression smooths out. "Call me, okay?"

Mercia bursts out laughing and takes a step away from the car. "Can you be any more desperate?" She pivots and walks toward the porch.

"Can you be any more of a bitch?" he calls back.

She flips him off, and disappears into the house, leaving Rachel alone with Greg. Rachel puts her hands behind her back and smiles, still acting like some lovesick idiot.

Mercia's nervous shout from within the house is enough to make her cut short whatever long goodbye Greg was waiting for.

"Gotta go, bye." She's already heading back to the house.

"Okay, bye."

She rushes up the steps and makes her way straight into the house. Rachel shuts the door behind her. The entryway is fine, but as she walks toward the living room, the issue becomes clear.

Rachel stands there staring at the destruction. The TV has been pulled off its wall mounts and lies in pieces on the floor. The coffee table is upended and two of the legs have been broken off. The sofa has been torn asunder and foam is spilling from the deep gashes. Even the curtains didn't survive, lying in large swathes on the floor. Confetti and glitter is strewn across the mess, which just feels like a slap in the face.

Her gaze moves up the scratched wall, deep gouges ruining the wallpaper and paint, toward a large hole in the ceiling.

"Where's my mother?"

"Hell if I know," Mercia snaps. "She climbed through the hole when I came in."

Rachel moves back to the staircase and takes the steps two at a time. "Mom," she calls, following the banging coming from somewhere on the second floor. The sound is muffled, though, coming from within the walls. "Mother?"

The bangs are replaced with a persistent scratching, like oversized rats scuttling about.

"Mom." Her voice grows more frantic as she runs to the hallway wall, pressing her ear against the smooth surface. She moves quickly past the bathroom, searching for Jenny.

Please don't get stuck in the wall. Please don't get stuck in the wall. Please don't get stuck in the—

A loud crash resounds, coming from inside her mother's bedroom. Laughter follows—manic laughter, in a high-pitched, creepy tone. Rachel runs for the bedroom and bursts inside, only to find her mother sitting on her haunches on the wall. Not against the wall, not in front of the wall. No, no. Jenny Clearly has to go and defy both logic and gravity by sitting *on* the wall. Vertically. In her hands, she's holding what appears to be some long dead critter, and there's a massive bite missing from its side. Her mother stares back at Rachel through glazed over eyes, eerie giggles interrupting the sound of chewing. Fur spills from her mother's lips, dropping to the floor.

"And I'm out." Mercia throws up her hands and backs out of the room. "I did not sign up for an exorcism, thank you very much."

"I did not sign up for an exorcism, thank you very much," her mother mimics Mercia in that same creepy high-pitched tone. She cackles, tears another piece of mummified flesh off the creature, and chews.

Rachel is too horrified to look away, only hears Mercia's retreat back downstairs.

"Wow," Greg says beside her. If it had been any other day, this might have startled her, but yeah. He's the least of her problems. "This is… Wow."

"Go find Mercia," Rachel says.

"She left as I came up," Greg answers. "I can't blame her."

Jenny drops her half-eaten dinner and lies back against the vertical wall, before she rolls up. She comes to a sudden stop. Jenny gets onto her hands and knees, climbs over the hindrance, and scuttle across the ceiling.

"Mom?" Rachel's voice quivers on the word.

"Mom," Jenny mocks, crawling over the ceiling, moving closer to the door where Rachel and Greg still stand in shock.

"Mommy—"

"*Mommy,*" Jenny interrupts in an unnerving whine.

A sob wiggles its way out of Rachel's throat as she follows her mother's movements, until Jenny comes to a halt above the doorway and busies herself with scratching at the wallpaper.

"Mom, get down from there this instant."

Jenny suddenly stands on the ceiling, coming face-to-face with Rachel, before an inhuman voice growls, "I'm *not* your mother."

Greg slams the door in Jenny's face, snapping Rachel out of her own fear. She spins on him and sees that his eyes are still fixed on the closed door. From how pale he is, she won't be surprised if he drops out of school and drinks himself to death.

"Greg?"

"Yes," he says.

"It's okay."

He blinks rapidly, before focusing on her. "That was not okay."

Rachel scratches the back of her neck, grimacing. "I'll admit it's weird, but I can fix this. I can—"

"You need to call a priest immediately. That's what you need to do." Greg turns around and walks down the hallway.

"I don't think a priest is going to be much help." Rachel follows him, glancing over her shoulder to make sure the door hasn't opened again. "I mean, I know what it looks like, but that's not exactly what's happening here. She's not possessed or anything of the sort."

He reaches the staircase and begins his descent. "Your mom literally climbed up the walls."

"Yeah." She can't argue with him on that particular point,

but this isn't a religious problem whatsoever. It's a Fae problem. A huge Fae problem. "Greg, wait."

He comes to a grinding halt at the bottom of the staircase and turns to look at her. She stops on the step above the ground, right in front of him, and reaches up to pinch the bridge of her nose. After Rachel has gathered her thoughts, she drops her arm and stares at him.

Red flashes in his pupils, almost imperceptible, but this time Rachel is certain she's seen it.

"What explanation can you possibly have for what's going on with your mom?" Greg says. "It's messed up beyond comprehension."

"Obviously," Rachel says, her mind reeling as she studies Greg, searching for whatever plagues him. "It's just—"

She stops speaking as she spots the broken mirror propped up against an armchair. Rachel feels the muscles in her forehead contract into a frown. She turns to look at the mirror, which reflects Mercia lying half-conscious against the sofa. Mercia opens her eyes and looks directly at Rachel through the mirror.

She snaps her attention back to Greg before he can figure out what she's seen.

"You're right," she says. She reaches out to hold on to the bannister. In her peripheral, she sees Mercia struggling to her feet.

"I'm glad you've come to your senses," he says. "Do you guys still have a landline or—"

"It's in the kitchen. We barely use it, but it works," Rachel says. "I could be wrong, but I doubt there's an Exorcisms 'R Us on the internet."

He smirks. "Leave it to you, Rachel Cleary, to make an inappropriate joke at the worst of times." Greg begins to turn, but she quickly grabs him by the shoulder and forces him to look back at her. "You okay?"

"No," she whispers.

It's not entirely a lie.

Rachel leans forward into him, wrapping her arms around his waist. Behind him, a royally pissed off Mercia stalks closer, a lamp in her hands. There's blood dripping down her forehead, matting her blonde hair to her head, and a bruise blooms on her temple.

Meanwhile, Greg wraps his arms around her shoulders, squeezing her tightly against his chest, whispering sweet nothings into her ear.

Mercia raises the lamp over her head and nods to Rachel, who pulls away from Greg.

"Greg," she says, gently running her hand over his cheek. He looks at her with those stormy eyes, so full of hope. Rachel smiles. "This thing between us …"

"Yes?"

"It's *so* over."

Mercia brings the lamp down over his head, smashing the porcelain into a thousand pieces. Bits rain onto the hardwood floor, tinkling as they touch the ground. He crumples to his knees and drops onto his side, unconscious, lying amongst the broken shards.

Mercia's foot connects with his side a couple of times before she spits onto his chest.

"That's what you get for knocking me out, you A-grade piece of—"

His eyes shoot open before she can finish her sentence. She shrieks and jumps back. This time, Rachel takes point and kicks him upside the head with as much force as she can muster.

"I'm getting real tired of guys acting like they can get away with treating girls like dirt," Rachel says through gritted teeth.

Greg goes limp and his eyelids shut a second time.

"We need to tie him up before he wakes again," Rachel says.

"No," Mercia says in a stern tone. "We need to get out of here now. We can go to my aunt's house and—"

"I'm not stopping you from leaving, Mercia. If you want to go, then leave."

Chapter Seventeen
Bad to the Bone

Rachel can't leave her mom by herself. Even if Jenny's current state scare the living daylights out of Rachel, she can't just go. Regardless of all the drama, the growing chasm between them, their crumbling relationship, she refuses to leave her mom to deal with this alone. If this is the decision of a sentimental fool, then so be it. She simply can't. Besides, if something dire happens to Jenny Cleary while she's re-enacting a scene from some independent exorcism film, Rachel won't ever be able to forgive herself.

Mercia calls her an idiot for making the decision, but leaves it at that.

Together, they tie Greg up—fixing his hands behind his back and his feet together—and half-drag, half-carry him into the destroyed living room.

"This isn't Greg," Rachel groans, straining as they lift him onto the sofa.

"I know," Mercia grumbles. She drops his lower body onto the floor. "Jeez, he's heavier than he looks." She wipes the sweat off her forehead with the back of her hand.

"Use magic on him the way you did with Mrs. Crenshaw?"

"I've already used too much today. My well is drying up fast, and I'll burn out if it empties out now. What I need is food and rest to replenish my reserves." She bends down and grabs hold of Greg's legs a second time and groans as she lifts him again. "Greg is probably going to think you tied him up so you could have your way with him." Mercia giggles. "Naughty minx."

Rachel grins, shakes her head. "I have no idea why he's so obsessed. We never got past second base."

"Some guys are into that." Mercia sets down his legs on the sofa, his knees folding over the ripped armrest. "Always wanting what they can't have. They're like a dog with a bone, can't stop themselves from wanting the fantasy they've built up in their head to spill into reality."

"You sound like you know a lot about it."

"I see how guys treat Holland."

"Oh," Rachel says.

They exit the living room together, and Rachel leads Mercia to the kitchen, where she scrounges up enough ingredients to make them each a couple of sandwiches. Rachel washes the meal down with coffee while Mercia sips on a glass of water. She watches as Mercia takes her goldmint pill and swallows it with the remainder of her drink.

A *bang* comes from upstairs and they both look up to the kitchen ceiling.

"I should probably go check on her," Rachel says. "Feed her something decent, before she decides to eat another dead rat or squirrel."

"Mind if I don't come along?" Mercia asks. "Someone needs to keep an eye on your stalker."

Rachel pulls the bread closer to make another couple of sandwiches for her mother.

"Your mom doesn't love you," Mercia says after a while. "She really wants to, but she doesn't."

"I figured as much," Rachel says, not looking up.

"It doesn't bother you or change anything?"

"I love her enough for the both of us," she says, cutting off the crust, the way her mother prefers. "Also, she's all I have left in this world."

"That's not true," Mercia whispers.

Dishing up her mother's meal on plastic would be better than providing her with anything breakable. She places the sandwiches on the plate, fills the cup with water, and walks out of the kitchen. Mercia's words doesn't bother her as much as they should—Rachel has suspected for years that her mother's feelings toward her aren't the typical motherly kind. It has driven a wedge between them even more, no doubt, but Rachel didn't lie about how she feels about Jenny Cleary. She does love her enough for the both of them.

She makes her way upstairs, back to her mother's bedroom, and knocks twice before opening the door.

Jenny is sitting in a corner, staring away from the door. Her hair is dirty, hanging in knotted strands over her slumping shoulders.

A tearing noise, like strips of paper being shredded, comes from her direction.

"Mom," Rachel says. She hesitates at the door. "I brought you dinner."

When her mother doesn't move, Rachel steps inside. Another pause. Rachel evaluates the situation, before she walks across the carpeted floor and stops a few feet away from her mother.

"It's not much, but—"

A croaking sound emits from her mother's throat. The sound stretches on for an impossibly long time, before Jenny sucks air into her lungs, wheezing loudly. She repeats this process a few more times. Rachel places the plate and cup on the floor behind Jenny after a while, deciding not to bother her.

Rachel backs up to the door again. "Try to eat something on the plate."

She closes the door and makes her way back downstairs, where she finds Mercia sitting on the armrest by Greg's feet, inspecting her nails.

As Rachel nears, she notices Greg is fully awake, and there's foam stuffed into his mouth to keep him quiet.

"What's this about?" she asks.

"He called me something I'd rather not repeat," Mercia says, holding her hand out to check her nails. "So he loses his talking privileges."

Muffled words escape the makeshift gag. Rachel looks down at Greg and shrugs before making her way to the other end of the living room. She takes a seat on an armchair across from them.

"We'll probably get in trouble for kidnapping him, holding him hostage, or something, right?"

"Nah, the Pearson family may have a lot of pull in this town, but the Holstein women rule it. Well, apart from Mrs. Crenshaw. That old lady is an institution even the Holstein witches regard sacred," she says, lowering her hand to her lap. "We just do it quietly, unlike this hotshot who thinks the sun goes down every time he takes a seat."

Rachel snickers.

"We're going to have to take shifts if we want to get any

sleep tonight. I know I took a nap this afternoon, but I'm dead on my feet. Can you take the first shift?"

"Sure," Rachel says. "My bedroom is—"

"I'm sleeping in the car," she quickly says.

"Okay, do you want a pillow or something?"

Mercia stands and shakes her head. "Nope, but thanks."

"All right, well, I won't lock the door. And if you see Ziggy, don't freak out."

Mercia exits the living room, and the door squeaks open before it closes behind her.

Rachel doesn't move, only watches Greg as he squirms around to lie on his side. It takes a while, but eventually he succeeds and stares back at her.

"I told you I didn't want anything serious, remember?" she says. "On several occasions, I told you it was just a summer fling, didn't I?"

He doesn't make a sound and doesn't move, but his eyes are clear and she's certain that he's listening closely to every word.

Rachel crosses her arms. "Greg, I really didn't want to be a jerk, but after today you've left me no choice. You were a Band-Aid, nothing more. I was lonely and you were willing to feel me up a bit so I could forget about my stupid life for a while. That's it."

He frowns.

"Yeah, I know," Rachel says, sighing. "I could have picked anyone for the catharsis you provided. I mean, none of the football players seem too picky. The difference between you and them is, you can actually challenge me intellectually. I'm sorry, but it's basically the only thing that sets you apart from all the other guys I may have considered for my summer fling."

Greg's eyes narrow.

"Judge me all you want, Pearson. You did the exact same thing." Rachel gets to her feet and crosses the room. She hunches down in front of the sofa. "Mercia told me all about how you had to pay girls to make me jealous. Sucks to be you, Greg, because I felt *nothing*."

Greg, who probably has a concussion and shouldn't be sleeping, falls into a deep sleep a few minutes later. Loud snores emanate from him, though, so he's definitely alive. The worst he'll have is a headache in the morning.

Meanwhile, Rachel passes the time by scanning through THE UNOFFICIAL HISTORY OF SHADOW GROVE, hoping to find further information on how to get the Bone Carver—*Ugh, couldn't Mrs. Crenshaw come up with something else to call it?*—off the streets. There's not much more to go on, other than the Golvath the Lonely entry.

I should have asked Orion to tell me his version of the story. She closes her laptop. *He might have had some insight into Golvath.*

Rachel places the laptop on the armrest and sits back, her gaze moving to the uncovered windows behind Greg. The night seems darker, lonelier, especially without Mrs. Crenshaw's porch light shining like a beacon.

Something flutters above her, and she looks up to see pieces of paper raining from the ceiling. Beyond the papers, there is a hole in the ceiling, and visible through the hole is her mother.

Her heart stalls for a beat or two. The hair on the back of Rachel's neck stand on end, goosebumps travel across her icy skin.

She stands, not looking away from her mother's demented eyes and vicious smile. It is an unbearable sight, maybe even unholy. But her mom is still in there somewhere. She has to be.

Jenny throws another handful of papers, and Rachel grabs one as it flutters down. She turns the heavy cardstock around and finds the surface smooth and glossy, the coloring bright. She snatches a second piece—this one larger than the last, and finds her suspicions are valid. Her face, or where her face should have been in the photo, has been scratched out. Rachel bends over to pick up another big piece and sees her mother and father's half-torn faces looking back. Another piece reveals one of Rachel's baby pictures, the face, once again, scratched out.

"Okay, what's your point?" Rachel looks back to the hole. Her mother is no longer there. "Fine, be that way." She tosses the pieces into the air and walks out of the living room.

Rachel exits the house and stands on the front porch, her heart aching. She inhales the fresh air deeply into her lungs, and pushes back the emotions threatening to consume her. Tears sting the corners of her eyes, but they won't spill. She won't allow it. Not yet, at least.

"You okay?" Mercia asks from somewhere on the dark lawn, startling Rachel in the process. "Sorry." Amusement laces her voice.

"I thought you were sleeping in your car," Rachel says to the darkness.

"I was," she says. "I came out to stretch my legs a bit before I went in to relieve you from babysitting Greg."

"He's out cold." Rachel waves her hand over her shoulder, as if she couldn't care less. "I think he has a concussion."

Mercia snorts as she walks into the light, her hair mussed and pillow lines creasing her right cheek. "Maybe you kicked some sense into him." She makes her way up to the porch and leans against the bannister. "I'm actually impressed, Rachel. Never thought you to be a badass."

A smile tugs at Rachel's lips.

"You should own it, girl," Mercia says. "Seriously, stop hiding who you truly are just because you're scared of what others think. You're so much more than the weird girl who lives near the forest."

"You're selling me short. I'm also the weird girl who always has her nose in a book."

"Yeah, well, I was trying to spare your feelings." Mercia winks. "What's the time, anyway?"

"Just past midnight." Rachel laughs under her breath. "Want some coffee?"

"Please."

Rachel gestures for Mercia to enter the house and follows her inside. She is instantly overcome by the oppressive atmosphere lingering in every corner, an unmistakable presence accompanying any Miser influence. It weighs her down, cloys at her skin and mind, every part of her screams at her to run away as far and fast as possible.

"The last time I felt anything so *off*, there was a poltergeist living it up in Holland's lake house." Mercia glances over her shoulder. "Holland had thought it would be funny to play with a Ouija board after some party I wasn't invited to."

"What happened?"

"What do you think happened? Things flew around the house the entire weekend we spent there." Mercia walks into the kitchen, and leans against the island.

"You didn't, like, clean out the place with magic?" Rachel reaches for the coffee machine.

Mercia barks a laugh and shakes her head. "Unlike some witches, I tend to steer clear of making contact with anything outside of this world. There are things out there—horrible things. You don't want to get too close to them."

Rachel switches on the coffee machine and readies the mugs.

"My magic hasn't settled yet," Mercia continues. "At this point, it's still volatile. I can do a bit of everything, but not much of anything either. And the brain injury isn't helping with the whole being a witch thing. I can, for example, use some elemental magic, but if I'm not careful, a simple rain spell can turn into a hurricane. Same goes for reaching out to the dead—I can communicate easily enough, but possession is a serious concern."

"Did you try finding Astraea Hayward after she went missing?" Rachel asks over the boiling water.

"The girl who vanished in front of Alice's Vintage Emporium?"

Rachel nods.

"No. It never occurred to me to try to find her." Mercia grimaces. "One thing I know for sure is that if Astraea Hayward was dead, my oumie would've said something. Anyone who dies in Shadow Grove goes to visit her after passing over."

"So, if she's not dead then where is she?"

Mercia shrugs. "I—"

A door slams shut, the sound resonating from somewhere on the first floor. Rachel and Mercia look at each other, eyes widening. Both spring to action, running out of the kitchen to find the front door firmly shut and the sofa empty. The sound of an engine starting reaches Rachel as she pulls the door open, and she sees Greg's Mercedes backing up dangerously fast, almost reversing all the way up Mrs. Crenshaw's driveway.

"How did he get out of those knots?" Rachel asks aloud.

The drawn-out croaking coming from the living room is answer enough.

Mercia punches the doorframe and makes an indignant noise of frustration. "Your mom is really getting on my nerves." She pushes her fingers through her hair.

Rachel pivots and marches to the living room where her mother sits on the armchair, staring at the empty sofa with her mouth open. Saliva dribbles down her chin and onto her chest. In her hands is a picture, a black scan of some kind. Rachel moves closer and sees the sonar scan of a fully developed baby in the womb. She raises an eyebrow.

"So you can tear up all the photographs in the house, but not the scan? What gives, huh, Mom?"

Her mother turns her head slowly to look at Rachel where she stands, still gaping. Only then does Rachel see the bold red letters on the back of the scan, spelling out a single word. *Mine.*

Rachel throws her hands in the air. "I give up."

She picks up her laptop from the armrest of the chair her mother now occupies, makes sure she has her cellphone in her pocket, and backs out of the living room, her eyes never leaving Jenny.

Mercia stands in the open doorway, waiting. As Rachel reaches it, she notices Ziggy's glow, no more than a speck in the dark, moving closer, quickly winding across the open field beside Mrs. Crenshaw's house.

Rachel gestures for Ziggy to enter the house before she closes the door on the world.

"Now what?" Mercia asks.

"I'm going to sleep."

Rachel seethes as she heads up the staircase, balling her hands into tight fists as she clutches her laptop against her chest, her teeth grinding together. It is entirely possible that this is a side-effect of whatever the Miser Fae is doing—after all, it seems like everyone in town is affected in some way or another—but there is only so much she can take.

Even Rachel Cleary has her limits.

Chapter Eighteen
We are the Hollowed Ones

Every evening, just before bed, Rachel asks Ziggy the question she yearns to hear her mother ask her. "Did you have a nice day?"

Tonight, Ziggy answers with two, not as bright, flashes.

Rachel sighs as she places her hand on the glowing sphere, causing the golden light to ripple down Ziggy's surface. "Yeah, me neither, Zigs. Tomorrow is another day, so let's get ready for bed and hope for better."

Ziggy doesn't seem as happy-go-lucky as usual. The Fae light simply drifts off and hops onto the pillow, before rolling underneath the covers and hiding in the most inconspicuous place on her bed—a winking emoji throw-pillow.

Rachel turns to her closet, searching for something more comfortable to sleep in. Shorts and a T-shirt seem inappropriate attire for the oncoming cold, but she's still unsure if she'll sleep comfortably by wearing winter pajamas. Besides, with her mother acting like a whack-job, she might have to go outside during the night on short notice.

Creak.

The soft sound infiltrates her busy mind.

Creak.

Closer this time. Rachel suspects it's the old house settling as the winter draws nearer. Nothing to get worried about. She hopes.

Creak.

The light goes out. Rachel spins around just as a clammy hand clasps over her mouth and nose. A heartbeat passes before she's slammed up against the wall and pain shoots through her shoulders. Whatever sound she wanted to make is lost in the back of her throat. Her eyes widen. Elongated fingers cover almost the entirety of her face, the index finger touching her ear. There is nothing in front of her, nothing at all. Panicking, yet physically paralyzed, she stares into the darkness as her lungs burn for oxygen.

Sour breath crashes against her face like a tidal wave.

"Mine."

The crackling whisper sends a jolt of fear through her body, far more insistent than the pain in her shoulders. She's barely able to roll her eyes to look to where the voice is, but manages a glimpse of bone white skin covered by ancient, filthy bandages.

"All mine," the husk of a voice continues. It sounds as if the owner hasn't spoken in years.

Another hand moves up her bare arm, making its way to her elbow. The devil begins whispering terrible things into her mind—warning her of what *could* happen. The caress turns darker as the creature grabs onto her forearm and wraps those impossibly long fingers around her wrist. The grip tightens, squeezing until her eyes water from the pain. The soft skin on the inside of her wrist ache as fingernails digs into her flesh, deeper and deeper, almost gouging at the muscles beneath.

To round the entire hellish situation off, Rachel's lungs

scream for air.

The unseen force keeps her pinned against the wall, while one hand remains fixed over her face and the other squeezes her arm even harder. If she could scream, she would, but even a whimper is an impossible feat. How long will it take her to suffocate when she's utterly defenseless? Not too long—a couple of minutes at most.

"*Forever.*"

Never in Rachel's life has a single word sounded so ominous, so terrifyingly final.

A ball of sunshine erupts from underneath the bedcover, illuminating the gloom with golden rays. Ziggy flies with such speed that the force of the impact makes the Fae light shatter into a million pieces. The hands disappear, and she slides down to the floor, gasping for breath

As Ziggy puts himself back together, Mercia steps into her bedroom. With a flick of her hand, the creature becomes fully visible and hurdles across the room.

A tall, emaciated body with elongated limbs wrapped in bandages is pinned against the opposite wall. Shiny, oversized black eyes bulge from a gap between the bandages, staring at her from across the room. If Rachel didn't know any better, she'd have thought the creature was an alien, not a Fae.

"What the hell are you supposed to be?" Mercia says, studying the figure.

A switchblade grin cuts across the Fae's face, revealing tiny, pointed teeth. Shuddering, Rachel scrambles to her feet, under the monster's unwavering gaze.

Mercia glances over her shoulder to Rachel. "You know this guy?"

"No."

"Cool," Mercia says, turning her attention back to the Fae.

"What is it?"

"Looks like a water spirit of the Fae variety," Mercia says. "They're usually harmless, but this one has been corrupted."

Before Rachel can fully come to grip with what's happening, the Fae spontaneously bursts into flames. A tiny, involuntary shriek escapes her as she watches in horror. Fire licks up the bandages, engulfing the frail being faster than she thought possible, turning it into ash. There isn't any smoke filling her bedroom, no scream accompanying what should be agony. Rachel expects, at the very least, panic and writhing as the blaze consumes the creature, but there's none. There's just the unnerving grin and amused stare.

A sickening crunch fills the otherwise quiet bedroom. The creature's neck twists by itself, stopping at an awkward angle, before the fire is extinguished by unseen forces. Bones snap and crack as the half-burned Fae folds in on itself, smaller and smaller.

"You didn't have to kill it right away," Rachel says. She stares at the unoccupied space where the midnight intruder had been.

"I didn't. He just kinda went …" Mercia turns around and gestures. "Poof."

A bloodcurdling scream pierces the night.

Rachel comes to her senses.

"I wouldn't go out there right this second if I were you," Mercia says.

"My mom, though." She frowns.

Mercia tilts her head. "Well, duh. Why else would there be phantom screaming coming from *outside* the house? Your mom's fine."

"I need to go," Rachel says. She takes a step toward the bedroom door.

"Ever think that maybe this is the real bad guy trying to lure you out into the open by preying on your weaknesses?"

"Caring isn't a weakness," she snaps back, but halts her advancement.

Mercia's eyes soften for a brief second, before cool calculation takes over. "Okay, listen up, Rach. Fae don't simply kill humans for the sake of killing humans. It's a sport. They toy with us for weeks, months, and in some situations—especially if it's one sick mofo doing the torturing—they'll draw the suffering out for years. Whatever's out there has its sights set on you, and if you're going to be predictable, you're as good as dead."

"But my mom is down there by herself. What if—?" Rachel gestures to the door.

"She's in the walls. Trust me, she's fine. I made sure to put her in a protective barrier," Mercia says. "Just take a break."

Rachel closes her eyes and shakes her head, defeat weighing her down. "We should, at least, find Orion."

"No, you need rest." Mercia makes elaborate movements with her hands as she whispers something under her breath. After the show, she simply says, "There. Your room is now guarded against the evil eye. Get into bed and sleep."

"What about you?" Rachel drags herself back to her bed.

Mercia's soft smile seems like a beacon of hope in an otherwise bleak existence. "I'm going to keep an eye on your mom and make sure Greg doesn't come back to do whatever he's set on doing to you."

"We need to find out where this Golvath is, Mercia. The town is tearing itself apart and this guy is doing all of it." Rachel squeezes her eyes shut. "What doesn't belong, huh? What is new all of a sudden? There's something out of place, I just know it."

"Sleep now. Think later. You want to beat this thing? Well, then you need to be at one-hundred percent." Mercia walks toward the door. "I mean it. Sleep."

Ziggy puts himself together, molten lava moving across the carpet like metal shavings being pulled by a magnet. The smaller, albeit shining golden sphere hovers back to bed, seemingly lackluster after having to protect her again.

"Okay, sheesh." Rachel climbs under the covers, and pulls them high up to her neck, before Mercia closes the door. Ziggy settles on her pillow. "There's no way I'm going to fall asleep," she whispers.

Two dim blinks, as if saying she should heed Mercia's advice.

Chapter Nineteen
Right in the Sternum

The next morning, after she's finished her morning rituals, Rachel heads downstairs, toward the kitchen where Mercia is feeding her mother grits. She studies the two at the table, surprised to see her mother's hair brushed and her clothing changed.

"You took care of her?" Rachel is unable to keep the emotions from her voice.

Mercia shrugs.

"Thank you," she says.

"I figured out how to handle her after you went to bed," Mercia says. She makes *choo-choo* noises as she brings the spoon of grits closer to Jenny's mouth. Her mother laughs and parts her lips wide. "There's breakfast for you on the stove."

Rachel moves to the stove, opens the pot of grits, and finds a bowl on the drying rack. She spoons enough breakfast in for herself, before adding some butter, sugar, and milk, and draws up a chair.

"My mom called this morning," Mercia says, still feeding Jenny. "Hawthorne is still under lockdown. Apparently the patients, and even some of the staff, have lost their minds. The handful who haven't been affected are holed up in some office.

That's not important, though."

Rachel looks up, bracing for bad news.

"They found ten different little bone sculptures in one of the rooms at Hawthorne, each one more heinous than the other, and they all depict a patient," Mercia says. "Two of those—I guess, one would call them omens—came true, according to my mom."

"That's not good," Rachel says.

"I told my mom the same thing."

"Phalanges," Jenny says. She raises her hands and wiggles her fingers, giggling. "Ten phalanges."

"Jenny, here comes the plane." Mercia whooshes as she makes the spoon fly.

Rachel takes another bite of her grits.

"Rachel, are ye home?" Dougal's voice comes from the front door. "By the Wee Man— What happened here? Rachel?"

"We're in the kitchen," Mercia calls.

Dougal rushes in, wearing the previous day's clothes. His hair is disheveled, bags are visible under his eyes, and his skin tone is paler than usual.

"Ye look like hell," he says to Rachel. His gaze moves across the scene before he fixes his stare on Jenny. "Yer ma looks worse."

Rachel shakes her head, shoulders already curving forward in defeat. The day hasn't even begun properly and she can easily go back to bed.

"You don't know the half of it," Mercia mumbles. "Food's on the stove. Help yourself."

"I don't know where ye come off actin' like it's yer house, but don't mind if I do." Dougal walks to the stove. "Nan said I should come check on ye. Good thin' I did."

"How is she?" Rachel asks.

"Better. The doc said she's recoverin' fine. He doesn't care for the way they handled her at the hospital here."

"Ten phalanges," Jenny barks out, her eyes darkening. "Ten metacarpalsssss."

"What's yer ma on about?" Dougal asks.

"Bones," Rachel says in a weak voice. "She probably knows there are more accidents about to occur."

Jenny bursts out laughing.

Mercia sighs loudly. "Why can't this Fae take a break?"

Dougal walks over and takes the last seat at the table. He glances at the wound on Mercia's head, which is already scabbed over, and asks, "What happened to yer head?"

"Greg," she says.

Dougal raises an eyebrow as he takes a bite. "I hope ye kicked him in the baws."

"The what?" Mercia asks.

"Ye know. He's family jewels."

"Balls," Rachel offers.

"Oh. Um, no, but I got a few good kicks in," Mercia says, shrugging.

Mercia's voice grows distant until it's non-existent. Rachel glances up, sees her mouth moving, watches as Dougal respond. Her mother meets her eyes, a crease forming on her brow. Meanwhile, the birds quieten outside, the world becomes voiceless.

"I need to find Orion," Rachel says the words, but can't hear herself speak. "I need … to—" She stands, blinking rapidly as the world spins. She moves a hand to her neck, but the pendant she's so used to sitting there is gone. She exhales through her nose, feeling something rummaging around in her head. Searching.

Searching. Wanting to know everything she knows, but there's a specific *something* it wants—no, *needs*.

The world shatters like a mirror being smashed. The shards drop around her, every tinkle a reminder that she is no longer in control of her own body. And then she's floating somewhere within herself. Hovering. It almost feels like she's outside of her body, but not quite.

There's someone inside her mind, an evil lurking just outside her reach. Drilling into her thoughts, deeper and deeper, the wanting growing desperate, the needing becoming unbearable.

Get out!

There's no response.

The unworldly violation continues as it sorts through her memories. She sees herself meeting Orion for the first time, remembers his apprehension to let her into his apartment. Rachel is transported back to her sophomore year, when Mrs. Crenshaw was the one cheering her on at a track meet and not her mother. Another memory comes out, this one of Rachel standing by her father's grave a few years after his death.

Liam Donovan Cleary
Beloved husband and father
August 20, 1979 – February 10, 2011

The memory shifts as the regression picks up speed. Emotions resurface. There's the immense heartache as she watches her mother's despondence turn to apathy. Before that, though, her father is alive, but still sickly. Then, the illness reverses, showing Liam Cleary as he looked before anyone even suspected he was sick. The memories stop at an unfamiliar scene.

She remembers the pure joy of spending the Fourth of July with her parents, watching the fireworks brighten up the sky, but parts are obscured. How old was she? Younger than eight, sure, but when was this? The image shifts before she can figure out when and where they were, playing back Christmases, birthdays, anniversaries, and less significant memories. All the while, Rachel is overcome with a myriad of emotions—happiness, sadness, anger. Everything flits through her mind, consumes every part of her being, until—

You want to play? Fine. Let's play.

Something inside her mind clicks, like rusty cogs being forced to turn after years of immobility, and then gives way. Too fast to fathom, she clashes into another, wholly different mind. How she's done it, she can't explain, but she grabs onto a sliver of darkness that doesn't belong and the intruder jerks back. She digs into the black tendril and doesn't let go, afraid of missing an opportunity to teach this Fae a lesson in boundaries.

A murky blur surrounds Rachel as she burrows deeper, assessing random thoughts that make zero sense, before finding what she supposes are its memories. Discerning faces is near impossible and the landmarks are completely distorted. At times, even the snippets of conversations are unintelligible, the language utterly alien.

Rachel finds a pinprick of light shining from an otherwise impenetrable wall of information, where a filthy little boy, no older than six, sits on a stony outcrop behind a quaint cottage in a picturesque valley. His eyes are on his constantly moving hands. He whittles away at a stick with a sharp knife.

Before she can see anything else, the invading mind seems to buck, tossing her consciousness into the wind, before Rachel's ethereal self falls first through nothingness and then past memories. She travels at lightning speed back through time, until she plummets into the here and now. The sole resident in her mind again, Rachel shoots her eyes open as residual tremors make their way through her limbs.

Her heart wildly pounds to an irregular beat as she looks around, finding herself still seated at the kitchen chair. Dougal and Mercia, oblivious to the battle she's just fought—and won— are conversing about Greg's intrusion the previous night.

Jenny, however, is looking directly at her.

Her mother's mouth pulls into an ugly, unrecognizable sneer while knowing eyes narrow into slits. Pupils dilate before a hint of red flashes.

Jenny moves faster than Rachel thought possible. By the time the kitchen chair actually hits the linoleum floor, her mother is already on the other side of the kitchen. Cutlery clatters across the countertops and spills into the sink. Grits splatter onto the table. Jenny spins around to face her mystified audience, holding a serrated steak knife against her own throat. She presses down hard, but luckily doesn't break the skin.

A chorus of flabbergasted, "Mrs. Cleary," adds to the horrified, "Mom," echoing through the kitchen.

"You're hiding something and I want to know what it is," Jenny says in a voice that isn't her own.

"I don't—"

Jenny presses the knife down, allowing a bead of blood to escape the tiny cut.

Rachel raises her hands, palms-up in surrender. "Okay, okay, what do you want to know?"

"Who are you *really*?"

"I'm Rachel Cleary?" The statement comes out as a question as her confusion grows.

"Are you? You don't sound too sure—"

"I've known Rachel my entire life," Mercia chimes in. "I swear on my life, the person in front of you *is* Rachel Cleary."

Slowly, Jenny turns back to Rachel. "You have a witch vouching for you while your own mother isn't certain? Curious."

"My mom's been through a lot," Rachel snaps at the intruder in her mother's body.

Jenny guffaws, or rather the thing inside her does. "Tell you what, Rachel Cleary. Either you figure out who or what you are or I'll take my displeasure out on your dearest mother."

"Give me five seconds and I'll go find my driving permit."

"Really, Rachel?" Mercia hisses. "Jokes?"

"I wasn't joking," Rachel growls back under her breath.

Jenny, or rather the thing inside her, slides the knife away from her neck and reaches back with her arm. With a simple flick of her wrist, Jenny releases the weapon. Hilt over blade, the knife cuts through the air and passes a hairsbreadth away from Rachel's face. The tip pins into a cupboard door behind Mercia and Dougal, before the serrated blade snaps in half and falls onto the counter.

Glass shatters next, pulling Rachel's attention away from the knife.

Shards crush beneath the soles of Rachel's shoes as she walks to the kitchen sink and stares through the broken window. Unable to do anything useful, she simply watches in horror as her mother sprints across the backyard, wearing little more than a shift and a robe.

"Where's Orion, Rach?" Dougal asks, placing a hand on her

shoulder.

Rachel gulps heavily before shaking her head.

"Yer ma needs him. We all do."

Thanks for stating the obvious.

Rachel turns on her heel and marches out of the kitchen, ready to turn her mother's room upside down if she has to. An answer should be somewhere in there—why else would this Fae be targeting her?

"Leave her," she hears Mercia say in the kitchen.

She stomps to the second floor, heads straight for her mother's bedroom, and finds all the destroyed photos on the floor where they'd been left the previous night. One by one, Rachel picks up the pieces and dumps them all onto the bed.

"What were you trying to tell me, Mom?" Rachel begins putting the pieces back together, her mind working overtime as she searches for answers.

An hour passes, but Rachel remains in the dark as to her mother's true intentions.

Mercia checks in on her, takes a seat on the edge of the bed.

Who am *I?*

Two weeks ago, Rachel had known the answer, but it isn't as forthcoming anymore. The SATs had thrown her off her game. Her journey into the Fae Realm left her reeling, confused, and uncertain. The situation with her mother, though …

As Rachel sits in her mother's bedroom, staring at the destroyed photographs, she can't bring herself to answer the simple question: Who am I? Jenny had subtly hinted at something, at an answer to this question, but those little nudges had formed a doubt in Rachel's beliefs. She grips the umbrella pendant, which she had found in the bathroom, where she had forgotten it that same morning after her shower.

"I don't look like either of my parents." She swallows down her emotions.

"Neither do I," Mercia says, waving as if it means nothing.

"Really?"

"Oh, yeah. My mom jokes and says I'm the UPS guy's kid. Truthfully, though, I may not necessarily look like them, but I inherited a lot of their traits." Mercia picks up two parts of a photo and holds them together before she magically bonds them into one piece again.

"My mom didn't seem too convinced about me being hers, though."

Mercia glances up at Rachel, sympathy in her eyes. "It's not necessarily about blood, Rach. Your mom—" She exhales through her nose and shifts around on the bed to get comfortable. "Okay, so, while I was in your mom's head, trying to break your mom from the Fae's clutches, I saw things I probably shouldn't have. When your mom was our age, she was the Holland Keith at Ridge Crest, except, she wasn't."

"What are you talking about?"

"Your mom wasn't *just* the captain of the cheerleading squad. Jenny was literally a beauty queen who got offered a big modeling contract by an international agency. She turned it down because Jason White told her he was going to marry her after they graduated," Mercia explains. "When he dropped her before their prom, it was too late, though. The agency had already moved on to sign another girl."

"Fine, but what does this have to do with me?" Rachel asks.

Mercia rolls her eyes. "Like your mom, you're not small town hot. You're the cover girl of French fashion magazines, the actress gracing our screen, the songbird on the stage, whatever. Here's the thing, though, Jenny knows she's gorgeous, whereas you probably don't care what you look like."

"I'm not sure if that's an insult or a compliment, but—"

"It's an observation," Mercia interrupts before Rachel can say more. "To people like Holland and your mother, you don't make any sense. You prefer books to people, making lists to wearing makeup, running track to cheerleading. The most ordinary thing anyone's ever seen you do is when you went out with Greg."

"In other words, my mom wanted a carbon copy of herself in order to live her life vicariously through me."

"Essentially, yes."

"No wonder we don't get along," Rachel murmurs.

"You get straight As—how did you not pick up on this earlier?" Mercia asks.

"I'm socially awkward, hello?"

A few beats of silence fills the space between them, before Rachel titters. Hesitant at first, Mercia only smiles, but releases an unexpected giggle. Spurred on by each other's giggles, the two girls soon rumble with laughter.

Their mirth eventually dies down, leaving Rachel hollow once more.

Rachel couldn't be who her mother wants her to be. No matter how hard she tries, she won't ever fit into the Jenny Cleary mold. So where does that leave them?

Will she and her mom forever be at odds or will they maybe someday find common ground? Jenny is a librarian, sure, but their taste in reading material doesn't match up whatsoever. Where Rachel loves genre fiction, her mom gravitates toward romance and literature. Jenny doesn't enjoy cooking whereas

Rachel does. They are simply too different, too at odds.

Who am I?

The question, still frustratingly unanswerable, pops into her head again. The fact is she doesn't know who she is—*does anyone?*—but she knows who she wants to be. Rachel wants to be kind and courageous, compassionate and humble. Popularity isn't something she has ever desired, but she would very much like it if she could someday be the person other people wanted to confide in. The question remains, though.

Who am I?

"What is this Fae actually looking for?" Rachel stares at the sonar picture her mother hadn't torn up. "Better question: What does it want from *me*?"

"I have no idea," Mercia says. "Are we even certain this is that Golvath guy?"

Rachel shrugs. "My instincts tell me it is, but I can't be sure." She picks up the sonar scan and studies the grainy image, searching for a clue. There's a reason why her mother didn't rip up this picture—there's a memory she needed to share. But what could it possibly mean?

"Rach?" Dougal's voice intrudes on her thoughts. "It's almost visitin' hours at th' hospital. Ye wanna come with me?"

"Mrs. Crenshaw doesn't want me seeing her like that," Rachel says.

Dougal grimaces then, nods. "Ye know why, yeah?"

"Yeah, it's because she loves me more than she loves you."

"Oi!"

Rachel grins. "I'm kidding."

"It *is* 'cause she loves ye, but also 'cause of pride."

"I know."

"Had to make sure ye know," he says. "I'll tell her ye said hi."

"Tell her I love her, too."

"Nan'll think ye're tryin' to be funny," he says, but smiles anyway. "I'll give her yer best." He pushes away from the door, but says, "Are ye two lasses gonna be all right by yerself?"

"I'm recharged and ready to go," Mercia says as she snaps her fingers and a bright flame dances on the tip of her thumbnail. "Don't worry about us."

"Don't get into trouble without me," Dougal says as he retreats.

"Don't get into trouble without me." Mercia nails his brogue with ease. Rachel snickers in response, earning a smile. "It's like he expects us to do something irresponsible."

"Speaking of being irresponsible, are you up for a recon mission?"

"Yeah, sure, why not," Mercia says. There's mischief twinkling in her storm-gray eyes and a grin playing at the corners of her lips. "Where are we heading?"

"To where this all began."

"Oh?"

Rachel stands and says, "Ever since the Fae's come out of hiding, I've been wondering what is new, what doesn't belong, and maybe we'll get lucky and find some answers there."

"I'm not going into the boiler room," Mercia says, standing.

"Would you believe me if I said that's not where the answers lie?"

Chapter Twenty
Calcification

The drive to school is not without its obligatory weirdness.

As Mercia turns onto Main Road, Shadow Grove's residents step into the open. Men, women, and children line up on the curb, standing shoulder-to-shoulder, watching the car pass with glazed-over eyes.

Rachel turns in her seat, expecting the onlookers to eventually disperse, but the people don't move. They just stand there, staring at the car.

"If that's not a threat, I don't know what is," Mercia whispers.

"What do you think the Fae will do with them?"

"Let's hope they don't follow us, for one," she says, turning off Main Road and opting to take a suburban route.

When they arrive at school, she parks in front of the main door.

"The area looks clear of any townies," Rachel says as she climbs out of the car.

"Don't jinx us."

They head up the stairs and enter the school.

The interior of Ridge Crest High is laced with abandon and disuse. Classrooms are in disarray. Lockers are emptied onto the floor, the doors standing wide open. The metal is riddled with dents, deep scratches, and locks are broken open and tossed aside. Overturned desks and books litter the floors, while obscene words and phrases are scrawled on the whiteboards or scratched into other surfaces. A faint yet undeniable rotting smell wafts through the stagnant hallways. Bone carvings lie among the clutter, discarded and broken remnants of whatever fate befell the students they represent.

Until now, Rachel hasn't taken the time to think about what had truly transpired while she was in the Fae Realm. Seeing the school like this, however, gives her an idea of the chaos she's missed.

Mercia hiccups back a sob.

Dust motes swirl in the air as they move through the abandoned building.

"Be glad you weren't here when everyone lost their minds," Mercia says, her voice emotional. "Those few who were lucky enough not to fall under the Fae's influence had to hole up in closets and bathrooms until the threat had passed. I almost got trampled in the process."

Rachel places a hand on Mercia's shoulder. "Who else, besides you, was left unaltered?"

"You mean who didn't go crazy?" Mercia mumbles. "Logan Breyer, Sylvia Cross, Xavier Eckstein, Polly Winston, the new guy, the lunch lady, and a couple of teachers."

Rachel frowns as she processes the information. "Why would they not be susceptible to the Fae's influence?"

"The same reason it doesn't work on me, I suppose." Mercia shrugs. "Logan, I know for sure, isn't entirely human."

"Okay, I'll bite. What is he?"

"Heck if I know." She hooks her curly blonde hair behind her ear. "It's not like I'm part of an exclusive club that gives out memberships to anyone classified as *not entirely human*. Besides, some of the non-humans I actually do know—"

A hinge squeals somewhere nearby, the sound deafening in the unnerving quiet. Both girls scuttle to the side of the hallway, searching the area. Mercia lifts her hand, ready to do some type of spell to deter an attack. Rachel bends down and picks up a discarded lacrosse stick, ready to defend them the only way she knows how.

With tentative steps, they move forward again, keeping close to the wall.

Mercia peers around the corner and her shoulders sag with relief.

"It's only Orion." Mercia lowers her hand.

Rachel peers around her to see Orion leaning against the lockers, arms crossed as he looks back at them.

"Just so you know, you both suck at sneaking around," he says by way of greeting.

Rachel lowers her weapon and steps out from behind Mercia.

"Anyway, I couldn't help but overhear your conversation. So, quick question," Orion says. He pins his gaze on Mercia as they come closer. "Are any of those non-humans who fell under the Fae's influence considered Fae, too?"

"Yes," she answers.

Orion pushes off the locker. "Well, it's more difficult to use influence on other magical beings, but other Fae and certain lower-level demons can be controlled by Intra-Canters almost as easily as humans."

"Demons?" Rachel chimes in. Her eyes widen. "Do demons

exist?"

"So, the Fae doing all of this is an Intra-Canter?" Mercia asks, ignoring Rachel.

"Without a doubt," Orion says. "My brother could learn a thing or two from this guy, to be honest."

"Rachel's right about it being Golvath the Lonely then?"

"My sources agree on the possibility, yes," Orion answers.

"Last question: Where's he hiding?" Mercia asks as they continue through the hallway.

"That's why I'm here, actually, to figure it out. What are you two doing here?"

"The dude's holding Rachel's mom hostage, so we're looking for clues or something."

"I seem to have missed a lot."

As Mercia explains what'd happened during his absence, Rachel tries coming to grips with the whole "demons exist" bombshell he'd dropped. She takes up the rear, holding the lacrosse stick firmly by her side, unsure how these creatures have managed to make this world their home. How do you *not* realize your neighbor is a demon?

What else is real? Is the Loch Ness Monster real? Are there aliens doing probes on people? Do dragons exist?

You're asking yourself the wrong questions. Focus on answering the one Golvath asked, the one that'll get your mom back: Who are you?

The answer still eludes her.

"Apparently Golvath's been at it for millennia," Orion says, breaking through Rachel's thoughts. "Every known realm has a story where Golvath's tried his luck in finding a bride, and from what I've heard, he always fails. Unfortunately, his plans have become more elaborate as time has passed, and he's become more vicious in his attempts."

"How exactly has he evolved? Rachel asks.

"Well, from the information I gathered, it seems Golvath used to only target the object of his affection. When that didn't work, he adapted his tactics. He started using influence on the girl's family members and friends in order to isolate her. That said, I don't know why or when he graduated to targeting entire villages."

"Ugh," Mercia grunts. "Golvath's behavior sounds similar to what elemental witches sometimes go through after a burn-out. It's like an addiction to power or something, and can be very destructive."

"Addiction is rare for Fae, in general, but it's not a bad theory," Orion says

Rachel puts together the puzzle pieces and slowly his mannerisms—how, since school had started, Cameron was always around her, present in some way or another—clicks into place. The evidence of Cameron being the perpetrator was a long shot, yes, but something about him just seemed wrong. She couldn't put her finger on why she felt that way, though.

He's as slimy as an eel. And eels are usually dangerous.

Everything about this guy suddenly makes sense. The epiphany, however, doesn't explain how they have to deal with him, but sorting out one problem is better in the long run.

Orion looks over his shoulder. "You're awfully quiet, Clarré."

"Mhmmm," she answers.

"If you're worried, I can confirm that demons aren't exactly the way Hollywood portrays them. They're *much* worse."

"I've compartmentalized that piece of information already,"

Rachel mumbles.

Orion turns around and walks backwards. "What is it then?"

"Something else," she says. "Something human."

"Vague much?" Mercia asks.

Rachel veers left, heading down the hallway that leads past the administration office.

"Where are you going? I thought— Oh, what the hell." Mercia harrumphs, earning a chuckle from Orion. "I don't understand the way her head works sometimes. It's like she hones in on something and nothing else matters."

"*She* can hear you," Rachel says. She opens the office door.

"Good," Mercia says. "Your hearing makes up for your serious lack of communication skills."

Ignoring Mercia's criticism, Rachel heads into Principal Hodgins' office, where metal cabinets line the wall behind his cluttered desk.

"Doesn't it bother you not knowing what Rachel's up to? What she's thinking? I've always found her mind fascinating, because I can't figure out her processes." Mercia says.

"Not really," Orion says. "I find it intriguing to watch her solve puzzles."

Rachel moves past the metal cabinets, searching the labels that mark each drawer until she gets to *M*. She tugs at the drawer once, twice, but it remains firmly sealed. As she turns around to search for a key in the principal's desk, she comes face-to-face with Orion, who gestures for her to move aside.

She takes a step back, allowing him access to the drawer.

Orion bites into his thumb until he draws blood then presses the wound to the lock. An audible click follows, and he reaches to the drawer to pull it open.

"Or you could've just asked me to open the drawer instead of mutilating yourself," Mercia says from the other side of the desk. "Just my opinion, though."

"You need to use your magic sparingly, Little Witch. If Golvath gets into my head, and you don't stop me, this town won't survive the onslaught," Orion says.

"Right. Okay. Tell me, how do you suppose I stop a Fae Prince, huh?"

"Get creative."

Meanwhile, Rachel moves her fingers across the files in the drawer, searching until she comes to one labeled: MAYER, C. "Ah-ha." She pulls the thin folder out of the cabinet, places it on the principal's desk, and opens it to find next-to-nothing inside. There are no transcripts, no previous address. Apart from a few recent entries regarding not so stellar grades and his current address, there's nothing to indicate who Cameron is or who he was before the start of the schoolyear. There is, however, a folded up note with RACHEL written in blocky red letters.

Rachel opens the note and reads the words carefully before she slams the piece of paper back onto the table. "I knew it. I freaking knew it was him."

"What?" She picks up the note and reads the message Golvath left her. "Oh."

More puzzle pieces fall into place.

She found Cameron attractive, alluring, even considered him her type. The carefully crafted persona spoke directly to her, and that bad boy façade he paraded around had made her take notice. If Cameron, or rather Golvath, had pursued her for a while longer, if he'd been just a little more patient, she would've been head over heels in no time. The disgusting part is, he knew as much from the get-go, and had ended it before she could reject him just so that he could play the victim.

"Are these the ravings of a lunatic?" Orion asks, holding up the note.

"Some may call it that," Mercia says. "I call it toxic masculinity."

Orion raises an eyebrow. "Even I could figure that part out, but what's up with him calling Rachel a Stacy? Who's Chad? And I don't understand the term 'femoid'."

"Golvath is the Fae equivalent of an incel," Rachel explains.

Orion's mouth forms into an 'O' as he glances at the note. He looks up again, his eyes seeming to sparkle with realization as he slaps the note with his other hand. "Well, that explains a *lot* about why Golvath never succeeds in finding a bride. He doesn't actually want to."

"That's not quite what incels are," Mercia sighs.

"No, I know what a human incel is, but this is a Fae we're talking about," Orion says. He places the note on the desk. "We don't react the same way humans do. For example, we struggle to come to grips with the concept of death, because we generally live incredibly long lives. And where humans make a big thing about sexuality, nudity, and monogamy versus polygamy, Fae find those restrictions comical."

"Your point being?"

"My point, Little Witch, is that Golvath is a deranged Fae, who's learned to reject his pursuits *before* they can reject him. He considers that he's the wronged party in these events, which leads to unnecessary revenge. Though, I'm aware it's not necessarily incel behavior for humans, it makes perfect sense for a Fae with some underlining psychological issues," Orion explains.

"So, how do we rectify the problem?" Mercia perches on the metal arm of a chair positioned in front of the desk.

Orion purses his lips and glimpses at Rachel. "Do you have a plan, Clarré?"

"My plan begins and ends with killing him," she says in a deadpan voice.

Mercia's eyes widen. "It's a bit of an extreme approach, don't you think? I'm all for condemning people for their actions, but you have to keep in mind we're dealing with a mentally unstable individual."

"Fine," Rachel turns her attention to Orion. "How do Fae deal with their mentally unstable kin?"

"It depends on the individual, the family, and whether there have been crimes perpetuated by the person in question. The criminally insane are usually sent to Leif Penitentiary, whereas the more manageable cases are handled by private institutions. Golvath, however, is more likely to be publically executed if he ever returns to the Fae Realm, because he does kill living, breathing beings in the most heinous ways imaginable," Orion answers.

Rachel chances a glance at Mercia. "There's your answer."

"That's all good and well, but how do you propose we actually kill the guy?" Mercia asks. "Orion's already said he's not strong enough to go head-to-head with Golvath. My powers are limited, too. And, I hate to say this, but you're only human, Rach."

Rachel opens her mouth to respond, but before she can utter a word, a door slams shut somewhere inside of the building. She shuts her mouth and grabs the lacrosse stick while her heartrate increases.

Mercia looks over her shoulder, stares into the larger part of the administration's office. She turns her attention back to Rachel and Orion, concern weighing down the corners of her lips.

Without a word, Orion gracefully moves around the desk, silently stepping over the mess on the floor.

There's an audible crack as something breaks outside the office. A different set of heavy footfalls move with purpose, growing louder as they near. Next, trainers squeak against the tiles, followed by clothes shifting. A cough sounds farther away. Clamor as something heavy is pushed.

"Come out, come out wherever you are," an unfamiliar voice calls.

Orion presses his finger against his lips, gesturing for them to remain silent, before he slips into the administration office. He returns a few beats later and motions for them to close in.

She squares her jaw as she quietly walks around the desk.

"I'm going to glisser you into the parking lot, one at a time." Orion's whisper is barely a breath. "Clarré, do you have your keys?"

Rachel nods.

"Oh, Rache-e-e-l." The voice drags her name out. Another door slams shut, something is thrown violently across a space. Laughter echoes.

Orion opens his arms for her and she steps into his embrace, readying herself for the mind-blowing and world-tilting that accompanies this way of transportation.

When nothing happens, she says, "Whenever you're ready."

Orion releases her and takes a step back. His frown is prominent as he looks at his raised arms as if they don't belong to him.

"You okay there?" Mercia asks.

"I can't glisser," Orion says. He turns his hands so he can

stare at his scarred palms. Faint flames runs up his arms, his magic seems to sputter as it struggles to ignite.

Mercia snaps her fingers and the witch flame dances on her thumbnail. "My magic appears unaff—" Her flame is smothered. "Crap."

"How?" The worry in his voice turns to confusion as he regards Mercia.

She shakes her head, staring in dumbfounded silence where the fire had been.

When neither of them spring into action, Rachel whispers, "Find a weapon."

Mercia blinks. "Are you telling me I have to do things the old fashioned way, the *human* way?"

"Yeah."

"Well, that sucks," Mercia grumbles.

She searches the principal's office for something to defend herself with. Orion looks like someone plucked off his ethereal wings.

"You can't hide forever," a female voice calls out, amusement thick in her tone.

With a heavy sigh, Rachel heads back to the principal's desk and opens the drawers in search of the legendary Big Black Box, which is purportedly full of confiscated items Principal Hodgins has collected from students over the years. Finding nothing of the sort, she quickly turns her attention to the cabinet beneath the window and slides one of the doors open. Behind a stack of paper and some miscellaneous stationary, Rachel finds an open bottle of whiskey and two glasses. In a wrapped copier paper box beside it await all types of confiscated goodies, including cigarettes, vapes, an unholy amount of lighters, knives, a few ancient cell phones and Gameboys, a scratched up hipflask, and plastic toys. She pockets a can of mace she finds beneath an expired packet of Marlboros and picks out a brass knuckle duster.

Rachel holds out the knuckle duster and hisses, "Mercia."

Mercia picks it up with her fingers and sneers at the offensive object. "I have so many questions right now."

"Just put it on and hope you don't have to use it," Rachel mumbles. She turns back to face the door. Orion, still staring at his ever-fading flames, is in a world of his own. "Orion," Rachel says a little louder to catch his attention. As he looks up, she hands him the lacrosse stick. "Imagine it's a sword, Faerie Boy." Rachel brushes past him, pulls the pepper spray out of her back pocket, and holds it steadily in her hand.

"Try not to spray us if you use it," Orion's warm breath touches the back of her neck.

"I can't make any promises."

He flashes her a grin as he steps ahead and peers around the door. He looks left then right, before returning to his original position.

"Where's the nearest exit?" he asks.

"Main door?" Mercia says, sounding unsure.

"Nuh huh, I've seen that movie and it didn't end well," Rachel says. "Let's maybe first try a window before we do anything stupid and get ourselves killed."

"You don't honestly think it'll be that easy, do you?"

Rachel shrugs. "Won't hurt to try," she says, walking over to the nearest window, which overlooks the courtyard. She strains to open it. When it doesn't budge, she makes her way back to the others.

"Well, you called it," she whispers. "We could try the old

schoolhouse's exit?"

"You want to go past the boiler room?" Mercia hisses.

"Would you rather face a horde of homicidal townies?" Rachel snaps back in a low voice. "These are people we know, and although they're innocent in all of this, at the end of the day we may have to hurt them to save ourselves."

Mercia considers this before she answers with a curt, albeit reluctant nod.

"Gotcha," the first unfamiliar voice shouts. A deafening crash resounds through the school, putting everyone on edge. "Damn it."

"One of you will have to take the lead, while I guard our rear. We move fast and quietly," Orion says. He leans back to check the hallway again. "The hallway is clear, so we've got to go now."

Rachel gestures to Mercia.

"Oh, hell no. This is your idea," she whispers.

Without another word, Rachel makes her way to the head of their party, glances out the door to find the hallway empty, and darts forward as quietly as she can. She navigates the path, careful not to step on the various objects littering the floor. The rancid smell grows stronger as they near the cafeteria.

"Where, oh where, can Rachel Cleary be?" the female sings, her voice farther away now. "Class is in session, young lady."

Rachel slows her approach upon reaching the intersecting hallway.

Glancing around the corner, she comes face-to-face with none other than Holland Keith.

Holland reaches out and grabs Rachel by her sleeve.

"I found her. I found her!"

Chapter Twenty-One
Body of Work

As Holland's excruciatingly high-pitched voice bounces off the walls, Rachel presses down on the mace spray's trigger, directing a steady stream of irritant at Ridge Crest High's queen bee.

Exultation turns to shrieks of agony as she falls to her knees. Holland paws at her eyes, rubbing the mace into her cheeks and temples. Her oily blonde hair tangles as she shakes her head.

The hunt begins.

Footsteps chase toward them, other voices join the ruckus.

Orion pushes Mercia in one direction, grabs Rachel by her arm, and says in a low tone, "Run."

Mercia spins on them. "I have an idea, but I need time," she says. "Lead them away from me. Keep them occupied."

There's no time to argue. Mercia sets off toward the old schoolhouse, leaving Rachel and Orion to rethink their escape plan. The others are closing in, though, running to Holland's aid as she continues to howl.

"The cafeteria," Rachel urges, breathless as adrenaline and fear course through her veins.

Orion gestures for her to take the lead, glancing over his shoulder.

Rachel rushes toward the godawful smell permeating from the lunchroom. Thick and unforgiving, the rotting stench lingers in the air, sticking to anything it touches. Still, she'd rather face the smell than whatever the townies have been tasked to do with her.

"Bar the doors," she instructs as they enter the cafeteria.

Orion pushes the broken lacrosse stick he'd been carrying through the handlebars.

"I need something else," he says.

She looks around. Empty food trays lie upside-down on the floor, their contents scattered across the surfaces of ripped up tables and upended chairs. Here and there, splotches of unidentifiable goop stick to the walls, like there had been a food fight nobody bothered to clean up. Trashcans are overturned, whatever litter they once carried strewn about and adding to the chaos, and the smell blanketed the entire lunchroom.

"That?" Rachel says, pointing at a heavy bench lying on its side.

"It's too heavy to maneuver into place in time," Orion answers. "Find me a broom or a mop or something that'll fit in between the handlebars to strengthen the hold."

Rachel steps across the filth, navigates her way behind the serving counter. Things don't look any better in the kitchen. Large stainless steel pots and pans have been pulled off the stoves and out of the ovens, the remnants of whatever the lunch ladies had been making spoiling in the open air. All the ingredients that'd been left out of the massive fridges are in a state of decay—meat, vegetables, fruit, milk. Oversized flies buzz around, sluggish from their feast while maggots crawl around.

A shudder crawls up her neck.

Don't think about it.

Rachel scans the kitchen. A broom lies amongst the wreckage, half-covered in what could have been lasagna. She hops across a particularly foul-looking puddle of gunk and crouches to reach for the handle.

Loud thumps and crashes sound from the door, accompanied by an authoritative, "Clarré."

"I'm coming," Rachel calls back, picking up the handle, disregarding the grossness of having to touch the squishy old food clinging to it. She gags as she rushes back, only to find Orion using his body to keep the doors shut.

"Quickly," he says, twisting slightly away from the door.

An almighty kick from the other side sends Orion skidding backwards, revealing two twisted, desperate faces in the gap between the opening doors. Rachel doesn't know the attackers, though she can recall seeing the woman around town now and then. Her face is streaked with dirt and her black hair is matted with dried, flaking blood. The man is in even worse condition—mud cakes his tattered clothes, while his skin is peppered in purple bruises.

What had happened to them while they'd awaited their orders?

Through sheer strength, Orion pushes them back into the hallway, aligning the handlebars once more.

Rachel shoves the broom into the small space, but the flimsy thing flexes with each impact, the wood splintering from the force.

"The broom won't hold for long." Rachel rubs her hands clean on her jeans. When he doesn't answer, she looks to where Orion had last stood and finds the space empty. "Faerie Boy?"

"Give me a second." Orion's voice travels from the other side of the cafeteria, where he is testing the glass doors one after the other. Nothing budges.

"Maybe try breaking the glass?"

"Won't work," Orion mumbles, giving up. "It's an ancient blanket spell, which basically acts like a fumigation tent where magic is concerned." He steps over an upturned chair, walking back to where Rachel waits. "We're trapped until Golvath decides differently."

She glances at the lacrosse stick and broom, both looking as if they'll snap at any moment. "What do we do about them in the meantime?"

He grimaces as he searches the cafeteria. Orion looks up at the ceiling, and his frown smooths out, the concern disappears from his eyes.

Rachel follows his gaze to the vent grille, which is large enough to fit them both if they can reach it. However, it would certainly not hold their combined weight.

Orion makes his way over to the nearest chair. He lifts the chair, flips it over, and with the subtlety of a wildebeest, drags the piece of furniture into position underneath the vent. Using the chair as a boost, Orion reaches to push his fingers through the grille's slats and tugs hard enough to break the vent cover from its hold. He drops the grille, the metal clattering loudly as it lands.

The blows against the door hesitate long enough for Orion to push a second chair across the floor before starting up with renewed vigor.

She realizes his game plan and smiles.

"And here I thought you were just another pretty face," she says, earning an unexpected guffaw.

241

Once he settles down, he whispers, "I need something small and round, with a bit of weight to it."

Rachel fishes the can of mace from her pocket. "This?"

"That'll do," he says.

The lacrosse stick buckles under the pressure. The wood cracks in half, the pieces rattle against the door, before falling onto the floor.

"Better get a move on, Faerie Boy," she says.

"Almost done," Orion says, stacking a third chair. He takes a few steps back to regard his work, and nods. "Okay, up you go, Rachel."

Rachel frowns as she cast a glance back at him.

"Play along," he hisses.

"Don't let me fall," she says louder than necessary, shrugging at her lame acting.

"I won't." He gestures for her to continue her performance, his eyes twinkling.

Rachel grunts repeatedly and over-exaggerates an *oomph*. "Come on, Orion, before they break down the door."

In response, the beating intensifies.

"Wait for me in the kitchen," he whispers. "Just go, Clarré. I'm right behind you," Orion says louder.

Rachel nods and makes the journey back to the kitchen. She peers around the entrance.

Orion waits to complete his ruse, looking between the cafeteria doors and the ceiling. After a few minutes, he pulls back his arm in order to throw the mace can into the vent, while he wraps his other hand around the leg of the highest chair.

Bang, bang, bang.

The broom handle splinter beneath the assault, weakening

242

with each hit.

Then, when Rachel is certain her nerves won't be able to take much more of this, he pulls the chair down and, at the same time, tosses the mace can into the vent. Orion turns and runs for the kitchen, jumping over the counter and slips down behind the surface, while the muffled thumping and rolling inside the air duct continues.

He's barely out of sight when the broom handle shatters and the door bursts open.

Rachel crouches and pokes her head out of the kitchen, only to find him with his back pressed against the counter, breathing hard.

Rachel mouths the words: "Come on."

"Gimme a boost," the woman's voice intrudes on their silent argument.

"You give *me* a boost," the man replies.

They laugh together, before the woman says again, "No, you give me a boost. I'm smaller and faster."

"Fine," the man agrees, still chuckling.

Orion's lip twitches and nose crinkle before he gives into her request. Rachel waits until he shifts onto all-fours and crawls across the sticky, soiled floor. She slips back inside and stands, waiting for him to get out of sight.

Once Orion is inside the kitchen, he can't get back to his feet quick enough. He finds a dish towel on a nearby surface and wipes his hands clean, clearly displeased about having to crawl through the muck. Rachel can't blame him. She's ready to bathe in bleach just to get rid of the smell.

Rachel crosses the kitchen to where the pantry is located, the door having been left ajar during the fray. The smell is worse in there, so much so that her eyes start burning and she has to swallow down bile. Still, it's a better hiding place than standing in the kitchen.

Rachel slowly opens the door to eliminate any chance of squeaking, and disturbs a swarm of fat flies feasting upon a second boneless corpse. Maggots crawl across the skin, pulsing in unison, making it appear as if the misshapen cadaver is actually breathing.

She dry heaves at the ghastly sight, tastes bile as acid burns its way up her throat.

Orion is there before she can make a sound, spinning her away from the pantry so that she can hide her face in his broad chest. With his free hand, he gently pushes the door shut again, but the smell doesn't dissipate. The image doesn't vanish.

Who was it? Who else had suffered Golvath's wrath?

The first time she'd come across one of Golvath's victims, she'd been too shocked to respond appropriately. Now, though, Rachel can't help the tears from stinging her eyes. It doesn't matter who had died by Golvath's hand—they'd still suffered an excruciating and needless death. And for what? Because an insane Fae had the hots for her but was too scared of being rejected? That wasn't a good enough reason to kill anyone.

Orion rubs small circles on her back to soothe her.

"You see anything?" the man in the cafeteria calls out.

"Nuh huh. You?"

"I see a hole," he says, chuckling. "I'll go check." Wandering footsteps crunch over debris, an out-of-tune whistle grows closer.

Rachel pulls away from Orion and looks up at him through bleary, widening eyes. She shakes her head, not willing to force herself into hiding alongside the decomposing body in the pantry.

In response, Orion moves his hands to rest on her shoulders, looking deep into her eyes, expressing without words: "Don't worry, I'm right here."

Rachel shakes her head more violently.

The whistling doesn't stop. Crunching footsteps nears the kitchen. It won't be long until—

Orion's hands make their way up to her cheeks, forcing her to stop shaking her head. "There is nowhere else," he whispers, his words mere breaths.

A tear rolls down her cheek. Of course he's right. The cupboards are too small to hide in, the fridges have glass doors, and there's no telling how thorough the guy will search. There are no other options than the walk-in pantry, body or no. She inhales deeply, the hand she has on his chest trembling, but she relents.

Orion opens the door again, just wide enough for them to slip inside, and gently nudges her to move forward.

Rachel pulls her shirt up over her nose and mouth as she reluctantly steps across the threshold. She tiptoes around the pulsing maggot-infested corpse, while kamikaze flies ricochets off her body.

Orion closes the door behind him, careful not to let it click, before he follows her deeper into the pantry.

It takes every iota of her strength not to give into the automatic bodily responses of being in an enclosed space with a decomposing corpse. Her stomach roils and her gag reflex contracts to the point of weakening her legs. She manages to walk to the farthest end of the pantry, passing rows and rows of metal shelves, where most of the dry goods and canned products remain undisturbed.

Rachel turns around, her back pressing up against the wall, as

Orion nears.

He evaluates her with a quick glance before averting his gaze to the shelves.

Things haven't been the same between them since the debacle in the Fae Realm. Yes, she screwed up big time. She's the reason hundreds of Halflings are dead, but she didn't even know what a Sluagh was before she'd come face-to-face with one. Surely he understands she didn't mean to lead them to the Halfling camp? Everything toppled over like dominoes. There is coldness between them, a broken trust of some kind.

Granted, he wasn't *this* guy in the Fae Realm—the kind, caring, somewhat rugged Fae prince. No, in the Fae Realm, he was a warrior, one who didn't have time for a teenage human girl's problems.

He reaches up to the top shelf near her head and wraps a hand around a small glass vial, full of purplish fluid.

"You don't trust me anymore," she whispers.

"It's not a matter of trust," he says in a low voice.

"Then what is it?"

"You're unpredictable and sometimes reckless."

Me, reckless? Ha! That's a first, she thinks as Orion twists the top off and takes a step closer, but doesn't say it out loud. He shows her the bottle's label. *Vanilla Essence.*

"It's better than nothing," he whispers.

Rachel nods, uncovers her nose and mouth and accepts the bottle. She douses her shirt in the vanilla essence, and shifts the fabric back to cover the bottom half of her face and breathes somewhat easier.

Orion does the same for himself.

The whistling outside continues, the guy halfheartedly

searching the kitchen for any trace of them, before seeming to travel back into the cafeteria. He shouts something unintelligible to the woman in the air duct and laughs loudly.

"What now?" Rachel whispers.

"We wait until they move on."

Chapter Twenty-Two
The Ghost Boy

Time passes too slowly for Rachel's liking.

She and Orion huddle in the pantry, often reapplying vanilla essence to their clothing to make their stay with the boneless corpse more bearable. Meanwhile, Orion listens for any movement in the cafeteria, whispering what's happening outside of their hiding place. The minutes tick on and her anxiety increases. Eventually, just when Rachel is ready to hand herself over to Golvath and his cronies, Orion lets her know that the woman is climbing out of the air duct.

They can finally leave the pantry from hell, but the relentless stench of decay follows. The smell is in her hair, on her clothes, tainting her very olfactory receptors. It's better than being in there with Golvath's victim, of being reminded of what could happen if they don't win this fight, but not by much.

"We need help," Rachel says.

They make their way out of the kitchen and carefully walk into the cafeteria.

"Who's going to help? There is nobody else. Everyone's under Golvath's control," Orion's voice is husky with fatigue. Not having magic to fight the bad guys has apparently taken its toll.

"We'll see." Rachel fishes her cell phone out of her pocket and dial Dougal's number.

"What didn't ye understand about stayin' out of trouble?" Dougal answers on the second ring. No *hello*, no *are you okay?*—just pure worry and criticism.

Rachel exhales loudly, before she says, "Lecture me later. Are you in town by any chance?"

"Aye," Dougal says. "Nan told me off for leavin' ye and Mercia by yerselves. Said I needed to come back right away, so here I am at yer empty house."

"Oh, good. That saves you a trip," Rachel says. "Bring Ziggy to the school and stay out of sight."

"Do I want to know what happened?"

"I'll tell you later. Just don't actually come into the school," Rachel explains.

"All right, see ye in ten," Dougal says and ends the call.

She pushes her phone back into her pocket and regards Orion. "You were saying, Faerie Boy?"

Orion shakes his head as he makes his way back to the doors leading into the building. "We need to find Mercia before they do."

A pang of irrational jealousy pushes to the forefront of her mind. An unfair thought pops into her mind: *He wasn't this worried about me in the Fae Realm.* This green monster doesn't feel like her, doesn't usually rear its ugly head inside her, but for some reason it's there. *What makes Mercia so special?*

Rachel tries ridding herself of the emotions. *This isn't me. I don't care what he does with his time or who he does it with.* She blinks, swallows down her envy.

Rachel carefully follows him, sidestepping shards of glass

249

near the overturned counter to avoid any preventable accidents. They travel into the deserted hallway, both keeping an eye out for any surprises. There are none, though, just as there is no sign of Mercia.

"Do you know where she'll hide?" Orion eventually asks.

Another bout of jealousy crawls through her body.

"I don't know her any more than you do," Rachel whispers back.

It's true, but—

She frowns and wraps her hand around the umbrella pendant. *What's going on with me?* Surely it's not possible for Golvath to bypass the Ronamy Stone? *No.* She doesn't feel anything weird rummaging through her mind. Rachel's just tired, she isn't her usual self. Stress can do that to a person.

Orion gives her an incredulous look. "I thought you two were friends."

"I bribed Mercia to help me with drugs she desperately needs. It's doubtful any type of friendship begins under such circumstances."

"You and I don't have a squeaky clean beginning either, yet I still consider you a friend."

"Even after the Sluaghs?"

"Yes." Orion's exasperation is evident in his sigh.

Regardless of the guilt she feels for causing so much heartache and hardship for the Halflings, she finds a way to smile at him.

"Truth be told, the Sluagh attack was bound to happen, whether you led them there or not. The army's morale was not improving after losing two battles in as many days, so it was just a matter of time until the Sluaghs sniffed us out," Orion says. He suddenly comes to a stop, tilts his head, closes his eyes, and seems to listen to something she can't hear. "Mercia's outside," he says. His brow furrows in confusion. "It sounds like she's somewhere above us, but she's definitely outside. Where could she be?"

"She headed to the old schoolhouse, so it's safe to assume she made her way to the bell tower." Rachel changes course, heading back to the old schoolhouse, hoping Mercia doesn't do anything stupid before they get there.

"You don't look pleased," he says. "Care to explain why?"

"Can you sense anyone nearby?"

"They're all searching for us on the other side of the school. Is everything okay?"

"I don't know. I feel weird," she mumbles. "More than that, though, I don't understand why Mercia would go up the bell tower by herself. If the stories are correct—"

"What stories?" Orion asks.

"During orientation week, every new batch of freshmen are told the story of the boy who fell. The tale's details change as to *how* he fell from the bell tower, but the rest essentially remains the same through every retelling.

"When Ridge Crest was still a three-classroom schoolhouse, and children of all ages attended, a fifteen-year old boy was tasked with ringing the school bell every morning and every afternoon. This chore was said to have been a great honor, because the schoolmaster at the time didn't hand out the responsibility to just anyone." She pauses as they turn the corner where Holland had waited for them. Once she's sure they're alone again, she continues, "One day, the boy walked up the rickety spiral steps to ring the afternoon bell. He shooed the nesting pigeons, and grabbed the rope to ring the bell. The bell tolled five times, and the children cleared out of the building. The boy, however, remained standing in the tower, staring at all of Shadow Grove."

"I suppose this was when there wasn't much of a town to look at?" Orion interrupts.

"Yup."

"So, what did he see?"

"Nobody knows, but it couldn't have been good. The story goes on to say he saw something so terrible it tore his mind apart and broke his will to live. When the bell stopped tolling, the boy screamed and screamed." Rachel looks up at Orion. "And then, during this madness, the boy fell from the top of the bell tower. Some say he slipped, others believe he was pushed, but some think he jumped. Apparently, he landed face first at the bottom of the steps that led into the schoolhouse."

Orion grimaces, an inquisitive eyebrow rising. "That's grim even by Shadow Grove's standards."

"The story doesn't end there, though. The tale does, however, always end the same way, *'The boy still walks the halls of the old schoolhouse, so whatever you do, don't approach him or you'll be driven mad.'* The thing is, the so-called Ghost Boy walking around the school is probably Golvath."

"Ah," Orion says. "Well, if it helps, I can't hear anyone else up there with her."

"It helps."

When they reach the T-junction in the hallway, she turns right, heading away from the boiler room and possible exit, moving deeper into the gloom of the old schoolhouse. The air feels thicker here, not alive or dead but something in-between.

"You would've made an excellent healer in my father's army," Orion breaks the silence. "The soldiers would've loved to hear your stories while they were losing their limbs or lives."

"I have a terrible bedside manner when it comes to people," Rachel mumbles.

"You weren't half-bad when I got stabbed by the Night Weaver's Fae light."

She grumbles an affirmative, but doesn't say more. A few steps later, they reach the stone archway. Beyond lies a small circular chamber with a questionable wooden spiral staircase that leads five stories up to the rusted bell.

"Mercia," Orion calls up the tower.

"Do you want the entire town to know we're here?" Rachel hisses.

"Look at those stairs." He gestures at the rotting, thin wooden slats that are already broken in some places, as well as the rickety handrail leaning precariously to the side. "No way am I climbing them."

"I could ha—"

"Not while I still have a breath in my body," he interrupts her. "Mercia."

"I'm sorry, but since when do you get to decide what I may or may not do?" Rachel crosses her arms.

"Since I gave up my entire existence in the Fae Realm just to make sure my brother didn't kill you," he snaps back. "*Mercia!*"

"Almost done," Mercia shouts back.

"Nova wouldn't have hurt me," Rachel scoffs.

Orion holds up his hands in a trickle of sunlight, showing off the crisscrossing scars that cover his fingers and palms. He turns his hands to show the rest of the ridges marring his skin. "I've seen those almost imperceptible flinches when you look at my hands, wondering what happened, what I did to deserve these scars. Well, let me tell you, my brother—the same one you think so highly of—did this to me when I was still a Faeling. Are you certain he wouldn't have done worse to you if he had the chance—a choice in the matter?"

"If he wanted to hurt me, he had ample opportunity."

Orion squares his jaw, shakes his head. "You don't know what you're talking about, Rachel."

"Oh, now I'm Rachel again."

"If I need to drive my point home, yes, then you're just Rachel."

"Well, *Orion*, that still doesn't give you the right to dictate my life for me. If I want to climb those stairs, I will."

He makes an animalistic sound of frustration in the back of his throat. "You're so … so …"

"I'm so what, huh?"

"So …"

Rachel grabs his hand and places it over the umbrella pendant around her neck, keeping a firm grip on his wrist. He struggles to pull away from her for a beat, before exhaling in relief and blinking a few times as he gets rid of the fugue in his mind.

"Do you feel better now?" she snaps at him.

Orion looks away from her.

She releases his wrist and places her hand on his unshaven cheek, nudging his head so their eyes can meet in the gloom. Rachel narrows her eyes at his icy stare, undaunted by the implied threat of bringing up what'd happened, what Orion had said. Bubbling rage cancels out fear and common sense. The tension coagulates. Electricity crackles in air the longer they stand there, their resolve unwavering.

There's a shift.

Anger, pain, and fear trickle away.

They close the space separating their bodies.

Rachel moves her hand away from Orion's cheek and feels her way around his neck, pulling him closer until their lips collide. She feels his free arm snaking around her waist, hand resting against the small of her back. Orion pulls her even nearer. When that doesn't satiate their desire for closeness, their mouths part and tongues dance. Their breaths combine, hearts seemingly beating to the same fast-paced rhythm. He takes a step forward and she backs up against the arched wall, before his hand changes direction again, finding her hip.

She pours herself into him—all of her ire, relief, desperation. Everything she's bottled up since he so unceremonious left Shadow Grove. In turn, she accepts his pain and dread and anger, every part he'd hidden away since she showed up in the Fae Realm. Rachel deepens the kiss.

Orion reluctantly pulls away, breathless, and rests his forehead against hers.

Her chest heaves as she searches for air, dizzy from the kiss. Her swollen lips still pulse, her skin remains tender where his stubble had scratched. The places his hands had lingered are warm, crackling with life.

They'd both needed someone. Probably anyone would've sufficed right then. She's not naïve enough to imagine the kiss being anything other than a desperate attempt to normalize an abnormal situation. But there is no denying their chemistry. She's still unwilling to label this *something* between them as anything other than companionship, or the increasingly sameness of their personalities, but it's there. That chemistry is real.

Normal people don't react like that. Dougal's words from

when he'd been influenced by Golvath rings through her mind, chastising her for her strange behavior in certain situations. *Freak out for God's sake!*

"You do know this thing between us won't end well."

Rachel grins, pushes onto the tips of her toes, and presses another kiss in the corner of his mouth. "We'll worry about that once it stops being so much fun." She lowers herself to the ground, reaches around the back of her neck, and unclasps the necklace.

"What are you doing?" Orion asks. "No. What if—?"

"I pushed Golvath out of my head this morning without the help of the Ronamy Stone. I'm sure I can do it again."

He reluctantly takes the pendant into his fist.

"Don't lose it."

He releases his hold on her and backs off.

"*Yes,*" Mercia's hiss of triumph echoes down the bell tower.

Orion's eyes widen as a golden flame flickers into existence, moving up to his wrist, enveloping his entire arm. "She did it," he says, looking at Rachel.

"Well, stop standing around then. Glisser Mercia out of here and then come back for me."

Orion extinguishes his flame and quickly fixes the necklace around his neck. A heartbeat later, he's gone, leaving Rachel alone in the dark against the stone archway.

"Finally. Some privacy."

Chapter Twenty-Three
A Royal Hunt

Cameron Mayer—or rather Golvath—steps out of the shadow, wearing a smirk that could easily curdle milk. He's dressed in the faded leather jacket she's seen him wear so often; his jeans are ripped at the knees, and the biker boots are scuffed up at the toes. Other than his familiar appearance, though, something about him is definitely different.

"It's the ears," he says, answering her unasked question before pushing his hair aside to reveal his elongated ear, which ends in a sharp tip. "I got tired of hiding them." He releases his hair and walks up to her, taking Orion's space. "Now why would you think about a prince when you are in the company of a king? Honestly, Rachel, stop being so mediocre."

"I'd much rather be mediocre than homicidal."

"He's not getting back in," Golvath says, rolling his eyes. "He's not coming back to save the pretty damsel, because he's not strong enough. Woe always you."

"What's your deal?" she asks, mentally placing one brick atop the other to protect her thoughts from his probing mind. "I've come up with countless theories and none of them really fits, so seriously, like, what's your problem?"

"You are m—"

"No, no," she interrupts, wagging her finger. "Don't put this on me, Golvath. From what I've heard, you've been pulling this same exact stunt for ages. You see a girl you like and then you build her up in your mind until she's some pure, untouchable goddess. Then—and *please* correct me if I'm wrong—you throw a hissy fit and turn the entire village into mindless minions because you've convinced yourself she's out of your league." Rachel drops her arms to her sides. "What is that about? I mean, you didn't even give me a chance to respond, and I'm actually not that hard to impress."

"Don't flatter yourself, Rachel Cleary; you're no goddess," he says. "If anything, you're Fae-bait."

Fae-bait?

"Well, screw you, too."

Golvath flinches, astonishment blanching his face.

Rachel pushes away from the stone archway and walks up to him, incensed and unafraid, until she's in his face. "You're pathetic."

The crack is as unexpected as the force behind his slap. Rachel stumbles back, covering her burning cheek with her hand. The glare she shoots him could easily penetrate Kevlar, but the maniacal laugh bubbling out of her throat is far more effective in unnerving the Fae than any weapon she could've wielded.

She moves back to her original position, unable to keep her sneer at bay. Rachel narrows her eyes and releases her cheek. "Do it again. I dare you."

Instead, he asks, "Who are you?"

"If Mrs. Crenshaw was around, she'd say you sound like a broken record," Rachel replies.

Golvath sneers. "Nancy Fraser? The same Nancy who dubbed

me The Bone Carver? Oh, I showed her."

"You put Mrs. Crenshaw out of commission for a couple of weeks at most. Be thankful you're dealing with me instead," Rachel hisses in defiance.

Golvath's eyes bulge, a throbbing vein appears on his forehead. "Who *are* you?"

"I am your worst nightmare."

As if summoned by her words, Ziggy flies into Golvath's face, effectively blinding him. Rachel seizes her opportunity and runs down the hallway as fast as her legs can carry her, forgetting all about pacing herself. Golvath bellows, his outrage making the entire building tremble.

"Ziggy!"

Ziggy flies to her side, flashing bright gold as he keeps up with her. His glow fades the farther he travels. The golden sphere dims and entire patches diminish. Soon, Ziggy fades to gunmetal.

Rachel can't bear to witness the Fae light lose its vibrant coloring or blinking out of existence altogether. "Are there any Sluaghs nearby?"

One flash.

"Close enough to the school?"

Ziggy flashes once more.

"It's not an entire horde, beca—"

Two flashes interrupt her.

"Bring it here as fast as you can," Rachel instructs.

Ziggy glides a few feet ahead before making an abrupt U-turn. The Fae light shoots back the way it'd come, quicker than she'd ever thought it could possibly move.

"Nobody outruns me," Golvath screams, his feet pounding the floor behind her. "Nobody escapes *me*."

"Go see a therapist, you creep." Rachel readies herself to slide into the upcoming hallway leading into the more modern parts of the school.

Golvath's rage turns feral as he roars obscenities, the thunderous sounds bouncing from one bare surface in the hallway to the next. His hatred catches up with her, slamming against the brick walls she's built around her mind. Parts of her wonder if he's right, if his vitriol is justified. Maybe she did treat him unfairly by not giving him a real shot. Perhaps she does deserve—

Without slowing down, Rachel squashes the weird thoughts—none of which belong to her—and mentally fixes the crack in the wall.

"That won't work on me again," she screams without glancing back.

His heavy footfalls slow ever so slightly as another enraged temper tantrum ensues.

Rachel puts out her hand to grab onto the wall. She propels herself around the corner and into the adjoining hallway.

You've successfully goaded a serial killer into chasing you, so now what? What's the plan? She has no idea what comes next. All she can think to do is to stay out of Golvath's reach until Ziggy lures a mythical creature back to her. Whether a Sluagh is any match for Golvath is a whole other story, one she prefers not to worry about while she's running for her life, but the concern is real. There's also the possibility of making a bad situation worse.

"You can't go anywhere." His voice sounds fainter, farther away, as if he's stopped running after her. "Eventually I'm going to find you."

"Bite me," she mumbles, passing the girls' bathroom where

she had found the bone carving of Mercia. How long has it been since then? Two weeks? More?

Think about the plan.

Nothing forthcoming is feasible in the long run, but—

She turns into the main hallway, slowing down considerably so as not to stumble when she rushes over the debris. One misstep is all it'll take to give Golvath the upper-hand. Rolling an ankle, spraining a foot, even breaking a toe can become a death sentence.

She won't give him the satisfaction of making it any easier.

Her phone vibrates in her pocket.

She runs away from the smell of the cafeteria, the decomposing body in the pantry, all while hoping Holland and the other two townies who're searching the school have preoccupied themselves somewhere else.

Rachel slows as she comes to the administration office's open door and slips inside. She walks around the receptionist's desk and into Principal Hodgins' office, before gently closing the door. Finally, Rachel pulls her phone out of her pocket and reads the messages sent from Dougal's phone.

R U OK?

Rachel slides down onto her haunches, leaning her head against the wall. She closes her eyes for a minute, catching her breath, before she musters the strength to respond.

Hiding in Hodgins' office. Could use help.

She moves as soon as the message is sent. Back to the Black Box in search of a weapon—she'll throw Golvath with a Gameboy or one of those really old Nokia 3310s if she has to. Maybe, if she targets his head, he'll get a concussion or something. Luckily, she remembers seeing some knives in there earlier. Rachel finds a makeshift shiv and places it on the cabinet's surface before spying Mercia and Dougal rushing toward the window.

"Hold on," Mercia says when she closes in, her voice muffled, like she's separated by water instead of glass.

Rachel nods, keeping herself from making too much unnecessary noise.

"Orion's trying to break in through the cafeteria," she continues. "It won't work, he knows it, but—"

Rachel points to her phone before quickly typing: *Stop talking. He'll find me.* She sends the message to Dougal, who shares it with Mercia.

She mouths, "Oh."

Rachel types again, telling them about sending sent Ziggy to find a Sluagh and how she and Dougal shouldn't be anywhere near here when it arrives.

Sluagh don't kill witches, Mercia's message reads.

Rachel raises an eyebrow and points to Dougal, mouthing, "Not a witch."

Mercia's shoulders drop as she says out loud, "I'll keep him safe."

Rachel looks at her phone again to begin her response when a sound just outside the principal's office catches her attention. She glances to the door, listening for a discernable sound, while locking her phone and slipping it back into her pocket. Blindly, Rachel picks up the shiv and hides the long hilt—made from a toothbrush's handle—against her wrist. With a quick glance at the window, she gestures for them to leave and takes slow, calculated steps toward the door.

Her heart races as she clutches the shiv for dear life.

Adrenaline pumps through her body, making her want to run, fight, or both. Logic tells her not to do anything stupid.

Wait, think, outsmart the enemy and use his weaknesses against him.

The intercom crackles to life overhead and screeches in that hollow, deafening way. Rachel grits her teeth as she stares at the door.

"Rachel Cleary, Rachel Cleary, please report to the office immediately," Golvath announces, keeping his voice level. "Or ..." There's a sigh on the other side of the door. "Or I'll have to debone your mother and make a spice rack from her spine."

The crackling intercom system dies, lending finality to his words. Rachel, however, doesn't move, hardly breathes. She simply listens to the on-goings in the administration office, waiting to make her next move.

Rachel has no idea what her next move is yet.

Survive. That's the plan.

The receptionist's swivel chair moves across the plastic floor protector while something heavy slams down on the wooden surface of her desk. There's a disgustingly loud slurp, followed by an equally loud gulp.

Rachel glimpses back at the window, but finds herself alone. She turns her attention to the door again, listening and waiting.

Golvath clearly doesn't hear as well as Orion does, otherwise he would have heard her moving around by now. This certainly works in her favor. Rachel is also sure he can't glisser. If he could, he would've caught up with her in the hallway. So, what can he do other than use human bones for his macabre art projects and dig around in peoples' heads?

He can cause accidents, can't he? Or is that just a byproduct of his intra-canter abilities?

The plastic wheels of the swivel chair rolls against the non-slip plastic protector, pulling her out of her thoughts. The chair exhales as his weight disappears from the seat, before the intercom screeches to life once more.

"I'm growing tired of these games," Golvath's voice booms overhead, the calmness gone. "If I have to drag you out of whatever hole you're hiding in, you're going to *wish* you'd come out when I said. Don't make me punish you, Rachel. You won't like it. Not one bit."

The announcement ends.

Those heavy biker boots walk one way across the tiles then return to the other side, all while he's speaking under his breath. It sounds almost like he's talking to someone else—probably to one of the people under his influence—but a second voice never joins in on the conversation.

It's just Golvath ranting to himself.

And although Rachel can't make out what he's saying, she's pretty sure he's not doling out praises for her hide-and-seek skills. The one-sided argument goes on for a few minutes, before he walks with purpose across the administration office. Soon, his footsteps fade completely, his rants going with him.

She waits behind Principal Hodgins' office door for a few more minutes, expecting him to return, thinking it may be a trick. Eventually, when it becomes apparent that he won't come back, Rachel decides not to tempt fate by staying in one place. Besides, the idea of being trapped in a confined area without an escape route doesn't sit well with her.

Rachel reaches for the doorknob and slowly turns it until the lock springs open. Inch by painstaking inch, she opens the door wide enough to look out. A steaming half-mug of coffee stands on the reception desk. She scans the rest of the area, before making her way to the next door. Rachel peers around the corner, looks down either side of the hallway and finds it empty. Quickly, quietly, she makes her way out of the administration office.

Hiding will only help her for so long. She needs a proper plan, one that doesn't involve rotting away in a pantry while Golvath plays with her bones for however long it takes him to find his next victim. Maybe it'll be years, perhaps centuries even. Who'll help her? Rachel is lucky to have allies, but the next girl might not. Cameron's next victim could be alone, confused by what's happening and helpless to save herself from this monster. Rachel can't let that happen. She won't.

Rachel walks down the hallway, glancing over her shoulder now and then to make sure nobody is sneaking up on her. She keeps the shiv ready, in case someone jumps out of a classroom. Rachel doesn't want to use the shiv on anybody, but she will if things spiral out of control.

Voices come from somewhere ahead, babbling on about how the vents are magical portals, because people disappear in them.

Rachel pauses then darts into the nearest open door just as Holland's tousled head comes into view and hears the three townsfolk under Cameron's influence coming closer. She glances at the interior of the room, where ruby red lockers are lined up against all the walls, and loose-standing rows fill the floor space. Long, slatted wooden benches are positioned between each block. Here and there lie dirty towels, some draped across the benches, while clothes are strewn about, and contents spill from a few open lockers. There's dampness in the air and shadows linger, made worse by the absence of artificial lighting. A faucet *drip, drip, drips* an eerie song.

"I'm telling you, those two are somewhere in the vents," the woman says.

Rachel slinks deeper into the locker room.

"They are not," the man exclaims. "You looked for them up there, didn't you? So, if they're not up there and they're not down here, they must've vanished by magic."

Holland giggles and says something incoherent, making the other two laugh along.

Rachel slips behind a block of lockers, out of immediate sight, and waits for them to pass. However, the three loiter in the hallway for some time, their voices carrying a hint of madness. They seem to move closer, seem to want to search the area. Holland says as much, though her intermittent giggling makes it hard to discern the true purpose of her exploration.

To avoid capture, and due to sheer desperation, Rachel backs up against the farthest wall of lockers, until she's cast in shadows.

Holland's tittering grows louder, her footsteps sound nearer.

Rachel navigates the shadows one step at a time, inching toward the showers. She breathes slowly, keeps calm, and tries not to bump into anything. Making the slightest noise now, with Holland creeping about, could spell the end of her journey.

"I'm *so* bored," the woman says, sounding almost as melodramatic as Holland sometimes does. "Let's go do some science."

"Ooh. Let's blow something up," Holland agrees, clapping her hands.

Rachel peers out of the shadows just as the woman grabs Holland's hand and basically drags her back to the hallway, their humor already improving. She hears them sprinting away, gives it another minute or two, before she begins her own trek back to the exit. With a quick scan of the area, she determines she's alone, and swiftly heads in the direction opposite of the laughter.

Past the water fountain, the football coach's office stands in ruin. Beyond that, several more classrooms are situated on either side of the hallway—some have been in use since the additions were made to Ridge Crest High, while others have become nothing more than storage rooms. Forgotten objects from years past have taken up residence in some of those classrooms, becoming lost in time.

Another turn comes up, where the back staircase is located. Only the music room is up there, on the other side of the school, while the rest of the second story is practically wasted space.

Her cell phone vibrates and Rachel pulls her lifeline into the open.

Go back 2 bell tower – M.

She returns her cell phone to her pocket and thanks the heavens for the labyrinth-loving architects, all of whom had decided quantity was better than quality when it came to building this forsaken school. From her current location, Rachel has plenty of options on how to get back to the hallway that leads to the old schoolhouse.

She eyes the staircase, wondering if she should take that route. *Too many variables at play. There are other ways, none of which pass by the science labs. Paths you know better.* Rachel changes course, retracing her steps.

By the time she gets back to the girls' locker room, she feels her energy levels fluctuate as her adrenaline wanes. Still, she doesn't stop. She keeps walking until she comes to a narrow corridor that leads back to the cafeteria. There are no doors here, no features whatsoever. The reason for its existence is merely to serve as a shortcut to the other side of the building, yet no student has ever favored this route.

She stares at the end of the corridor, which inspires a bout of claustrophobia. From her perspective, the walls and ceiling close in bit by bit, until the opening on the other side looks barely big enough for a child to crawl through. She hesitates momentarily. There are other ways, longer routes, more treacherous paths, but time is ticking and Golvath has had centuries to hone his craft of hunting down victims.

Rachel sucks in a lungful of air and steps forward.

Chapter Twenty-Four
Death Knell

Every part of Rachel feels like jelly by the time she exits the corridor. Her pulse races ferociously. A trickle of sweat runs down her neck, soaking her collar.

The adrenaline injection is exactly what she needed, though.

She passes the cafeteria, finds no trace of Golvath or his influenced cronies who're looking for her. She navigates her way through the debris, heading back to the old school building.

Stop. Wait. Listen.

Nothing.

When she comes up to the T-junction and finds it similarly empty, her synapses fire warnings.

Too easy, she thinks. She turns full circle, searching for anything out of the ordinary, and purses her lips. *No way is it this easy.*

Rachel stares into the dimly lit hallway, which ends at the bell tower, and recalls all the slasher films she's watched. This is usually the part in the movie where the final girl gets lulled into a false sense of security, a time when stupid, preventable mistakes are often made. But what other choice does she have?

I might as well get it over with while I still have some fight left in me.

Gripping the shiv tighter, she musters all of her courage, and walks into the shadows with purpose. She could have tried skulking around in the half-light, should have probably been less conspicuous, but then she would be wasting precious energy. No. All of that would have been futile, anyway.

She squares her shoulders and holds her head up high as the gloom intensifies, fearless of the Fae lurking about.

"I know you're here, Golvath," Rachel says. "I can feel you watching me."

"Funny." Golvath's voice turns her blood to ice as he wraps his arms around her, pinning her biceps against her sides. "I've been watching you for months and you never noticed before," he whispers triumphantly in her ear, his hot coffee breath blowing against her neck and cheek.

Rachel strains forward before jerking backward as hard as she can. Her skull collides with his forehead harder than she expects, and white hot pain shoots directly into her brain. A starburst of light enters her vision, pinpricking her line of sight. Still, the blow is enough for Golvath to loosen his grip. While he moans, Rachel sprints out of his hold, down the ever-darkening hallway. She ignores the migraine blooming behind her right eye, disregards the possibility of having a concussion, and pays little attention to Golvath's howl of frustration.

Focusing on her strides, she pushes herself into full speed, desperate to get as much space between herself and her murderous stalker as possible. Rachel darts through the darkness, forcing her legs to work harder, move faster.

"You'll pay for that," Golvath shouts somewhere behind her. He stalks forward.

She slows to an easier speed as a trickle of light brightens the stone archway, and makes the sharp turn into the bell tower without coming to a complete stop. Navigating the treacherous spiral stairs is, however, not as simple. Each step creaks when she places her weight on it, some even buckle. Now and then, there's a precarious crack underfoot, driving her forward or making her freeze.

The spiral structure trembles and questionable handrail shakes as Golvath bounds up the staircase. Each step he takes reverberates up her legs and spine. Rachel doesn't look back, can't stop. She propels herself forward, no longer worrying about falling through an iffy, rotten step. There's no time to worry.

A black tendril caresses the back of her mind, whispering sweet nothings as it searches for a way through the mental wall. Whenever that darkness senses a weakening in her defenses, it probes deeper or strikes unexpectedly. The mental attacks leave behind something akin to a thick, sticky, poisonous residue.

—and kill you—

Golvath's—thankfully distorted—thought pops into her head.

Rachel falters and grabs onto the tilting handrail to steady herself. She chances a look behind her, only to see the Fae charging up. With every huff, his nostrils flare.

"You should think about getting a gym membership!"

The red-faced Fae releases a scream of fury through his labored breaths, before he starts taking two steps at a time to catch up to her.

"Oh, crap."

Rachel stops taunting and runs up the remainder of the stairs, hoping Mercia, Orion, and Dougal have some type of plan to get her safely down from the bell tower before Golvath can sink his claws into her.

Rickety wood gives way to stone as she runs onto the narrow walkway that surrounds the suspended rusting bell in the center. She leans over the side, searching for a familiar face on the ground.

"You think you're *so* smart, but you've literally trapped yourself for me," Golvath says.

Rachel pivots, still holding onto the stone sidewall, and circles the bell. There are only so many places she can go from here.

"Oh, have you run out of witticisms now?" He calmly walks around the walkway, his gaze never wavering from hers. Golvath licks his lips, grins. "I'm going to take my sweet time with you, Rachel Cleary."

He darts forward, outstretched arms and long fingers grabbing at her. His one hand becomes entangled in her hair, the other takes hold of her shirt. She screams as he jerks her back to him, ripping strands of hair from her skull.

Rachel twists around, brings her elbow up, and hits him square in the face. At the same time, she lifts her leg with as much force as she can muster and knees him right in the groin.

Golvath howls. He releases her a second time, then drops onto his knees. Rachel rushes out of his grasp, backing away as he falls forward and rolls onto his side, writhing in pain.

"You bitch," he bites out.

A few seconds, a minute at most, is all the time she's bought herself. Rachel shifts the shiv, preparing to use it, as she turns around and searches the ground again. Mercia stands there, a speck on the pavement below, staring back at her. She screams something up at Rachel, something indecipherable through the magic surrounding the school.

"*What?*"

Mercia's silent scream is accompanied by hand gestures.

Rachel shakes her head. "I can't hear you."

"Stupid mistake." Golvath's breath hits her face.

Rachel spins around, thinking she still has a few seconds to get out of his reach, but he's right behind her. So close. Too close.

She gasps just as he wraps his hands around her neck.

Golvath leans closer, until there's no space between their bodies and they're both half-lying over the sidewall. His fingers press against her windpipe, blocking off her air. Spite fills his blue eyes; a vindictive smile mars his otherwise handsome face.

Rachel reaches with her free hand and rakes her nails down his cheek.

His skin breaks in places, angry red welts appear almost immediately. He hisses, but doesn't relent, only squeezes her neck harder, pushes her back with more force.

Her lungs are on fire. She gapes like a fish as she searches for oxygen, just a single breath, but nothing passes through.

"I'm going to watch the life leave you."

With no other card to play, she shifts the shiv forward and pulls her arm back as far as she can. The world seems to slow down as she uses all of her remaining might to thrust the sharp, metal tip toward Golvath's jugular vein. Rachel watches the shiv move closer, closer, closer, and then stop a hairsbreadth from reaching her intended target.

Golvath's smile broadens as she struggles against the invisible hand keeping her arm in midair.

"*Did you think you could keep me out forever?*" His voice rings through her mind, the dark tendril breaking down the mental wall, brick by brick. *"Drop it."*

Her hand opens at his order, fingers splay, and her arm relaxes. The shiv drops, rolls, and probably disappears down the bell tower. Her only weapon, only hope of survival, falls out of her reach.

Golvath looks past her and shouts, "You're not strong enough to break through my spells, Prince. The best you can do is to watch her die."

Rachel's eyes roll back as she attempts to catch a glimpse of Orion.

Using what little strength remains, she forces her hands up to her neck, scratching and gouging and pulling at his fingers.

Air. Need air.

Golvath laughs at her futile attempts.

The edges of Rachel's blurry vision darken.

Suddenly she's in a meadow, the moonlight shining down on a girl in a white nightdress with her golden hair gently blowing in a soft breeze. Tears streak her face as she picks up a red and yellow can by her feet.

"Please don't do this." Her voice quivers almost as much as her hands tremble. *"Please."* She lifts the can over her head and tilts it until clear liquid runs out of the spout. The girl cries louder as she douses herself. Her golden hair goes limp, nightdress sticks to her body. The sharp, distinct smell of gasoline fills the night sky as the breeze changes course.

Rachel realizes this must be Mary Wentworth, the girl who set herself on fire in the 1950s.

"I don't want to die." She throws the can aside and falls to her knees, shivering and crying and begging.

Golvath's voice enters the memory. *"Then you should have loved me."*

He looks down at his hands as he strikes a match. The phosphorous tip sizzles to life, the orange flame growing stronger.

The abject horror Rachel feels at having to watch this scene play out is nothing compared to this girl's suffering.

Without another word, Golvath tosses the match toward the helpless girl, setting her ablaze.

Unable to look away, powerless to help, the most Rachel can do is mentally scream while flames lick at the girl's body. The smell of rotten eggs, sulfur, wafts through the sky as her golden locks burn away, replaced by the pronounced, sickening sweet stench of cooking fat.

The scene changes abruptly as another memory takes shape.

This time the girl is facing away, as if she's staring at the beautiful horizon beyond. Her long, raven-colored hair cascades down her shoulders like a silky curtain. She glances back, her dark eyes red and bronze skin blotchy. There's something exotic about her, something that's not entirely human shines through.

The breathtakingly beautiful girl walks forward, pleading without words for some type of release from the spell she's under.

"Fly away little bird," Golvath says, unable to keep the amusement from his tone.

He watches as she swan-dives off an unrecognizable cliff, so graceful, so elegant.

A telling *thump* rings across the plains, the sound reverberating in Rachel's heart until she shatters.

Golvath peers over the edge at the girl's broken body where she lies cradled in a cluster of sharp rocks. Blood already pools around her, staining the boulders.

Gone. Just like that.

The memories flit through her mind of all the girls he's loved and the various ways he essentially murdered them. He stabbed one girl to death—over and over until his muscles ached from exertion. The act was done with such brutality that even Golvath had been disgusted with the end result.

"Too messy," Golvath says into her mind. *"I won't do that again."*

Another girl walked into the ocean on his command and never resurfaced after a wave went over her head. Then there was the girl who ran out in front of a horse-drawn carriage, a death by trampling.

The most horrifying of all his kills, however, was when he'd forced a girl to starve herself to death. He'd enjoyed seeing her wither away, enjoyed her suffering as she tried explaining that yes, she wanted to eat, but she literally couldn't swallow a morsel without his say-so. They'd thought her mad and sent her off to— what Rachel believes may have been—a convent, while Golvath had continued tormenting her with food for almost a year.

Dozens of teenage girls of all races, from completely different worlds, had died because of his infatuation and cruelty.

"You'll be my first strangulation." There's smugness in his almost-victorious thought.

Her limbs go numb. Parts of her brain shut down, due to the lack of oxygen. The sensation of needles and pins pricking her fingers and toes comes next. Her lips tingle, her tongue feels swollen. Is her heart slowing? She can't tell.

Ziggy flits into her line of sight, hovering for a few crucial seconds behind Golvath's head before torpedoing straight for the unsuspecting Fae. The golden sphere smashes into the side of his face, throwing him off-kilter. Flesh burns under Ziggy's touch, bubbles and sears to the bone.

Golvath stumbles to the side. It's enough for him to loosen his hands from around her neck.

Rachel sucks precious oxygen into her lungs, inhaling and exhaling rapidly, replenishing what Golvath denied her. She twists to take some pressure off her back, dizzy from the rush of blood to her brain. Rachel hangs onto the sidewall, mostly to keep herself on her feet.

She looks back.

Golvath is uselessly swatting at Ziggy as he hurls crass insults at the Fae light. More importantly, she notices the disfigured, gray-toned face on the other side of the bell tower. Tufts of oily hair are plastered against its skull, his nose is missing, and one ear hangs on by a piece of skin. One half-decomposed hand presses onto the sidewall, finger bones on display wherever the skin has withered away.

The Sluagh's milky eyes survey the situation on the bell tower, then turns his full attention on Golvath.

He throws his leg over the sidewall, torn pants flapping in the wind, entire patches of skin missing from his limb. The second hand appears, holding a rusty broadsword. The Sluagh flops over the sidewall, onto the walkway, and slowly gets back to his feet.

Rachel looks around until she finds Orion hovering in the sky near her. His large flaming wings drip molten lava, supernova eyes gazes back at her. Although his mouth is moving, his voice is lost through the spell.

An unholy cry fills the air. Rachel shoots her attention to Golvath, who's finally noticed the approaching Sluagh. The sword rises above the Fae's head. Ziggy flies off then, just in time to avoid the blade slicing down into Golvath's shoulder, past his collarbone, and stops somewhere near the top of his ribcage. Blood spurts across the bell tower, staining the stone and covering the rusty bell.

"*Jump*," Mercia's scream suddenly finds its way to Rachel, the spell broken with Golvath's far too quick death.

The Sluagh uses an inhuman amount of strength to lift Golvath's limp corpse off the floor. He shakes the body like a rag doll, struggling to release his blade. Golvath's corpse strikes the bell—a deafening clangor rolls through the town. Rachel's molars vibrate from the knell and her skull pounds. The Sluagh tries to loosen his broadsword by tugging at his weapon. He lifts Golvath into the air again.

Shake, shake, shake. *Dong!*

Rachel throws her leg over the sidewall, gritting her teeth as she battles her own body, the exhaustion and pain almost unbearable at this point. She takes one last big breath before rolling off the edge.

As she plummets back to earth this time, she isn't looking at the ground. Her eyes are fixed on the diorama heavens, where fluffy white clouds float in an almost three dimensional formation. The sun shines brightly, warming her face, while a cool breeze gently flows through the town. For Shadow Grove, especially in autumn, the day is lovely—perfect to spend outside before the big chill hits.

Her hair whips and her shirt billows around her body. After almost being strangled to death, screaming is out of the question.

Before she can even come to grip with the fact that she's willingly fallen off a five-story tower, Orion swoops in to save her.

Her breath hitches as he catches her in his arms, carrying her like a bride. Orion gradually descends back to the ground.

"This is becoming a habit," he says, a ghost of a smile in the corner of his mouth.

Her throat is raw, the bruises around her neck are tender, and she's simply too tired to respond. So, Rachel does the only thing she still has energy for: she closes her eyes and drifts away.

Chapter Twenty-Five
Sticks and Stones

The front door slams shut with such force, the glass panes rattle in their frames.

"Mrs. Cleary?" Mercia's voice travels upstairs, full of nervous angst. "Rachel's asleep if you— Mrs. Cleary?"

There are footsteps on the stairs, the gait forceful, albeit not unfamiliar. Rachel climbs out of bed and walk toward her bedroom door, which was left ajar by whoever last checked on her. She peers out of her bedroom.

Her mother stands on the second-floor landing looking back at her.

Her larynx is still swollen after her ordeal with Golvath, but Rachel manages to croak, "Mom?" She opens the door wider.

Jenny stares at Rachel for another long moment, before she turns toward her own bedroom without saying a word. The nightdress Jenny's worn since she jumped out through the kitchen window and ran off that morning is unimaginably dirty, like she's been swimming through mud, and her bare feet is crusted with heaven knows what. Still, she appears to be fine physically. Mentally, however, she might not be all right.

The main bedroom's door closes, leaving Rachel both concerned and dumbfounded.

She'll be better in the morning, Rachel tries convincing herself, but it's useless. There's no telling what Golvath did to her mother's mind, no saying what venom he spewed. Whatever hope there may have been to reconcile their strenuous relationship could be forever lost.

Mercia climbs the stairs, her expression reiterating Rachel's own worries.

"You should be in bed," Mercia says when she notices Rachel standing in the dark.

"My m—"

"I'll handle whatever problem this is," Mercia interrupts. "And I told you to rest your voice."

Rachel halfheartedly salutes her.

Mercia and Orion had tended to her, healing whatever damage they could, and the bruises were already fading around her neck. Internally, however—especially mentally and emotionally—Rachel's tenderness remains distinct. She waits as Mercia walks off to the main bedroom and watches as the young witch softly knocks on the door.

"Mrs. Cleary, can I come in?"

There's no answer.

"Mrs. Cleary? I just want to make sure you're okay."

"I'm fine," her mother responds. "Leave me be."

There's a pause, before Mercia says, "Are you sure?"

Rachel hides in the shadows as she watches Mercia attempt to fix the situation. How can anyone fix something that might be broken beyond repair, though?

"I'm sure you are confused, but if you just—"

The door swings open and an intimidating figure resembling Jenny Cleary fills the entrance. Steel eyes stares Mercia down, an

281

uncharacteristic resolve resides in Jenny's jaw. There's coldness in her now, a severity Rachel has never known.

"I've never been more lucid in my life, child," Jenny says. "Run along home before your mother finds out you're at the infamous MacCleary house." She says nothing explicitly hostile, but the threat is clear. *Leave or I'll make you leave.*

Mercia glances over her shoulder, concern evident in her expression. "I'll be back at first light to check on Rachel."

"You do that." Jenny shuts the door in Mercia's face.

Rachel moves out of the shadows as Mercia crosses the distance of the hallway, whose face has turned ashen.

"What was that about?" Rachel whispers, her voice as brittle.

"Her mind seems fine," Mercia responds in the same quiet voice, not answering the question. "The only weirdness I sensed was a rage at *everything.*"

Rachel nods. She is angry, too, after all. How had the universe allowed a being as heinous as Golvath to exist for so long? It's unfair to all of his victims and their families.

"I'd lock my bedroom door if I were you, just in case your mom's rage needs an outlet," she continues. "Or would you rather want to come home with me? We can do that. My mom has her misgivings about the Clearys, but she won't mind when I explain the situation, I promise."

Rachel smiles as she rests a hand on Mercia's shoulder. She shakes her head. With Ziggy by her side to keep her safe, nothing in this house will harm her. The Fae light won't allow it. Besides, this is her mother. Jenny doesn't have a violent bone in her body. Her mother can be indifferent at times, yes, but never physically abusive.

"Okay, well, you have my number if you need me," Mercia

whispers. "And Dougal's right across the street, too."

"The worst is over," Rachel says. "I'll be all right."

Though every part of her aches in ways she never thought imaginable, Rachel finds the strength to see Mercia to her car. It's the least she can do after everything they've been through. Nevertheless, Mercia's reluctance is as obvious as the moon is bright. Eventually, Mercia does take her leave, and Rachel returns to her bedroom.

She locks the door ... just in case.

Rachel gets back into bed and pulls the cover up to her chin. She listens for anything untoward, wondering if she'll ever have a good night's rest again. Silence is her only company tonight. That and an exhausted Fae light. Poor Ziggy. His shimmer has been completely lost, the brilliant gold slowly fading into a dull color.

Her eyelids grow heavier, limbs become lead. How deep is her exhaustion? The surrounding darkness is a sweet seductress, tempting Rachel back to where Golvath's victims live on forever.

Rachel gives in and drifts off, visiting the sisters she couldn't save, but who are finally free.

Sunlight spills through cracks between the curtains, pooling on Rachel's bed, the carpet, and painting the walls. She groans as she blindly reaches for the emoji pillow and pulls it over her eyes, hoping to fall asleep again. Rachel lies there for a few minutes, unmoving, before throwing the pillow aside.

Wide awake, she lifts the covers and looks down to where Ziggy is resting by her feet.

"You're sleeping in, aren't you?" she half-croaks.

A single, dim flash answers her.

"So unfair."

Rachel sits upright and stretches, her bones creaking and

popping after her dreamless sleep. After a long soak in the bath to soothe her aching muscles, she has a plan to get her life back to a semblance of normalcy. First, Mrs. Crenshaw will be returning home soon and they still haven't moved her things from the upstairs bedroom to a more accessible location on the ground floor. Then, Rachel needs to figure out if she can retake the SATs—after defeating Golvath, a standardized test will be a piece of cake. Also, there were some college applications still waiting to be submitted.

Getting back into her usual routine won't hurt.

She stands, yawns, and drags her feet toward her bedroom door where her toes touch the smooth surface of something that doesn't belong at the edge of the rug. Rachel looks down, her mind not yet running at its full capacity, and finds a white manila envelope lying in a pool of sunshine. She picks it up, stifling another yawn as she tears open the top and pulls out the contents.

A scribbled yellow Post-It note is attached to a heavier folded-up piece of paper, reading:

I can't do this anymore.

Rachel shakes her head, blinks a few times before unfolding the larger document. A blue frame surrounds the official contents of the certificate. Her name is typed into the first horizontal block, her gender beside it, along with her date of birth in the next space. She's seen her birth certificate countless times before, so why would her mother—? *Wait. This can't be right. There must be a mistake.*

"Mom, what the hell is this?"

Rachel wills the typed letters to reconstruct themselves and change back to how she remembers them.

She reaches out to steady herself against the door, her heart sinking to her stomach as she stares at the document.

"No," she whispers, unwilling to accept what she's seeing. She reaches up to touch the umbrella pendant, which Orion had returned to her the previous day, before she unbolts her bedroom door.

It's a lie, another trick. Golvath must've survived. That's the only explanation.

Her mother's bedroom door is wide open, the bed never having been slept in. Even from a distance, she can see the destroyed photographs still littering the bed. Anxiety threatens to take over, to tear apart her already-fragile mind.

"Mom?" she croaks. Rachel marches down the hallway, ready to demand answers. "Mom, what's the meaning—?" She cuts herself off as she enters the room and finds the wardrobe doors hanging open, empty.

Rachel glances at the dressing table. The drawers are all lying on the floor empty. Jenny's jewelry box isn't where it usually stands either and her hairbrush is gone. A quick search of the en-suite bathroom divulges a similar picture—the toothbrush is absent, the bottles of shampoo and conditioner are missing, the medicine cabinet is empty of anything essential.

She pivots and rushes back into the bedroom, out into the hallway. Rachel bounds down the stairs, her physical ailments forgotten, and searches for her mother. Clutching the offensive piece of paper, Rachel regards the remnants in the living room. In the corner of her eye, Rachel's gaze falls upon the open front door, where the morning sun brightens the outside world.

Nausea twists her stomach into knots.

She couldn't have gone far.

The most naïve part of her believes her mother is sitting on the porch, coffee in hand, beginning her day as she usually does. Rachel steps closer to the door, her heart drumming hard in her chest.

"Mom?"

The two wicker chairs are vacant. Rachel moves off the porch, searching the lawn and hoping to find her crouched in the garden, pulling weeds from the earth or tending to the hedges. It's not impossible, just highly unlikely.

"Mommy?" Rachel manages to call out, turning her attention to the empty driveway.

Her legs give way, and Rachel crumples onto the thick, green lawn. She stares at the space where the white Hyundai i10 usually waits, wishing it back.

Rachel prays to the universe to take pity on her and return her life to what it had been before she'd crossed paths with the Bone Carver, before he'd poisoned her hometown. She wants to go back to before she learned of the Night Weaver preying upon the children of Shadow Grove, hurting those who were already in so much pain. All she wants—no, *needs*—is to return to living a life of ignorant bliss.

The despair is too much for her to bear. Time has no meaning anymore, life makes no sense. The creased birth certificate in her hands took everything away. Everything Rachel had ever thought true about herself, about her very existence, is gone.

It's okay. Everything's going to be all right.

More lies.

Things will never be okay again.

As soon as she laid her eyes on Misty Robins' name on her birth certificate, in the place where Jenny Cleary's name should have been, she *knew* nothing will ever be the same again.

If this birth certificate is authentic, then Rachel is the progeny of a Halfling noblewoman who'd sworn revenge against the Nebulius dynasty. She is the daughter of a woman who's indirectly responsible for the death Orion and Nova's father—King Auberon.

Who else knows the truth? Does Mrs. Crenshaw know she isn't Jenny's daughter? Does the town council have a hand in hiding her real parentage?

It doesn't matter.

Liam Cleary, the father she'd lost so many years ago, the man she'd worshipped even in death, had been the biggest liar of all. Yes, Rachel can blame Jenny for systematically withdrawing affection toward her, for shunning her responsibilities as a parent, even for her callous departure. But Jenny Cleary, the woman who'd essentially raised her, is as much a victim of her father's deception as Rachel. She had tried telling Rachel the truth while under Golvath's influence, but it'd fallen on deaf ears.

"There's a monster in that house. I'm not your mother."

Yes, Rachel must be a monster if she's in any way related to Liam Cleary. There's no question about it anymore. As for Misty, she can't forget the allegations that've been made against her, can't shake the image of what horrible things she purportedly did to Orion's father.

Misty Robins had killed two guards at the Royal Vaults and emptied out the treasury of anything she could use against the Nebulius royals. She'd handed out some of those artefacts to the prisoners she'd helped escape from Leif Penitentiary. The Night Weaver got the Akrah cloak—a sentient cloak that fed on darkness. Another artefact, the Travolis Ring, had been used to kill King Auberon. No, not just kill. Disembowel.

That's Rachel's legacy now.

Come to think of it, Rachel's already living up to Misty's reputation—three-hundred-and-twelve Halflings' died because of her rushing through the Fae Realm without a plan in place. Like mother like daughter, right?

"How could he do this to us?" Rachel asks. "I thought he loved my— I thought he loved her." She looks up at the clear blue sky through blurry eyes and a curtain of tangled hair, searching for an answer.

It's completely possible he didn't even remember the truth. Who knows? But whether Liam remembered or not, it still takes two to tango, and he'd betrayed his wife. He would forever be responsible for his own actions, just as Rachel will forever have to live with the consequences.

My father is a liar and a cheater. My birth mother is a traitor and a murderer. What does that make me?

Rachel pushes herself to her feet, wiping away tears with the back of her hand. She turns in place and marches up to the house, her mind spinning with questions she can't begin to answer. Will Jenny ever be able to forgive her? How is she going to tell Orion that she is actually the biological daughter of the woman who killed—or rather disemboweled—his father? Should she try and find Misty?

Who am I?

A more terrifying thought takes shape in her mind, one she never thought she'd have to ask herself.

What *am I?*

Chapter Twenty-Six
We Are What We Are

There's a peculiar somberness in Shadow Grove in the days that follow. When Rachel passes people in the street, she senses shame, self-pity, and guilt. They try their best to act normal in public—this is Shadow Grove, after all—but there's been a shift in the tightknit community. People had gotten badly hurt, some had even died. None of this has gone unnoticed. So, the town council can spew their propaganda as much as they like, put the blame on a supposed town-wide gas leak if they want, but Golvath's memory lived on in everyone.

Two bodies had been found in the school—Mr. Gambini, the janitor, and Ms. Jones, one of the new lunch ladies. The media didn't report on their bodies being boneless, simply said they had succumbed during the major, town-wide gas leak. Nobody's recovered their bones yet, and there is no telling if they ever will. What Golvath planned to do with all those bones, Rachel couldn't say. The third body belongs to Golvath, or rather Cameron Mayer as people knew him, who'd supposedly fallen to his death from the bell tower. There's no mention of how he was almost cut in half, no talk of the fact that he had no parents to call and no residence in Pine Hill, or anything about his unusual ears. Nope. He's just another casualty, which works for the cover-story the town council chose to go with.

Things return to normal as usual, though, or as normal as possible. The school opens its doors once more, the shops fix the damage and clean the sidewalks, services resume as if nothing's happened.

People move on. *Life* goes on.

The day after the vigil, just as Rachel readied to leave to get Mrs. Crenshaw's house ready for her return, there's a knock on the door. She walks into the foyer, opens the door, and finds Greg standing on her doorstep, looking more disheveled than she's ever seen him. Though he wore his usual ensemble—white shirt, jeans, blazer rolled up to his elbows—there are dark rings under his eyes, and his shoulders slumps.

"Are you okay?" Rachel asks in way of greeting.

He exhales a humorless laugh. "Shouldn't I be asking you that?"

Rachel stares at him, unsure how to answer.

"Rach, I don't expect you to forgive me, but I need to explain—" He holds up a hand to silence her before she can interrupt. "Let me finish, please."

Rachel shuts her mouth and nods.

"I literally wasn't myself, but I remember what I'd said and I can't forget what I did to you." Greg squeezes his eyes shut. He reaches up to pinch the bridge of his nose for a moment, before sighing loudly as his arm drop back to his side. "And you can deny it all you want, but I saw how scared you were of me …"

"I know it wasn't you, Greg," Rachel says.

When he meets her gaze, Rachel sees the unshed tears gleaming in his eyes.

"What I did to you is inexcusable. What that other …" He

swallows hard, and then shakes his head. "I had to battle against something in my head to keep myself from hurting you."

She takes a step toward him, places her hand on his cheek, and says, "It wasn't *you.*" The stubble against his cheek scratched the palm of her hand. "I said things to you, too. Horrible things that weren't entirely true."

Greg nods. "Yeah, but I deserved it."

"No, you didn't," Rachel says. "Greg, I will always love you, but I can't love you the way you want me to."

He closes his eyes again, nods. "I know," he whispers.

Rachel stands on the tips of her toes and presses a chaste kiss against his cheek. Arms wrap around her, draws her closer. She feels Greg lips against the top of her head, hears him breathe in deeply as he nuzzles her hair.

"I'm sorry," Rachel whispers.

"Me too."

He releases her and takes a step away. "If you ever need anything, call me, okay?"

She smiles and wipes at her damp cheeks. "Promise."

Greg reaches out and brushes his thumb over her cheek, catching a stray tear. "See you around."

"Yeah."

Rachel walks out on the porch as Greg leaves, and watches Griswold Road long after his Mercedes had disappeared.

As Rachel put the final touches to Mrs. Crenshaw's living room, where a banner shouts *WELCOME HOME* and colorful balloons float against the ceiling, Mercia hisses, "They're coming," from the window.

Orion walks out of the dining room and halts beside Rachel, wiping his hands on a dishcloth. "Are they back already?"

Mercia scrambles away from the window and toward Orion and Rachel. "Happy faces," she whispers.

The *click-click-click* of the walker grows closer, moving with determination.

"Nan, lemme help ye up the stairs."

"Stop hovering, Dougal," she snaps. "I'm not a damn invalid yet."

"She sounds fine," Orion whispers to Rachel.

"Break a hip and suddenly even a teenage boy is helpful," Mrs. Crenshaw mumbles.

Rachel stifles her laugh by biting the inside of her cheek.

The front door opens and Dougal steps inside, out of the way, before the walker come into view. Rachel has to admit she looks much healthier today, in her own clothes, than she had in the hospital. With her hair meticulously done into a tight bun, and the apples of her cheeks shining with rouge, Mrs. Crenshaw's walker seems more like a prop than a helper.

"Dougal's dawdling suddenly makes sense," Mrs. Crenshaw says, suppressing a smile as she sees the decorations. Her gaze falls on Orion. "I'd curtsy, but my doctor advised me against strenuous activities."

Orion guffaws. "I'm sure he did. Welcome back, Nancy."

Mrs. Crenshaw's almost imperceptible nod is accompanied by a small smirk. She turns her attention to Mercia. "A Holstein witch made the journey to this side of town? Well, you lot must've thought I was really at my end then. I still have a few years left in me, girl. Don't you worry."

"Actually, Nan," Dougal says, and clears his throat. "She's my guest."

Electric blue eyes turn on him, widening. "I thought your mother said you were batting for the other team."

"That's Alex, Nan. The middle brother?"

Mrs. Crenshaw waves her hand through the air as if it's inconsequential. "All you Mackays look alike to me."

Rachel bursts out laughing, joy bubbling through every part of her body. She crosses the distance and leans over the walker to wrap her arms around the fragile woman.

"I missed you," Rachel says and means it.

Mrs. Crenshaw tentatively puts one arm around Rachel and pats her shoulder. "I missed you, too," she whispers back.

Rachel releases her and steps out of the way.

Mrs. Crenshaw backtracks out of the front door. "Dougal, bring me a blanket. I want to get some fresh air into these old lungs before the winter comes."

The party files onto the porch.

Mercia and Dougal move onto the lawn, where she conjures a kaleidoscope of butterflies. They talk among themselves, laughing at whatever private jokes they share. Orion sits across from Mrs. Crenshaw, who pokes fun at him often. He smiles, sometimes laughs at his own expense.

"Show some respect to your elders, Nancy," he says, much to Mrs. Crenshaw's delight. It's probably been ages since she's been called young, after all.

Regardless of how Golvath affected Shadow Grove, at the end of Griswold Road, there's mirth in the air. Rachel's almost sure even the faeries and pixies and knockers in the forest are happy that Mrs. Crenshaw is back.

Rachel excuses herself from her company and makes her way to the kitchen, where the cupcakes she's baked had cooled off enough to be frosted.

This is normal. This *is home.*

Rachel can't broach the subject of her parentage with Mrs. Crenshaw yet. She probably won't for a while, but for the first time in weeks she's happy. Of course, she can't hide the fact that her mother—no, it's just Jenny now—isn't at home. Mrs. Crenshaw hasn't said anything, but Dougal must've told her what happened. People have, after all, already speculated over Jenny's whereabouts, always gossiping and coming up with wild theories. Nobody blames her for leaving, though. Some simply envy her for having the courage to put this place behind her.

When the pink frosted cupcakes are done, Rachel arranges them onto a tray, and carries the treats outside.

"If this is about me and Rachel—"

Rachel stops in the living room.

"Whatever you and Rachel get up to is none of my business," Mrs. Crenshaw cuts Orion off. "I've never worried about my girl. If you hurt her she'll chew you up and spit you out, anyway, so that's the least of my concerns."

"So, what is it then?" Orion sounds confused.

"You and I both know Fae needs stability. You can't be living with one leg in this world and with the other leg in the Fae Realm. It'll rip you apart," she says, the seriousness in her voice unmistakable. "We've both seen it happen."

There's a pause, before Orion says, "You want me to choose now?"

"I don't want you to do anything, Princeling. I just need you to understand that if you're not careful, you may turn into something you don't recognize in the mirror, and it'll fall on Rachel and Dougal's shoulders to put you down."

"It won't come to that."

"See that it doesn't, especially *if* you and Rachel become more than friends with benefits," Mrs. Crenshaw says.

Rachel walks to the front door. "Who's ready for cake?"

The conversation ends abruptly and the merriment continues. Dougal and Mercia return to the porch, still chatting, hands accidentally grazing, secret smiles being shared. It's sweet to see Dougal's rough edges smoothed out.

"Isn't Holland going to be annoyed because you're spending so much time here?" Rachel asks as she licks a drop of frosting from her thumb.

Mercia shrugs.

"I don't think I can handle her wrath," Rachel says.

"In all honesty, I think Holland is glad I'm not around her place as much anymore. She remembers more than she wants to admit, and she knows I remember what she did," Mercia says. "Suits me, too."

Rachel grins. "Oh, really? Pray tell *why?*"

"Och! Ye can stop playin' dumb, Rach," Dougal says. "Ye know why."

"Do I, though?" Rachel snickers.

Orion says something in Gaelic to Dougal, which makes the Scotsman blush. He laughs, earning a brusque response.

"Don't make me put a no-Gaelic sign up," Mrs. Crenshaw mutters, picking at crumbs on her blanket.

"Why don't you tell us about you and Orion instead?" Mercia says, leaning back in her chair. Game, set, match.

Rachel's humor fades. She's been keeping Orion at arm's length with good reason. There's no telling how he'll react when he finds out she's related to Misty Robins.

Their eyes meet, and she feels like she's falling from the bell tower all over again. Rachel doesn't want to lose this yet. She doesn't want him to hate her *now*. He peers at her through his long, dark eyelashes, seeming to want an answer as much as Mercia does.

"What about me?" Mrs. Crenshaw comes to Rachel's rescue. "Nobody's asked me if I met a rich gentleman during my hospital visit."

Dougal's eyes widen. "Surely, ye haven't, Nan."

"Ha!" Mrs. Crenshaw barks a laugh. "You underestimate me, Dougal. One day, I might just bring you a new granddaddy home."

Dougal visibly shudders, which brings about another bout of laughter.

For the first time in what feels like forever, Rachel decides to forget about everything that's happened in the past and whatever troubles the future may bring, and simply focus on the present. Today is a gift, after all.

Ziggy greets her as she arrives at home, zooming this way and that, conveying his excitement by blinking dull gold. Rachel giggles as she tickles the Fae light's surface, the sphere's flashes turning to ripples.

"I told you to come along. Mrs. Crenshaw would've enjoyed

seeing you," she says, ignoring the loneliness that clings to every piece of furniture and wraps the entire place in gloom.

She could have asked Mercia to sleep over another night, could have embraced her inner-vixen and even brought Orion home with her, or she could have stayed the night across the road. But she doesn't have the strength to fake her way through another round of questions. Every time someone asks her if she's okay, she wants to throttle them.

No, she's not fine. Nobody would be all right after being stalked by a serial killer and then being abandoned by the only mother they ever knew. Nothing about her is *fine* or *okay* or *all right*. She smiles and acts like she can't be fazed, because she doesn't want to relive those moments for the rest of her life. She's too grateful she's alive. Too happy to have Mrs. Crenshaw back where she belongs.

Rachel locks the front door behind her, throws the keys into the bowl on the side-table, and kicks off one shoe. Ziggy shoots toward the staircase, taking along his light.

"Hold on, Zigs." Rachel hops forward as she takes off her other shoe.

Ziggy waits until she's caught up before ascending to the second-story at a gradual pace.

Rachel takes off her jacket and tosses it onto the swivel chair in her bedroom. She slumps down on the edge of her bed as Ziggy plays around her.

"Not tonight," she says, inhaling deeply through her nose. "I'm worn out."

Ziggy settles down on the emoji pillow as Rachel leans forward, reaching down between her legs, her fingertips searching beneath the bed for the keepsake box she keeps hidden there.

After a few anxious seconds, she touches the autumn leaves decoupage that covers the exterior of the shoe box. She pulls the box out into the open and lifts the lid, sets it aside on the bed. Rachel picks up the card lying at the very top of all her collected memories, and reclines, reciting the words out loud without needing to read the card:

> *I was born into the Court of Light, but;*
> *My world is cast in perpetual gray.*
> *Shadows are my friends, and;*
> *Darkness will be my legacy.*
>
> —*Nova*

Oh, how she relates to that. Now more than ever.

Ziggy flashes once beside her, and she lazily looks his way.

"You don't approve of my reading material?" Rachel asks in a humorless tone.

There's hesitation before Ziggy rolls closer and nestles into her side, dimming ever so slightly.

"I'm not depressed, Zigs." Rachel absently tickles Ziggy's surface, staring at the card she knows by heart. "Orion isn't going to take the news well. On the other hand, revealing my heritage will probably help him to make up with Nova. So, there's a bright side to the whole situation."

Ziggy doesn't respond.

"What do you think Nova means with this poem, huh? Is it some kind of admission of his allegiance with the Miser Fae?"

Ziggy shoots away without reason, hovers near her bedroom door, and the gold fades away until he's a nuclear blinding light.

"What the—?" Rachel sits upright, blinking in surprise.

"Ziggy?"

The Fae light becomes an anamorphous blob, suspended in the air.

"Zigs," she repeats, throwing her legs off the bed. "What's the matter? What's happening to you?"

Suddenly, a small creature runs into her room, disregarding the Fae light completely, and slides to a stop in front of her feet. The knocker—the kind of faeries that mostly live underground in mines and sewers—huffs air and pushes his graying hair out of his face. She hasn't seen this one before. He is older, and looks somewhat grumpier. Cheeks red, eyes wide, he stares up at Rachel.

"Err … Hello?" she says. "You okay there?"

The knocker moves to rummage around in a miniature leather bag, before producing a card. He holds it out to her, standing on the tips of his toes.

Rachel leans forward and accepts the message. She turns the card around, studying the blank back before spinning it the other way.

"Okay," she says, glancing back at the knocker. "There's nothing on here."

He gestures for her to look back at the card, insists by waving his hand violently through the air.

"Fine, but who sent this?"

The knocker's shoulders slump, and he rolls his eyes. His hands go up to his head, fingers splay, before he mimes putting a crown on his head.

"Nova?"

Vigorous nodding in response.

Rachel looks back as ink bleeds into the card. Random letters are spelled out, coming into existence in no particular order. Her heart races as the message takes shape, a four-word warning.

You are in danger.

Rachel sighs heavily. "Yeah, tell me something I don't know."

Acknowledgments

I always feel wholly inept when it comes to expressing my immense gratitude for everyone who've dedicated months of their time to producing my books, as well as those who showed their unwavering support and friendship throughout the journey. A simple 'thank you' seems inadequate for all the hard work and effort everyone's put into *The Bone Carver*.

To my unparalleled and marvelous team at Vesuvian Books, all of whom went above and beyond to make *The Bone Carver* shine, I can't begin to express my appreciation. I can try, but you all deserve so much more …

A super thank you goes out to Holly for editing *The Bone Carver* (a.k.a. cleaning up my messes).

Massive thanks and hugs are owed to LK for being a superhero—few people could step up the way you have during a global pandemic. You are amazing!

Thank you so much to the other Vesuvian authors who've supported me from the first day. You've all systematically turned into my international family, and I appreciate each and every one of you dearly.

Then there's Marcela Bolívar, who's responsible for the gorgeous cover. Thank you so very much for creating such beautiful, striking art. I am awed by your talent.

Michael, from MJC Imageworks, thank you for making my title pop like nobody's business (I still love the flies so freaking much!). You are a rock star!

Without everyone's subtle nudges, input, and expertise at Vesuvian Books, *The Bone Carver* wouldn't exist, so thank you again from the bottom of my heart.

I don't even know where to start saying thanks when it comes to Italia Gandolfo. Not only are you a great agent, but you're a wonderful friend. Thank you for taking a chance on me and my books, thank you for always being around for a little chat, and thank you for always being my cheerleader. Love your bones!

To my wonderful husband, whom I love with all my heart, words often fail me when it comes to how much I appreciate your support, friendship, and love. Since the beginning, you've done the impossible when it comes to making sure I have what I need to blossom. Without you, I wouldn't be half the person I am. I love you!

I would also like to thank my family—my mom, aunt, and sister—as well as my in-laws for all their love and support. I know I can be difficult at times, and yeah, my work/sleep schedule is weird, but somehow you still put up with me anyway. Thank you so much for always being so understanding. I love you all to bits.

Lastly, I would like to thank you, the reader. You are the reason why I keep writing stories. Without your constant support, I would never have gotten where I am today. So, I just want to thank you for always motivating me to be the best I can be.

About the Author

Monique Snyman's mind is a confusing bedlam of glitter and death, where candy-coated gore is found in abundance and homicidal unicorns thrive. Sorting out the mess in her head is particularly irksome before she's ingested a specific amount of coffee, which is equal to half the recommended intake of water for humans per day. When she's not playing referee to her imaginary friends or trying to overdose on caffeine, she's doing something with words—be it writing, reading, or fixing all the words.

Monique Snyman lives outside Johannesburg, South Africa, with her husband and an adorable Chihuahua. She's the author of the Bram Stoker Award® nominated novel, *The Night Weaver*, which is the first installment in The Night Weaver dark fantasy series for young adults.

www.MoniqueSnyman.com